IN THE LAIR OF LEGENDS

DAVID BUZAN

Black Rose Writing | Texas

ISBN: 978-1-68513-250-7 (Paperback); 978-1-68513-331-3 (Hardcover)
PUBLISHED BY BLACK ROSE WRITING
www.blackrosewriting.com

Printed in the United States of America
Suggested Retail Price (SRP) $21.95 (Paperback); $26.95 (Hardcover)

In the Lair of Legends is printed in Garamond Premier Pro

*As a planet-friendly publisher, Black Rose Writing does its best to eliminate unnecessary waste to reduce paper usage and energy costs, while never compromising the reading experience. As a result, the final word count vs. page count may not meet common expectations.

PRAISE FOR
IN THE LAIR OF LEGENDS

"Set in post-Civil War America, *In the Lair of Legends* is a well-crafted adventure thriller that delivers on every front. The protagonist, Winterhawk, is a Native American, a cavalryman, and a war hero. The villain, a horrific, man-eating monster. I was drawn into the story from the first chapter. The characters are relatable and complex. The sometimes-gruesome action scenes kept me on the edge of my seat! *In the Lair of Legends* is a page-turner I couldn't put down."
–Randolph Harrison, MEd, author of *A Guide for Aging Heroes: 30 Days to owning the Second Half of Life*

"Buzan pulls the reader into a non-stop, action thriller from the very first pages. Jolon Winterhawk's secret mission to escort a rail shipment of gold in 1873 Oregon is bursting with energy and brutal adventure. The story takes the reader through an epic train ambush and life-and-death battles with violent Army conspirators, all under the narrative dialog of a Native-American warrior from this period. Simultaneously, Winterhawk wages war with towering mythical beasts of the Northwest, and this deadly struggle is both exhilarating and tragic. You won't be able to put this book down."
–Michael Fletcher, author of *To Hunt a Holy Man*

"*In the Lair of Legends* is a non-stop action-packed story, told mostly through the point-of-view of Jolon Winterhawk, a Nez Perce warrior and returning US Cavalry soldier, with one last mission before he can finally go home. Everything that can go wrong does as he comes up against racism, traitors, greed, and the Gigantors of native legend. Nothing can stop Winterhawk from fighting with every breath to return to his family and their love."
–Lena Gibson, author of *The Edge of Life*

"*In the Lair of Legends* is a fast-paced action novel that kept me on the edge of my seat. From epic fight scenes to near death experiences, this page turner kept me begging for more about Winterhawk and if he would make it back to his family safely. A hearty well-done to Dave Buzan on this exhilarating read!"

–Michelle Weinfeld, author of *From Generation to Generation: A Memoir of Food, Family, and Identity in the Aftermath of the Shoah*

"Once you start reading *In the Lair of Legends*, I hope you don't have plans to do anything else. It's an action-packed historical novel that pulls you into its pages and puts you in the middle of the action, refusing to let go. Driven by mythology and world events, its warrior hero perseveres against amazing odds, propelled by the most important of all things... family. Dave Buzan has crafted an exciting and original adventure for the ages. Don't miss it!"

–Jeffrey Jay Levin, author of *Watching*

"Jolon Winterhawk has more lives than Indiana Jones's black cat, and he needs every one of them as he wages a one-man war against the forces of evil. *In the Lair of Legends* is a morality tale for the ages. There's danger and peril around every turn. You won't be disappointed!"

–Karen Brees, author of *Crosswind*

"In *The Lair of Legends* is a brilliant first novel by the writer David Buzan. It is a historical novel set in the Northwest Territories of the post-civil war America. It's main character, a Native American Union war hero named Jolon Winterhawk is as resourceful as heroes come, and his fortitude is buttressed by unwavering his love for his wife and daughter. The writer creates a clever story line that pits Winterhawk against the worst of mankind, as well as the most brutal of fantastical creatures. It is non-stop action carefully unfolded over the length of this novel. With this genre of novel, the devil is in the details and David Buzan masterfully brings all of those details to bear in creating one hell of a novel. He's also left enough of a thread to support a sequel should he so desire. Congrats David, you've written a winner."

–Tom McCaffrey, bestselling author of *The Claire Trilogy*

IN THE
LAIR
OF
LEGENDS

PROLOGUE

Cascade Mountain Range
Buncombe, Oregon
1873

It had been several hours since a jigsaw of dark storm clouds had completely obliterated the sun. Within minutes, the torrential rainfall had transformed the afternoon light into a sickly gray sheet that loomed heavy over the expansive Oregon forest. Beneath the dense canopy of foliage, it was as if the inky blackness of midnight had already descended.

Breath hitched coldly in his lungs, Thon squatted against a toppled fir tree, its bark sheared and blackened by a lightning strike. Pregnant rain droplets were smashing through the surrounding covering of branches around him, sounding like a hail of cannon fire.

He peered intently into the thicket of shadows that flanked his position, mouth set in a harsh grimace. His stomach was knotted with tension. The gritty taste of bile had collected around his tongue in a thick clump.

Beneath his feet lay the root cause of this abject fear.

Grizzly tracks embedded deep into the mud.

For three hours he had methodically tracked the animal east; now, the tracks faced due west.

That meant it had somehow caught his scent.

The grizzly was hunting *him* now.

Thon wrapped a hand around the massive stock of the Zieg A-8, the famed Australian hunting rifle that had been specially designed to use so-called Bunyan shells: triple buckshot.

He thought of it as the world's first carnivorous firearm. Just pull the trigger, and the Zieg would pick the meat clean off the bones.

Thon crept stealthily away from the fallen tree, navigating his way carefully through the tangled underbrush. He settled beside a large boulder, sinking low, weary joints in both knees sounding off like twin gunshots.

He focused on every sound, dissected every shadow.

The grizzly was somewhere out there.

Waiting.

Thon had been tracking this particular bear for the last two days, methodically following its movements throughout this dense section of the Cascade Mountains. Somewhere along the line, he had made a mistake. He must have gotten too careless. He assumed that he had somehow gotten downwind, allowing the bear to--

His heart began to hammer.

Twenty feet away, a dark shape was moving fast.

Thon hefted the Zieg up against his shoulder, rapidly swinging the barrel around, finger curled around the trigger.

A small, black form darted from out of the underbrush, mouth outstretched to display a row of jagged teeth. A pair of reddish eyes peered out from beneath a matted jumble of dark hair as it scurried towards the relative safety of the shadows.

The small animal had to be a bear cub.

That meant the den was nearby.

Thon had been tracking a female. Killing her cub would bring the grizzly out of hiding, and into full range of the powerful Zieg. With any luck, the adult male grizzly would also be nearby. It was a chance to triple his earnings in a single hunt.

Thon didn't hesitate.

He pulled the trigger.

Amplified against the heavy basin of trees, the subsequent blast was enormous. Thon's heavily muscled arms absorbed the massive recoil of the rifle as a long tongue of fire curled out from the barrel.

The A-8 hit the creature with deadly accuracy, lifting it off its feet, slamming it back against a tree with bone-crunching force. Falling hard to the ground, it writhed in a deepening pool of its own blood.

Thon's eyes flicked wide with shock.

The animal that he had fired upon...

It hadn't been a cub.

In fact, it wasn't a bear at all.

Thon lowered the rifle and stepped forward, features contorted. The horror he felt didn't come from the sickening carnage he was presently viewing, it came from something he had *already* seen.

In the hellish flicker of light given off by the blast, he'd seen something which burned into his brain like a hot poker burrowing deep into wax.

It had been staring at him.

True.

But...

The small creature had also been –

Standing.

Thon sensed it before he saw anything, his survival instincts primed by a lifetime spent in the woods. There was sudden movement from above. He leaped sideways, shoulder slamming hard into the mud, rolling hard.

The grizzly he'd been tracking walloped to the ground a foot behind him. The lower portion of its jaw had been torn off, a strand of entrails snaking out from a massive gash along its lower torso.

Thon heaved himself backwards as the ravaged carcass of the grizzly slowly rolled over. He could see that both of the bear's front legs had been savagely torn from its body.

The rifle dropped from his grasp, panic overwhelming him.

Something had pulled the grizzly up into those trees.

Thon scrambled desperately to his feet.

Something with enormous strength.

His boots slipped precariously across the mud, arms pinwheeling wildly for balance. He began clawing frantically against a tree for leverage, the bark cutting the tips of his fingers to shreds.

Something similar to that small creature he had shot.

Thon pushed himself away from the tree, the slashing rain effectively blinding his vision.

Only, this one had to be –

A gigantic shadow dropped to the ground in front of him.

BIGGER.

The creature appeared massive enough to nearly eclipse the sky. Its broad shoulders seemingly a mile across, thick limbs as round as the largest tree, and a gaping mouth that appeared like it could swallow the entire world with a single, savage bite.

Inhaling its rotted and decaying breath, Thon lost control of his bowels. He slipped in the mud, arms flailing helplessly.

The monster's crimson eyes centered on him.

Emitting an unholy roar, it swiped an arm downwards, tearing open Thon's upper chest, revealing shockingly white bone amidst a geyser of blood. His high-pitched scream echoed throughout the forest as the massive creature pounced atop his thrashing body.

As he felt the white-hot stab of pain consuming him, Thon had time for one final, horrifying thought.

He was being eaten alive...

PART I
The Demise of the Golden Goose

CHAPTER 1

CloudTrail Railway Pass
Cascade Mountain Range
Southern Oregon
1873

"Sometimes," the old man hissed, impenetrable facial wrinkles shifting to display a cruel mouth fissure, "the Devil answers prayers, too."

Lieutenant Jolon Winterhawk shifted uncomfortably in the creaky dining chair. Although he typically cast a shadow across most men, his large stature appeared to be dwarfed by the military prestige of the elder statesman seated across the table from him.

Excited by the prospect of a captive audience, Colonel Smythe leaned forward, shoulder blades pitched like a bone tent. He had both hands pressed down on the dining table for balance as the speeding dining car heaved precariously around a sharp bend in the tracks.

"The 11TH Regiment had fallen before midday," Smythe said. "General Lee's secondary battalion had cut them to pieces. By the time I arrived with the 21st, the entire prairie was bathed in blood. You kept death close that day because it filled your lungs with each breath."

Colonel Smythe paused just long enough in his narrative to shovel a large forkful of fried eggs into his mouth. He began chewing sloppily, grunting with satisfaction.

Winterhawk pushed his unfinished breakfast plate away and sat heavily back against the rickety dining chair. The incessantly loud noise of the train wheels was beginning to embed into his senses like a jagged knife being scraped across a blackboard.

The two men were riding onboard the USMRR LV-426, an armored steam train operated by the Army's Transportation Corps. It was the last remaining train still sanctioned by the U.S. Military Railroad after the end of the Civil War. The train itself comprised of six cars: engine, coal, dining, passenger, boxcar, and an unmanned caboose. There were twelve Cavalry soldiers onboard protecting its valuable cargo.

The sole purpose of the LV-426 was to transport millions of dollars of unrefined gold ore from dozens of private mines throughout California and Oregon. The confiscated ore was then taken to the White Salmon Blockhouse, a heavily fortified Army outpost hidden deep in the Oregon Cascade Mountains. After being smelted and turned into bars, the gold would then hop from train-to-train until it ultimately reached its final destination: the Treasury Building in New York.

The impenetrable storage facilities secreted deep within the Treasury Building acted ostensibly as a proxy cashier's vault for the Treasurer of the United States. In fact, several million dollars might be contained in those vaults at any given time. Bags of paper notes, gold coins, and bullion were often stacked from floor to ceiling.

Because of the ruinous economic collapse that would occur within the United States infrastructure if those vaults were breached and its contents stolen, twenty armed guards were assigned to protect each vault on around-the-clock watches.

With the entire country teetering on the financial brink a decade after the Civil War, the government was hungry for as much gold as they could excavate... or confiscate. Gold was thought of as being the best defense against the next impending war. This time, it was a universal hope that freedom might be bought instead of fought.

Do you know what those federal boys should really do? They ought to hope in one hand, and vomit in the other. See which one fills up first.

Because of the extreme risk of robbery, the precise transport dates were kept secret until the last possible moment of departure. Its routes were kept hidden from all but a handful of top U.S. Army officials. It was a lengthy, often treacherous journey across a United States that still found itself fractured even a decade after the Civil War.

Sometime over the intervening years, a jokester from the Army brass had hung a crass nickname on this particular train: the *Golden Goose*. It was a humorous name that seemed to stick with the Cavalry grunts assigned to protect it.

The Golden Goose. That's a real knee-slapper, amigo. In terms of belly laughs, it's probably right up there with those negotiations with the Native Nations in 1862 when American officials promised that the reservations would always belong to the tribes. Sometimes things are so funny that they just hurt, *you know?*

Winterhawk firmly set his jaw.

Although every soldier riding the rails was told that protecting the valuable cargo on the *Goose* was the most important military operation in the western United States, the truth was that Winterhawk had been on outhouse details that had felt more dangerous.

Nice touch of irony there, right, chief? Whatever job those Army boys give you, walking away with shit on your hands is their plum guarantee.

Not that any of that truly mattered; not to him, not anymore.

After ten years of distinguished service with the United States Cavalry, this was going to be his last assignment. He had the discharge papers burning a hole in his pocket to prove it.

The final mission was one that he had already completed numerous times: ensuring that the gold shipment reached the White Salmon Blockhouse.

Safely delivering the gold ore had become much more to him than just dutifully following orders. It had turned into a way to bring honor to the memory of his own father's ultimate sacrifice.

That's a mighty fine answer you got there, hombre. But the hard lesson that your father learned all those years ago is a truth you still haven't quite grasped yet. In a war, you can fight everything but *the money.*

Winterhawk felt the Cavalry uniform constricting over his muscular torso like it was a second skin. The observation was a pointed one. He wondered what his ancestors would have thought if they could have foreseen that the son of a Nez Perce warrior would one day become the highest-ranking Indian in the United States Cavalry.

They'd probably have the same opinion of you that the tribal members of today share. Many of those simple-minded prairie dwellers back at the Malheur Reservation still refer to you as an "apple." You're red on the outside, but white on the inside. And just like a real apple, you didn't fall far from the tree. Just ask your father about it. Oh—wait! You can't. He's dead.

Winterhawk pushed the thought away, and once again turned his attention to the man seated across from him in the dining car. His penetrating eyes canvassed every nook and cranny of the military relic before him.

Sitting on the wrong side of sixty, Colonel Smythe wore his advancing age with the same oblivious pride as a border whore flaunting her emaciated bosom. The man was a decorated Civil War hero; thus, shelving the proper military decorum of retirement in favor of a forced extension of service.

In a calculated political move, it had been decided by the top Army brass that Colonel Smythe would continue his sworn duties by acting as a proxy representative for the North. It was thought that Smythe's distinguished record of service could somehow persuade those Americans who still kept misgivings about the bloody outcome of the war.

While some say that it is the victors of a war who ultimately write history, Winterhawk knew that the real truth is forever buried with its victims. The politicians count on men like Colonel Smythe to erase the screams of the dying and transform them into the cries of righteousness.

You'd better jump off of that particular soapbox, Geronimo. Do you really think any of that dung makes you any different? Let's call a spade a spade, shall we? Doesn't the Army use you in exactly the same way?

Colonel Smythe flashed a wide grin. A solitary strand of egg yolk dripped from a cracked yellow tooth, moistening his bottom lip.

"If you spend enough time in the trenches," Smythe said, "there'll come a time when you don't even take notice of all that enemy gunfire whizzing past your ass."

Winterhawk understood that all too well. The feeling of invincibility that permeates the subconscious after repeated combat survival on the battlefield. You get careless; lose focus. Become—

Like your father?

Winterhawk winced.

No. Definitely *not* like his father. But at least that man had died on his feet; fighting to the end, not cowering in fear.

Your father died on his feet. No arguing with that. But guess what, chief? That's because he was running.

Winterhawk squeezed his eyes shut.

Of course, his feet were just about the only chunk of him left after those nasty Confederate boys blasted him into little pieces. Jack be nimble, Jack be quick, Jack got his ass blown up by a dynamite stick.

"On the day I arrived with the 21st Regiment was the same day that General Pike lost his head," Smythe continued, eyes twinkling. "If you had asked any man there about Pike, you'd hear the same thing: that man could ride a horse like King David could fling a stone.

"Pike was riding just ahead of me, so I got a prime view when that cannon blast sheared off his head. He was swatting a fat mosquito from his neck when that lead ball from a Parrott 20-pounder finished the job for him. But that wasn't the worst of it. What I saw next would have made Lot himself take an extra helping of salt with his soup."

Winterhawk sensed the six other Cavalry soldiers in the dining car leaning forward in their chairs, listening intently to this gruesome account.

"For damn near fifty yards of trail, Colonel Pike continued to ride on his horse, torso bobbing up and down in the saddle, looking just as comfortable as you please while blood pumped out of the fresh hole on his neck."

Winterhawk had seen that sort of thing during combat. He'd seen a whole lot worse, too.

"But what made me wretch a Sunday duck was getting a real good glimpse at the reins. It was his *hands*, Lieutenant Winterhawk. They were still clenching onto the leather, knuckles white with the effort. Even at the very end, General Pike proved he was born to die in the saddle."

Disgusted murmurs were exchanged between the other hardened soldiers in the dining car.

Winterhawk wondered how the Army would react if *this* particular story ever hit the newspapers. The antics of a galloping, headless soldier would not cause a stampede of new enlistments.

But that was the root of the whole problem. When there was no more war to fight, the Army was forced to engage in combat inside the arena of public opinion. It was a battle they couldn't afford to lose.

The country had continued to be divided after the Civil War. It was thought the people needed heroes; brave men who had fought with honor and decorum. Soldiers on both sides of the Great Conflict who had risked everything, whose heroic stories of survival would fill newspapers from Boston to San Francisco.

To this end, they had carefully molded Colonel Smythe into some sort of military exhibit. There were many men like him, of course. Soldiers who had forgotten that any other type of life had existed for them before the war.

Then we've come full circle, haven't we? Once again, how does any of this make you any different? You're not a traveling monument, boy-o, but you're sure as shit are a circus freak.

Winterhawk could find little of that thought to argue with. He knew that most of the men he had fought alongside didn't really think of him as a soldier. They considered him to be more like an *exception*. To them, he was just a flesh-and-blood olive branch extended to an entire race of people.

Smythe sat back in his chair, unfocused eyes taking in the wilderness rushing past the dining car windows. "All of that seems so long ago now. If I didn't have the nightmares, I would almost swear the whole damn war had never even happened."

Winterhawk felt a sudden wave of pity for the man. If his own father had lived long enough, would he have turned out any differently? That's the truth about regrets. They only haunt the living.

Smythe cast him a steely glance from across the table. "I read reports about your involvement in the War of the Rebellion."

"I dodged a few bullets."

"Don't be so modest, Lieutenant Winterhawk. I've glanced at your files. Reconnaissance for the Army's 3rd Armored Cavalry Regiment in Virginia during the Battle of Cold Harbor. You single-handedly saved the lives of a dozen soldiers during the skirmish at the Chickahominy River. They should have awarded you the Medal of Honor for what you did."

"They don't give out medals to Indians, Colonel."

Winterhawk could feel his chest involuntarily constrict as the memory flooded over him. He remembered the final screams of the men who had died near the Chickahominy. For a moment, he found it difficult to breathe.

"That's a damn shame," Smythe said. "Where did you find yourself after the war ended, Lieutenant?"

"I became a fort frog," Winterhawk replied. "Hopped from one outpost to the next. After a while, they gave me this cushy job riding the *Goose*. How about you, sir?"

"When the war ended, some Army peckerheads tried to convince me to retire. I tried it for a spell, but I grew tired of polishing a rocking chair with my ass. But I've finally grown tired of all the political bullshit. Hitching a ride home with you boys so I can put myself out to pasture. This sightseeing trip will be my last assignment."

"We have that in common, sir."

"Discharge papers?"

Winterhawk nodded. "Once we deliver the gold ore to the White Salmon Blockhouse, then my time playing in this sandbox is over."

Smythe began studying Winterhawk's uniform with all the subtlety of a roving searchlight probing every nook and cranny of a moss-covered prison wall.

"Thunder Rolling Down the Mountain must have tremendous faith in you, son."

Winterhawk narrowed his eyes with suspicion. "You know Chief Joseph's name?"

Smythe nodded. "Joseph's own grandfather was among the tribal leaders of Nez Perce. Those people offered hospitality and sustenance to Lewis and Clark's near-starving party when it staggered like a drunken mule down Idaho's Clearwater River Canyon back in 1805. My very own father was a member of the Corps of Discovery. Perhaps you've heard of them?"

"They were a specially-established unit of the United States Army," Winterhawk answered. "They formed the foundation of the Lewis and Clark Expedition. The Corps of Discovery spent more time among the Nez Perce than any other tribe they encountered in their entire journey."

Now it was Colonel Smythe's turn to show surprise. "That's absolutely right, Lieutenant. I didn't realize your military education was so far-reaching."

Education? It's more like embracing that age-old mantra: Know Thy Enemy.

Winterhawk shrugged. "I've always been fascinated by military history."

"Well, Lieutenant, when my own family history began knocking at death's door, the lineage of Joseph and the Nez Perce tribe resuscitated them from the dung heap. Without their direct intervention, the Lewis and Clark expedition would have certainly failed. And my father would have starved in the wilderness."

Isn't that the same type of blind trust in the West that your own father had? Making a pact with the Devil seems to run in the family, doesn't it?

Winterhawk felt a flash of anger coil in his stomach.

"Decades later," Smythe added, "Chief Joseph's own father, Tuekakas, continued with that same spirit of generosity by insisting in 1863 that a handful of his men from Nez Perce—"

"Ten," Winterhawk said. "Not a handful. Chief Joseph handpicked ten warriors to enlist in the war."

Sounds like a nice campfire ditty to me! "Too afraid to fight, and too afraid to run! I'm gonna play like the white man. I'm gonna be a soldier in Ory-gun!"

Smythe smiled. "And in doing so, those *ten* representatives of Nez Perce joined nearly three hundred thousand warriors from other Indian tribes across North America by enlisting in the United States military to end the barbarism of slavery."

That means that we're all just one big, happy family! Oh, and speaking of family, I'm sure your wife and daughter have had nothing to worry about while you've been off gallantly protecting the white man's precious gold.

Winterhawk glanced at his left hand, staring down at the battered silver locket fastened tightly to his wrist.

Inside of the locket was a picture of his wife and seven-year-old daughter. The photo of Kaya and Chenoa was taken last year at the Malheur Indian Reservation while he had been on an extended leave.

You know the saying that a picture is worth a thousand words? I hate to be the one to break it to you, Jolon, but I think that picture of your family is saying just two things: "fuck" and "you."

He shook the thought away.

In the beginning, Kaya might not have appreciated all of the reasons behind his decision to enlist. But he knew now that she finally understood.

The Cavalry service was to provide his family with safety and security. They had been promised a protected homestead. Both Tuekakas and Chief Joseph had given him their solemn word on this. If he served the Nez Perce nation proudly, he and his family would be granted land that would never be taken away from them. It was a promise that he had believed.

If you honestly believe that, then I've got a thousand acres of golden maize in the Promised Land to sell you.

Smythe took notice of the locket, motioning towards it.

"Have a picture of your family in there?"

"Yes. My wife...and my daughter."

"That's real nice, Lieutenant. Every soldier needs someone besides the undertaker hoping to see them again."

Winterhawk resisted the urge to open the locket; instead, he pulled his gaze up and stared hard at Smythe.

"Hope ain't the half of it, sir."

Smythe flashed a wide grin. "I would show you a picture of *my* family, but the scarlet ladies don't like standing still for those damn flashbulbs."

Winterhawk could not attempt a smile in return. He was too weary to pretend any further acts of cordiality. This final *Goose* trip had been an ordeal of manners, as well as a true test of patience.

And for now, this conversation was over.

Winterhawk stood from the table. "It was a pleasure having breakfast with you, Colonel."

"Thank you, Lieutenant."

Smythe barely afforded him a glance. He had already returned his gaze to the windows, eyes fogging over with boredom.

Winterhawk started towards the back of the dining car. He was anxious to retrieve the worn weapons satchel he had stashed beneath one of the empty tables.

Good manners, Jolon. It's rude to bring weapons to the table while you're eating. Especially when some of them are stained with your father's own blood. You might have to strain your eyes pretty hard to see anything on them after all these years, but the blood is still there, just the same.

Winterhawk thought once again of how freedom awaited him when this train finally arrived at the White Salmon Blockhouse. In less than twelve hours, the *Goose* would be finished winding its way through the Cascade Mountains and the gold ore will have been delivered.

Soon, no more enduring life as a soldier. He could finally return to being a husband and a father.

He almost felt giddy at the thought.

"Lieutenant Winterhawk?!"

There was something unnatural in the tone of that voice that caused a great knot of fear to burst open inside his stomach. He whirled around, and once again faced his breakfast companion.

Colonel Smythe had turned from the window. His face was now a sickly shade of white, wide eyes showing a depth of terror that Winterhawk had never seen away from the battlefield.

"What is it, Colonel?"

Smythe stared hard at him. "Lieutenant, I do not believe that any of us are going to make it off this train alive."

Winterhawk started forward in the swaying car, eyes slit. "What the hell are you talking about?"

And then he saw it, too.

Through the dining car windows.

On both sides of the train.

Death.

Coming for them fast.

Moments later, his whole world exploded in fire.

CHAPTER 2

For General Ramón Cornadez, the most fascinating moment in death was the Gasper's Prayer: those final seconds of life when a man literally said the very last thing that was on his mind.

Ramón had first begun keeping a record of the Gasper's Prayer well over twenty years ago. It had been on the historic night of the Cornadez militia's successful raid against Hector Schivaz, a land baron who had acted as a ruthless tyrant in northern Mexico. The man had been responsible for the financial ruination of dozens of farmsteads, including the one in Sonora owned by Ramón's father, who had committed suicide after his land was taken from him.

Several days later, Hector Schivaz was killed.

While the militia had him drawn and quartered, Ramón had taken revenge for his father by brutally murdering Schivaz's oldest daughter. He had savagely slashed open her chest, sawing so hard that the blade had become lodged in her breastbone.

The daughter had focused her dying eyes on him. She had then whispered something so softly that Ramón had to get down on his knees beside her in order to hear. It was her final words ("...there are flowers...") that eventually became the inaugural entry in his journal.

Over the intervening years, he had completely dedicated himself to this task, dutifully scribbling down each entry in the leather-bound journal. No matter how big ("...the bark looked like the sun...") or small ("...shoes...")

those final words happened to be, they would all be recorded for prosperity in the journal.

For Cornadez, the Gasper's Prayer was not just an obsession.

It had become an absolution.

In some twisted sense, he considered himself to be a Father Confessor. Of course, once you stepped into *his* confessional box, the only meaningful penance offered was death.

Take, for instance, the plight of Lieutenant Colonel Arch Newberry.

Newberry had been the senior Army official designated with plotting the course of the USMRR LV-426 through the northwest territories. His duties were one of the best-kept secrets in the U.S. Government. But every scrap of knowledge in this world--including *anyone* who secreted away that knowledge--had a price.

The robbery of the military train had been in the planning stages for well over two years now. Cornadez had begun formulating it after overhearing a fantastical tale of the *Golden Goose* from a drunken Cavalry soldier bragging to a painted lady in a Texas saloon.

"Ever heard the story about a *Goose* that laid a golden egg?" the soldier had asked the whore, slurping his beer, eyes drunkenly transfixed on her ample bosom.

"No," she had replied, hands busying themselves on his lap beneath the table, "but I'd love to tell you the one about a giant beanstalk."

Later that same evening, Cornadez had abducted the hapless soldier from his drunken sleep and taken him to a remote desert rock alcove. The man had been forced to share all that he knew about the train as Cornadez performed an agonizingly slow castration with scissors.

After that night, Cornadez had chased the legend of the *Golden Goose* all across the West. For the next two years, the Army train that secretly transported a million dollars in gold became his life's obsession.

Until recently.

When he had happened across an Army informer, the obsession became a reality. Cornadez had paid this traitor handsomely for the information that led him directly to Newberry's homestead in California.

With the aid of his militia, Newberry and his new bride had been abducted and taken to a barren stretch of field miles away.

After watching his wife being skinned alive, Newberry had decided to talk. He had known exactly when the next shipment was. Better yet, he had revealed the precise route the *Goose* would be taking.

The Lieutenant had ended up begging for his life as Cornadez methodically unplugged his bowels with a hunting knife. Newberry had shivered in the last throes of death as Ramón had leaned in close.

"We..." Newberry had whispered, shaking hands slowly going limp, "... saw the Moon."

Cornadez had smiled triumphantly at those last words, scribbling them down furiously in his notebook.

And as always, absolution was nowhere to be found.

THE TRAIN ROBBERY had been in the planning stages for years, and now the day had finally arrived.

Soon, Cornadez would be able to strike a near-fatal blow to the tyrants of North America. He would take the reclaimed gold back to Mexico and free his own family from a lifetime of poverty, breaking those generational chains of hopelessness forever.

And all of that would begin happening *today*.

The trap had been set on a section of the CloudTrail Railroad Pass, where a stretch of curved track made way for an uphill straightaway needed for momentum to carry the train safely across a bridge that spanned the Rogue River.

Before the train even made it close to the bridge, Cornadez would greet it with the small army he had brought along to this surprise party.

Stationed on a hill overlooking the west side of the tracks were four French mercenaries. These high-priced Zouave sharpshooters were armed with Spencer repeating rifles, the most accurate sniper weapon used during the Civil War.

Members of his own private militia flanked the east side of the tracks. They were stationed behind five Model 1861 Parrott 10-pounder mountain brass ground cannons.

For General Cornadez himself, he had brought a stolen Army case filled with three-pound Ketchum Grenades. The grenades were created to detonate upon impact, making them ideal for close-quarters combat.

As if sensing the large-scale slaughter that was about to occur, the horses tethered to three large transport wagons neighed nervously in the distant forest.

Hidden behind a large boulder a hundred feet north from the tracks, Cornadez took a final look around. Everyone was in their positions. Both sides of the track were completely flanked.

A train whistle sounded.

The trail of black coal smoke stained the sky.

General Cornadez couldn't help but grin.

It was time for the *Golden Goose* to get cooked.

CHAPTER 3

"Ambush!"

It took Jolon Winterhawk a moment to recognize the soldier who had just shouted that frantic warning inside the dining car. The ragged voice he had heard had been his own.

He winced as the ghastly shriek of the locomotive's blaring whistle filled the air like a tombstone symphony.

This train can certainly whistle, but it can't carry a tune.

The wheels of the train began to screech.

He lurched forward, hands gripping one of the dining chairs for support as the conductor engaged the emergency brake.

This was all wrong.

Stopping the train?

The conductor should be attempting to speed up the *Goose*. He needed to get them far away from the ambush, not allowing them all to become sitting ducks.

There must be something up ahead on the tracks that he hadn't seen yet. Whatever had frightened the conductor, he would find out what it was soon enough.

Now, he had more immediate problems to contend with.

Like what he had just seen out of the west side of the window.

Four riflemen standing on a grassy hill next to the moving train. Each man had been holding Spenser repeating rifles, barrels aimed at the dining car. The men were adorned with distinctive matching uniforms: bright red chasseur caps, light blue shirts, dark blue jackets, red sashes, red trousers, and white belts.

The Zouave Brigade.

The annals of European war had made them legendary.

Jacque Pierre Zouave had originally been a loyal commander in Napoleon Bonaparte's fierce Crimson Brigade. It was Zouave's unique combination of close combat techniques and stealth warfare that would eventually be adopted by the Colonialists during the Revolutionary War.

After the Napoleonic War officially ended in 1815, the original Crimson Brigade was systematically disbanded, but the soldiers decided to adopt their leader's namesake: the Zouave Brigade.

Following their French army counterparts over to America, Zouave's now second-generation brigade--dubbed the "Tiger Rifles" during the battle of Gettysburg--had further splintered into dozens of separate regiments scattered throughout the country.

Winterhawk had previously encountered them at the Battle of Cold Harbor. Expert marksmen employed by the Confederates as snipers to take out high-ranking Union targets. What made them so dangerous is that the Zouave were no longer soldiers. They had become mercenaries.

That's a terrific history lesson there, amigo. Good to know exactly who'll be responsible for putting that bullet in your brain today.

Given how fast the train had been going before the conductor had pulled the emergency brake, he calculated it would take at least another three thousand feet before they came to a full stop.

He had to do something before that happened.

Winterhawk pushed away from the chair, waving his arms frantically at the other soldiers huddled inside the dining car. "Get down! You have to get down!"

The soldiers ignored him as they looked out the windows in dull fascination at the coordinated ambush being launched against them.

Several of the windows shattered as a volley of rifle slugs peppered the interior of the dining car.

One of the men closest to Colonel Smythe let loose a gargled cry. He careened backwards, hands reflexively clutching his head, or what remained of it. Bullets had carved a large section off of the man's skull, leaving behind a gaping crimson cavity.

That's the best part of traveling by rail, ain't it, chief? You get to appreciate all of the Good Lord's magnificent scenery.

The surviving soldiers clumsily stepped away from the windows of the dining car, scrambling to unholster their sidearms.

Smythe reached for the hand-forged M-1860 Light Cavalry Saber strapped to his belt. "When I'm done with these sons of bitches, there won't be enough pieces left of 'em to even snore."

Gunfire could now be heard emanating from the passenger car fastened directly behind them as a half-dozen Cavalry troops took aim at their attackers through the windows of their sleeping quarters.

Those soldiers could return fire fast enough to pick off several of the attackers. They could even drop enough of those bastards to square the odds.

Don't get your hopes up, boy-o. Those poor boys couldn't hit the broad side of a redwood with their own piss even if they were scraping the bark with their one-eyed organ grinders.

This had to be part of the ambusher's trap. The French mercenaries were expert marksmen, but Winterhawk was convinced that they were being used as something else entirely.

Decoys.

The Zouave weren't operating as a coordinated sniper unit picking off selected targets within the carriages. They were firing a wild barrage of lead from their position due west in order to draw the attention of the soldiers away from the east side of the train.

Winterhawk was convinced this was true because of something else he had seen out of the dining car windows.

The sight had chilled his blood.

There was a row of Parrott mountain cannons lined up flush against the tracks, with a five-man Mexican militia group stationed behind each one.

Given their proximity to the oncoming train, the placement of all that heavy field artillery wasn't meant to inflict casualties.

Those Parrotts were going to be used to derail the *Goose.*

As if on cue, the roaring thunderclap of cannon fire sounded out. The noise was deafening inside the dining car as the east side of the train was pummeled by a barrage of 10-pound canister shots.

The combined impact of the cannons rocked the *Goose*, causing the train to lurch haphazardly under the cannon fire, nearly forcing the locomotive off the rails.

The militia would be reloading those cannons now. They would be ready to fire again on the train in just a matter of minutes.

Winterhawk felt a rush of cold air on his face. He whipped his head around, frantically searching for the source.

One of the cannon shots had ripped its way completely inside the dining car, exposing a large section of the carriage.

He then saw something else.

Colonel Smythe. Jostled by the tremendous impact of the cannon blasts. Careening backwards, arms pin-wheeling wildly for balance.

Smythe cried out in pain as his right side impacted hard against the cabin wall. His left shoulder dipped precariously through the exposed gash left by the cannon blast, the wind threatening to pull him through the jagged hole.

Smythe reached out with his right arm, grabbing one ragged edge of the hole in the cabin for support. His knuckles were white with exertion as he fought against the inertia threatening to pull him out of the train.

Smythe was now just heartbeats away from being sucked out through the hole in the dining car. He would never survive that fall.

"Colonel!"

Winterhawk propelled himself atop the nearest dining table, flinging his body into the air.

Smythe's feeble grip finally let loose. He fell backwards through the hole in the cabin, body twisting through the air as the ground rushed towards him.

Winterhawk soared out through the jagged hole in the dining car, his body impacting with the Colonel's in a spectacular mid-air tackle.

Grabbing Smythe around the waist, Winterhawk pulled him tightly against his own body, twisting his torso around a split second before they impacted with the ground.

Winterhawk grunted as he landed on his back, effectively shielding Smythe from the fall, sliding them both behind the shelter of a nearby cluster of large rocks.

For several agonizing moments, he waited for the sound of gunfire to unload in their direction. He was all but certain that the marksmen would be attempting to pick them off at any moment.

But that didn't happen.

The combined smoke from the cannon blasts and the steam engine's firebox had shielded their escape. The enemy had not seen them jumping off of the train. For now, they were both safe.

Right on, amigo. I guess only the finest and bravest soldiers cower behind rocks these days.

Winterhawk pushed the weight of Smythe off of him. "Are you alright, Colonel? Are you injured?"

His breath coming in ragged gulps, Smythe shook his head. "Nope. That was a still damn smoother ride than my first wedding night."

The frantic shouting of the conductor could be heard echoing across the field.

It was a single word, repeated over and over again.

"What the hell is that idiot screaming about?" Smythe asked, struggling to stand. He unholstered a Colt Army Model .44 from his belt, his hateful gaze focused on the Zouave riflemen stationed only a few hundred feet away from them.

Winterhawk had heard exactly what the conductor had shouted.

He rolled to his feet, staring up ahead at an unusual pyramid structure piled high onto the tracks directly in front of the barreling train.

He now understood why the emergency brake had been pulled.

The conductor cried out again, and this time everyone on the field of battle could hear what he was screaming.

"Landmines!"

CHAPTER 4

Coal torpedoes.

Originally invented by Captain Thomas Edgeworth Courtenay of the Confederate Secret Service, the coal torpedo was a hollow iron casting filled with explosives that functioned as a powerful landmine.

To construct them was relatively simple. Artillery castings would first need to be shaped like actual hunks of coal. While the walls of these coal shells are thick, a hollow space was left inside sufficient to hold four-ounces of gunpowder. After being filled, each shell was dipped in melted beeswax, and then rolled in coal dust. This created the false appearance of a harmless lump of coal.

Similar to a 6-pound artillery shell, a single coal torpedo had been known to obliterate a ship's boiler, sinking even the largest naval vessel within just a few minutes.

But after an oncoming steam train hurtling down the rails at over 40 miles-per-hour impacts with a collection of twelve of them...

Winterhawk had barely enough time to wonder how the ambushers had gotten hold of so many before he saw the conductor launch himself out of the engine car.

As he crashed to the ground, a volley of slugs from the Zouave sharpshooters cracked through the air. Blood geysers erupted in a half-dozen places along the conductor's torso as his lifeless body bounced wildly away from the speeding train.

Seconds later, the *Goose* plowed into the pile of coal torpedoes. The lethal stack detonated immediately upon impact, the thunderclap of a dozen exploding landmines reverberating across the valley.

The *Goose* let loose a metallic scream as the front of the train plowed forward into the crater left by the explosion. With the track ahead now missing, the wheels of the train had nowhere to go but down.

The fender of the train kissed the scorched earth, driving over 5,000 tons directly into the ground. For a split second, the *Goose* looked like a bucking iron horse attempting to dismount its passengers.

And just as suddenly, the train was rolling off the tracks. The explosion had forced a detour as the wheels touched dirt and began pushing itself onto the grass. The *Goose* began tipping dangerously, wobbling onto its right side as it continued its forward momentum.

Another round of thunderous explosions shredded the air.

Winterhawk staggered backwards, his mind racing.

Had the train just hit another placement of landmines?

Think again. If you want to live to die another day, you had best be sorting out things a whole helluva lot faster than this.

He then understood the source of the second huge round of explosions. The Parrott cannons.

The deafening noise of the cannons was soon overshadowed by the metallic death roar emanating from the train as the barrage of 10-pound shells delivered their fatal blow.

The *Golden Goose* was temporarily launched airborne as all six runaway cars were blown completely sideways off the track.

Panicked screams echoed through the valley as the Cavalry troops holed up in the passenger car were tossed about like a mouse being torn apart inside the jaws of a feral cat.

In that split second of flight, the dining car uncoupled from the passenger car, leaving it still attached to the steam engine and the coal car.

The walloping impact shook the ground like a small earthquake as the train landed onto its side. Both halves of the train slid across the prairie in opposite directions for fifty feet before coming to a stop.

While plumes of dark coal smoke poured from the dying steam engine, an eruption of excited hollers could be heard coming from the ambushers.

They were cheering because the *Golden Goose* had just been executed.

A sudden flash of movement caught Winterhawk's attention.

There was now a solitary figure sprinting along the tracks. The man was heading towards the overturned passenger car, holding onto a pair of objects in both hands.

Smythe raised his Colt, aiming at the group of Zouave marksmen. "If I'm gonna die today, then I'm taking a few of those bastards with me."

But the Tiger Rifles hadn't seen them yet.

Their attention was focused on the passenger car.

And the man gaining fast on it.

Winterhawk roughly shoved Smythe, knocking him backwards before he could squeeze off a shot.

"Lieutenant! What in the hell do you think you're doing?!"

Winterhawk whirled around and faced him. "In the next few minutes, you and I will be the only survivors of this ambush. Unless you want to be buried ass-up in your dress blues today, you'd better keep your ugly face kissing the dirt."

Nodding, Smythe begrudgingly took a knee behind the grouping of rocks that continued to shield them from the enemy's sight.

Winterhawk turned his attention back to the overturned passenger car. Specifically, on the man sprinting along the tracks towards it.

He narrowed his eyes with recognition.

Colonel Smythe had seen him, too. "Either I'm going blind, or God just developed a wicked sense of humor. Isn't that—?"

Winterhawk nodded grimly. "General Cornadez."

The criminal exploits of Ramón Cornadez were well known within the ranks of the United States Army. A notorious military ambush artist and war profiteer, his face was plastered on posters from Fort Collins to Fort Stevens. Cornadez was wanted for taking the lives of twenty soldiers during assorted attacks on military targets. He was suspected to be behind the killing of at least two dozen more.

"General Cornadez commands a small-time Mexican militia," Smythe hissed. "How the hell did he get access to a brigade of Zouave snipers and Army field cannons?"

Winterhawk thought that was an excellent question.

Since the assassination of President Lincoln, post-war profiteering had become a lucrative business. While well-financed organizations such as the Knights of the Golden Circle were operating under an ideological desire to keep the flames of Confederacy burning bright, most military racketeering was being done by smaller fringe elements working within the criminal underworld.

And then there were certified lunatics like Ramón Cornadez.

Behind every assassination and coup attempt, there was the hope that his efforts would somehow strike a fatal blow against America. Whatever General Cornadez stole, he would justify it as reclaiming what had already been stripped from Mexico by foreigners across the centuries. And he didn't mind shedding innocent blood to achieve exactly what he wanted.

It has a ring of familiarity to it, doesn't it? Almost like you've heard that little song-and-dance number before. That's because it's a familiar tune to any race of people who've been forced to march under the cadence of "white makes right." Just make sure you never learn those lyrics, chief. You can tap your toe along with it from time to time, but never let yourself get caught singing a duet.

Agonized screams brought his attention back to the overturned train. Two soldiers were attempting to pull themselves out of the broken windows of the passenger car. A second later, their heads exploded with twin pops as the Spenser rifles sounded off.

General Cornadez had now reached the passenger car.

Winterhawk could now make out what the man was holding.

Ketchum grenades.

Created for close-quarter combat, the three-pound explosives detonate upon impact. They were nothing but weaponized meat grinders.

Cornadez flung a pair of Ketchum grenades high into the air. They flew end-over-end towards the car, disappearing through one of the broken windows.

A brief flash of light emanated from inside the bowels of the car as the grenades detonated. A grotesque geyser of gore escaped through the windows as red chunks splattered inside the car.

Cornadez began running back towards the front of the train, heading to collect more of the lethal grenades.

Another few of those lobbed into the passenger car would finish the job of cutting down the soldiers still trapped inside. Then, the Zouave marksmen would systematically take out any last survivors.

Winterhawk could hear the anguished screams coming from the mortally wounded soldiers trapped inside the *Goose*.

He felt a hot flash of rage. He knew he had to do something.

"I've got to get back to the dining car, Colonel. I need my weapons."

For the first time since after the ambush began, Smythe looked genuinely frightened. "It's no good, son. We'll have a better chance now if we just cut and run. We'll hunt these bastards down another day."

Winterhawk squinted through the thick coal smoke that continued wafting up towards them from the dying steam engine.

The four Zouave snipers were a hundred yards to the left of them, rifles aimed at the passenger car. They were focused on taking out any potential survivors crawling out of the windows. Besides, they wouldn't be expecting anyone to make a run *towards* the train, only away from it.

On the east side of the tracks, Winterhawk could see that the five Mexican militia members were still flanking their Parrotts. The residual cannon smoke was effectively concealing much of their forward line of site.

General Cornadez had already returned to his stash of Ketchum grenades stored somewhere near the front of the overturned engine car.

There wouldn't be a better opportunity than this.

"I'm going for it, Colonel."

Smythe shook his head. "That's damn near ten-against-one odds down there, Lieutenant. What do you think you can possibly do?"

"Whatever I can," Winterhawk answered.

A Cavalry soldier appeared through one of the broken windows of the crumpled passenger car. His screams of rage were soon joined by blasts from his .44 Colts as he began firing wildly at the Tiger Rifles.

Using this distraction to his advantage, Winterhawk bolted out from behind the protective cover of the rocks. He began sprinting towards the dining car that was two hundred yards away.

He would be totally exposed to the Zouave for the next thirty seconds. More than enough time for one of those French snipers to see him, and take him down with a single shot.

A barrage of Spenser slugs tore into the passenger car. The bullets punched forcefully into the Cavalry soldier, shredding his torso to bits.

100 yards remaining.

The area directly in front of the dining car had a clear patch where the smoke hadn't yet obliterated the view. He would have to run directly through it in order to reach the train. That meant, for at least a full fifteen seconds, he would be totally visible to the ruthless ambushers.

A burst of excited shouts came from the group of Zouave riflemen.

"Poilu! Poilu! Poilu!"

You learned enough French back in school at Malheur to recognize what those frog eaters are screaming about, right?

Poilu.

In French, it meant soldier.

The Zouave must have seen him.

The marksmen would now be shifting their aim, centering those Spenser rifles directly on his back. They had a high vantage point. No obstructions. A perfect line of site.

Winterhawk glanced over his shoulder as he ran, hoping to somehow get a sense of the bullet trajectories that would be raining down on him any second.

He braced himself for the sound of gunfire.

Amazingly enough, no rifle blasts sounded off.

But he *did* hear something else.

Singing.

The Zouave mercenaries had indeed seen a soldier, but it hadn't been Winterhawk.

It was Colonel Smythe.

He had stepped out from behind the safety of the rocks and had climbed onto the largest one. Smythe had unfastened his weapons belt, letting the Colt and his saber drop harmlessly to the ground.

Incredibly, he had both arms raised high in the air as he faced the Zouave riflemen. He began to bellow out George Frederick Root's well-known *Battle Cry of Freedom,* looking to all the world like he was leading some crazed Baptist tent revival.

"Yes, we'll rally round the flag, boys; we'll rally once again! We'll gather from the plain, shouting the battle cry of freedom!"

The Tiger Rifles traded looks of incredulity amongst one another.

Winterhawk felt a burst of anger. He had told Smythe to keep his head down. What the hell did that lunatic think he was doing?

From the look of things, amigo, it would appear that the old man just decided to save your sorry ass.

The sound of a solitary rifle blast tore through the air.

Winterhawk took a running leap onto the edge of the dining car and somersaulted through the torn opening. Before he dropped from sight, he could hear the echo of Smythe's distinctive voice.

The man wasn't singing this time.

He was screaming.

CHAPTER 5

Wiping out the American forces had been deceptively easy.

The decoy landmines placed onto the tracks had worked better than Ramón Cornadez had expected. Those coal torpedoes were meant to only slow the train down; instead, their impact became its fatal wound.

Before the ambush started, General Cornadez had guessed that it would have taken the combined impact of the five Parrott cannons to derail the train. But the landmines alone had taken care of that. The cannons had just become the catalyst for that spectacular airborne jump from the tracks.

The response from the Cavalry soldiers onboard the train had been nothing but predictable. They had taken the decoy bait from the Zouave shooters, not seeing the cannons until it had been far too late.

Now, it was just a matter of eliminating the rest of the survivors.

He looked down at the two Ketchum grenades in his hands. The first pair had wiped out half of the men trapped inside the passenger car. The second volley would forever silence the remaining soldiers.

Yes, it was all too easy.

He knew that it's what would come after all the smoke had settled that should concern him now.

When the *Golden Goose* failed to reach its destination, the Army would send out search parties to locate their missing train. When they found the site of today's ambush, they needed to be properly convinced that there had been no survivors.

To achieve this, his own militia would unknowingly need to be sacrificed. Once he gave the signal, the Zouave had been given orders to cut them down. Afterwards, their corpses would be strategically placed around the battlefield. It needed to look like the militia and the American soldiers had killed each other during the fierce fighting.

Those men had been incredibly loyal to him over the years, but Cornadez didn't feel any remorse about what needed to happen to them.

These days, death was just the price of doing business.

And in this instance, the cost of doing business also meant leaving a half-million dollars of unrefined gold ore behind. It was a tragically absurd tactic, but a wholly necessary one.

While the gold itself could never be damaged under the heat generated from a normal wood fire, the temperature and toxicity of burning coal was more than enough to melt the unrefined gold ore into an unrecognizable mass of blackened sludge.

That was the second valuable treasure the *Goose* had been transporting: the coal car. After some of that coal had been tossed into the boxcar and ignited by the leftover Ketchum grenades, the resulting fire would burn hot enough to leave only confusion behind.

A grenade explosion would burn the contents of the boxcar straight to the ground. Discovered later in the rubble would be hundreds of pounds of torched gold ore. Enough gold left behind that nobody sifting through the remnants would suspect that any of the confiscated treasure had actually gone missing.

Cornadez and the Zouave would unload half the unrefined gold ore from the boxcar into the waiting transport wagons and take it across the border into Mexico. There was a smelting facility on his father's land in Agua Prieta that had once been operated by Spanish invaders. It was there that he would transform the ore into bars of gold. Then, he would finally reclaim all of his family's stolen land in Sonora.

To ensure his personal safety and to guarantee the valuable ore made it unmolested to Mexico, Cornadez would allow the Zouave mercenaries to accompany him on the journey back home. They would act as his informal bodyguards.

Of course, the promise of eventually splitting the gold with them was purely a fabrication. Those loyal French marksmen already had unmarked graves waiting for them across the border.

General Cornadez could only grin at the audacity of it all.

He had truly thought of everything.

Everything except what was happening now.

At first, Cornadez didn't quite believe what he was hearing. The sound was as unmistakable as it was unbelievable. He turned towards the source of the noise. He blinked in astonishment.

He saw an elderly soldier standing on a high rock, unarmed, arms stretched wide, bravely facing the Zouave marksmen. But this soldier wasn't attempting to fight his attackers. He wasn't screaming for mercy, wasn't begging for his life.

The old fool was singing.

The Zouave point shooter glanced over at Cornadez, a look of utter bewilderment stretched across his face.

Cornadez slowly shook his head.

The shooter nodded in understanding.

The old man was to be kept alive.

The Zouave sniper brought the Spenser up to his shoulder and pulled the trigger.

The elderly soldier cried out as the bullet impacted against his left shoulder. The force of the blast lifted him off his feet and dropped him hard to the ground.

The French mercenaries moved towards him, covering the ground fast in order to subdue their wounded prisoner.

Satisfied, Cornadez turned his attention back to the passenger car. He could hear the surviving soldiers inside praying for mercy.

"Sorry," Cornadez muttered, tossing the Ketchum grenades in a high arc above the car. "I'm not hearing any petitions today."

The grenades dropped through the passenger car's shattered windows. The subsequent explosion was concussive, the car momentarily shaking as the blast tore through the steel coffin.

And then there was only silence.

GENERAL CORNADEZ BEGAN lighting up a large celebratory cigar, the tip burning brightly as he expelled a huge lungful of smoke.

After the last of the soldiers holed up inside the passenger car had been slaughtered by the grenades, the Zouave had dragged their wounded prisoner to join Cornadez on the east side of the tracks.

The five members of his loyal militia had stepped away from the Parrott cannons. They were awaiting their next round of orders.

Ramón gestured impatiently at the tree line, motioning towards the area where the horses and transport carts had been kept hidden.

"Get the horses so we can start unloading the ore. Hurry up, fools! We don't have much time."

The men turned away, sprinting towards the distant horses.

General Cornadez turned solemnly to the four Zouave marksmen.

"Retire them."

The Zouave shouldered their rifles, rapidly firing, cutting the men down with a series of precision shots.

Surveying the massacre, the old man from the train began to laugh. "I'll be cow shit on the heel of my boot," he said. "I guess serving in your sorry-ass brigade is just like being in our Army: no good deed goes unpunished."

Grinding his teeth against his cigar with irritation, Cornadez turned towards the man. The wounded soldier was wobbling on both feet, face a ghastly white. His right hand was clasped tightly around the bullet wound on his shoulder, blood seeping through his fingers.

Cornadez pulled out the Gasper's Prayer from his coat. He opened up the journal, flipping through the pages until he found the place that marked the last entry.

"What's your name?"

The Zouave mercenaries took a step forward, aiming their rifles directly at the man's head. Their fingers were twitching impatiently around the triggers.

The old man stared at the Tiger Rifles for a long moment before turning his attention back to Ramón.

"Colonel Peter Smythe. United States Army, 21st Cavalry Division."

"Smythe," Cornadez said, furiously scribbling an entry into the blood-stained journal. "How do you spell that?"

"Correctly," Smythe answered.

Cornadez chewed once again on the cigar, fighting to control his anger. Such foolish arrogance! He glanced over at the French riflemen, giving them a consenting nod.

With his execution imminent, Smythe turned his back to them. He obviously wasn't going to give them the satisfaction of looking them in the eye while they cut him down.

Smythe began staring intently off in the distance. There was a brief flash of recognition in his eyes before a smile slowly formed in the corners of his mouth.

And then, the old man saluted.

Cornadez made a slashing movement with his left arm, signaling the Zouave to fire. They did so without hesitation, unloading their rifles mercilessly into the back of their prisoner.

As Colonel Smythe dropped dead to the ground, Ramón took a long draw from his cigar, blowing out a thick cloud of smoke.

In his final moments, why had that old fool saluted?

Cornadez suddenly squinted.

His heart hammered.

He was looking back at the smoldering train. Through the haze, he could make out a dark shape straddling the top of the dining car.

It was another soldier.

The man was aiming something directly at him.

It was a bow.

Cornadez took a step back in panic, the cigar dangling precariously from his lips.

He heard the unmistakable *whoosh* of an arrow.

Ironically, it would be General Cornadez himself who would utter the final entry in the Gasper's Prayer.

"Oh, shit..."

CHAPTER 6

With his breath heaving raggedly through his lungs, Jolon Winterhawk surveyed the inside of the capsized dining car.

The interior looked like it had been shaken like a child's bag of marbles. All the tables and chairs had broken apart; dozens of large furniture splinters now intermixed with hundreds of glass shards. Blood was dripping off the walls in thick clumps, formulating gruesome crimson patterns all across the floor.

I'm afraid that all the King's horses and all the King's men won't be able to do much about any of this.

He began scanning the area for his weapons. He knew he only had seconds to find the satchel before—

Winterhawk heard an anguished cry coming from somewhere just outside of the dining car.

It was Colonel Smythe.

The old man was still alive.

Those Zouave snipers wouldn't have missed such a stationary target; that meant they intended to only wound him. The Tiger Rifles had decided they needed a hostage. More likely, it had been General Cornadez who had given them that order.

He frowned with momentary confusion. Taking a United States Army colonel as a hostage wasn't the most intelligent tactical decision, but it seemed Napoleonic compared with the audacity of robbing a military train.

When it comes to brains, Cornadez is definitely proving that his family tree is a shrub. But just in case you haven't been keeping up with current smoke signals, that half-assed brigade managed to take down this entire train, and all the bootlickers riding it. And that might still include you, hombre.

Regardless of the reasoning, knowing Colonel Smythe was still breathing meant that there remained a slim chance of getting both of them out of here alive.

The low rumble of another dual explosion shook the floor. More Ketchum grenades. Cornadez must have hit the passenger car again.

Winterhawk resumed his frantic search for the weapons satchel, eyes roving across every broken nook and cranny inside the dining car.

He saw something that stopped him cold.

A soldier was pressed up against a corner of the compartment, his mangled body folded at an unnatural angle. Blood was seeping out of both of his eyes. His hands were bunched in front of his chest, fingers fanning the air like he was swatting at invisible insects.

Protruding from the center of the man's abdomen was a broken piece of one of the dining tables. During the crash the soldier had somehow gotten himself impaled on the jagged wood tip. He was bleeding out fast.

Winterhawk pulled the soldier's name from his memory.

Briggs. The young man had recently enlisted; hadn't been serving in the Cavalry for more than a few months.

Winterhawk looked closely at the piece of wood sticking out from the man's guts. He noticed something wet dangling from the sheared tip: his liver.

Briggs was still barely alive, but another man propped up a few feet away was very much dead.

This second soldier had been partially decapitated by a long sheet of broken window glass. The glass had pushed clean through his mouth, severing the upper half of his head from the rest of his body. Everything from the lower jaw down had been left intact.

Winterhawk glanced at the floor near the man's body. The soldier's partially severed head rested on the same piece of glass that had originally taken it off. He felt his gorge rise as he saw the dead man's eyes reflected against it. From this angle, it looked like those terrified eyes were staring directly up at him.

The eyes were pleading, crying out for help.

Help? This poor bastard's about a peso short and a day too late for that. But you could have helped him instead of leaping to the rescue of that old man. I suppose father figures come in many different colors these days. Something about Smythe must have reminded you how your daddy used to bounce you on his knee; that is, of course, when he still had both of his legs.

"Winterhawk..."

Frowning, he turned his attention back to Briggs. Staring up at him, the impaled soldier writhed with agony.

Winterhawk kneeled beside him. "I'm here, Briggs."

Briggs convulsed, muttering incoherently. Winterhawk leaned in close, gently resting a hand on the man's shoulder. He purposefully didn't look at the liver that was now dangling just inches from his own face.

"...don't let them steal..."

Briggs let out another moan before his head dropped heavily down against his chest. His body remained mercifully still, his suffering over.

Briggs had left him a present: his dying wish.

The man had succumbed while protecting the gold ore. With his last breath, Briggs had wanted to ensure that he hadn't died for nothing. His death needed to have some type of meaning.

You go right ahead and tell that to those kindred spirits who marched the Trail of Tears. Forget all about those yahoos that just ambushed you, amigo. It's blind faith that'll get you killed.

He understood the legacy that the Trail of Tears represented.

Chief Joseph had believed in finding some meaning in what had happened to those five tribes that had been removed from their ancestral homes in the 1840s, and forced to march to their own destruction. Joseph was acting on behalf of the Nez Perce people, negotiating a nebulous truce with the prominent white leaders of the western states.

Winterhawk was a large part of that truce. His impressive Cavalry rank was tangible proof of the serious trust that both sides had put into these negotiations.

But no matter how many battles you fight in that uniform, they *still don't exactly trust you. Neither side really does. The trouble is, you keep acting like they do.*

Five rifle shots cracked through the air.

It sounded like a firing squad.

His first panicked thought was that Colonel Smythe had just been executed. But he quickly disregarded it. If the Zouave had wanted him dead, they would have already done it.

No, this had to be something else.

There had been *five* distinct shots.

He thought of the Mexican militia he had seen operating the Parrot mountain cannons. There had been five of them. Cornadez had probably given the order for those Zouave riflemen to cut them all down.

It made much more practical sense.

With a myriad of corpses strewn all across the prairie, it would appear like everyone had died during the fighting. And with less of the brigade left alive, there would be more of the loot for the survivors to split amongst themselves.

But you don't ambush a military train and expect to waltz away with a million dollars in gold specifically earmarked for the Federal Reserve. After what transpired here today, the United States Army would pursue Ramón Cornadez to all four corners of the map. And they would never stop.

Unless they thought there was no gold left to chase.

Winterhawk considered the incredible abundance of ordnance that had been used in the train attack. Explosives could be used for much more than derailing a train. They could also be used to burn all tangible traces of the robbery into oblivion.

The Ketchum grenades could detonate the flammable stockpile of ore. Once the boxcar completely burned, there wouldn't be any way to know for sure what had gone missing.

The Army wouldn't waste time chasing criminals who were thought to have died during the ambush, nor would they allocate resources tracking down gold they didn't believe had ever been stolen.

He thought of the infamous Wells Fargo stagecoach incident that had happened in San Francisco back in 1870. The coach and its quarter-million dollars of currency had never reached its destination. The stagecoach was discovered three months later by bank investigators, found at the bottom of a deep ravine. The bodies of the coach driver and the two guards assigned to protect the wagon had been found among mounds of currency.

Or so it had seemed.

What had actually transpired was that those three men had staged the entire thing. They had dug up several corpses from a cemetery and put their uniforms on them. They'd even left a sizeable amount of money behind to make it look like the crash had been some unfortunate accident.

The group had eventually been caught and killed by Texas Rangers in a shootout that had made the front pages of newspapers across five western states. It had been a clever idea for a robbery; it had almost worked.

Winterhawk thought the same strategy was unfolding here.

With a myriad of corpses strewn all across the prairie, it would appear to the Army like everyone had died during the fighting. With the boxcar burned to the ground, there would be no way to know if any of the ore had truly been stolen.

General Cornadez had proven himself to be quite a brilliant tactician.

But there was one glaring, inescapable flaw with the entire plan: Winterhawk was going to kill them all.

He continued tracking his eyes across the inside of the dining car, finally spying his weapons. The quiver and bow case had slid against one of the far walls, while the gun belt and weapons satchel had been pinned beneath a cracked table.

Winterhawk reached for the satchel first, slinging it against his left leg, cinching the leather band tight.

Sheathed inside was a 12-inch gunstock war club crafted from an Italian Girandoni rifle that had been personally given to his great-grandfather by Meriwether Lewis. The club had been further modified by fitting the edged underside with razor-sharp whale bone.

It was a formidably dangerous weapon.

Winterhawk grabbed the gun belt next, which holstered a Model 1858 New Army Buffalo .44 Caliber single-action revolver. It had a solid-brass frame, walnut grip, octagonal barrel, and replaceable cylinders.

He cinched the gun belt firmly around his waist.

Next, he picked up the quiver and bow case, slinging it over his shoulder.

The bow itself was crafted from an Oregon Hornbeam harvested from a Malheur tree grove. Referred to as "ironwood" because of its remarkable strength, the arduous process of carving a bow from a Hornbeam required equal measures of resiliency and patience. Fitted with a bow string made from the sinew of a turtle's neck, the Hornbeam was capable of enormous power and accuracy.

Winterhawk darted back to the jagged blast hole in the dining car. Firmly grabbing the ceiling's ledge, he hoisted himself back outside the train.

General Cornadez and his hired killers had brought a fight to them today. Now, it was time for Winterhawk to bring these men a war.

CHAPTER 7

Winterhawk took in several large gulps of fresh air before the coal smoke from the steam engine invaded his lungs.

Keeping low, he ran across the top of the overturned dining car, eyes scanning the prairie for any sign of Colonel Smythe. He immediately sighted the distinctive Zouave shooters 200 yards off in the distance, their colorful wardrobe standing out against the lush green grassland.

Winterhawk could also make out the bullet-riddled corpses of the Mexican militia laid out on the prairie. It appeared to have been a one-sided slaughter.

General Cornadez was puffing energetically on a large cigar, gesturing wildly with a journal. The row of Parrott cannons was behind him, their open maws so invitingly close that he could have probably used one of them as an ashtray.

Colonel Smythe had his back turned to the ambushers. He was stoically facing the *Golden Goose*. Standing directly behind him, the Zouave sharpshooters had raised their rifles, taking careful aim.

Some rescue. At this point, it might be safe to assume that the English translation of your ancestral name should be, "Too Little, Too Late."

Winterhawk reached into the quiver and pulled out one of the five copper-tipped arrows. He stood fast atop the dining car, nocking the arrow against the bow.

Finally seeing him, Colonel Smythe saluted.

Winterhawk pulled back hard on the bow string.

The loud report of the Spenser rifles sounded like a thunderstorm going off in the prairie. The multiple blasts spun Smythe completely around, his lifeless arms whipping through the air like the limbs of a scarecrow caught in a tornado.

Cornadez guffawed loudly, taking a lengthy drag from his cigar, the crimson tip glowing brightly.

Winterhawk took aim with the arrow.

Cornadez glanced up and saw him. His eyes went wide with shock as he took an involuntary step back towards the cannons.

"Adios," Winterhawk muttered.

He released the arrow.

When fired from the 50-pound draw weight of the Hornbeam bow, a typical copper-tipped dogwood arrow shaft could travel 100- yards with targeted accuracy. But that was predicated on perfect conditions.

In this instance, the target was standing almost 200-yards away. Apart from the distance, the difficulty of the shot itself was further compounded by the ten-degree wind gust pushing directly against the arrow. That it had been fired from an elevated position meant that the arrow also needed to fly on a perfect downward trajectory without gravity driving it straight into the ground.

And then there was the target himself.

Instead of presenting himself in a directly forward line of sight that would have helped offset some of these accuracy difficulties, Ramón was positioned 200-yards southwest of the *Goose*.

The target was also in motion.

After seeing Winterhawk perched atop the train, Cornadez had taken several steps backwards, effectively throwing off the aim of any shooter who'd been counting on a stationary target.

Even factoring in all of those shifting variables, a well-trained archer could conceivably hit such a target; however, a kill shot would almost definitely be built upon old-fashioned luck.

But Winterhawk hadn't been looking for a kill shot.

He hadn't even been aiming directly at Cornadez.

And while the arrow had missed, the shot itself was perfect.

It was a bullseye.

The deadly arrow had streaked through the air and passed an inch from Cornadez's cheek. The copper tip impaled itself through the large cigar dangling from his mouth, ripping it forcefully away from his face. The arrow then flew directly inside the barrel of the nearest Parrot cannon and embedded the smoking cigar deep inside.

Cornadez realized the arrow hadn't even grazed him. Waves of relief washed over him. Before he could shout commands to the Zouave snipers, something unusual caught his full attention.

The loud *sizzle* of burning gunpowder.

And there was something else now.

The Parrott cannon that had swallowed the arrow and his cigar...

The barrel was ferociously smoking.

General Cornadez was standing directly in front of the cannon when it fired. The resulting blast vaporized his torso, limbs scattering in all directions like the seeds of a dandelion being taken apart by a strong gust of wind.

The Gasper's Prayer spun around in the air, pages fluttering like the wings of a wounded bird.

The Tiger Rifles shouted out with disgust as a crimson shower drenched their faces. Reacting quickly, they looked over to where the kill shot had originated from.

Winterhawk had already notched a second arrow on the Hornbeam and was aiming it directly at them.

Scattering like roaches from beneath an overturned rock, the Zouave began fanning out in all directions.

Winterhawk released the bow string.

One of the Zouave shooters screamed out as the arrow punctured the back of his head, the shaft pushing through his throat.

The shot knocked the man off his feet. Landing facedown, he began clawing at the arrow protruding from his neck. He started making grotesque gargling sounds, choking on his own blood.

The three remaining Zouave had stopped running. In tandem motion, each man dropped to one knee, shouldering their rifles.

Winterhawk was expecting them to return fire immediately. But they didn't. In fact, the Tiger Rifles weren't aiming at him at all. Instead, the shooters had centered their rifles on a spot somewhere to the north of the dining car.

"La boîte! La boîte!"

La boîte had an English translation.

The men were shouting about a box.

He whipped his head around, searching frantically for their new target.

What had he missed?

What box?!

And then he saw it.

The wooden case of Ketchum grenades that had been left beside the tracks. They had been placed directly in front of the overturned coal car, which was still coupled to the dining car he was standing on.

An explosion can occur inside a coal mine whenever heat reaches an air pocket that contains at least five percent methane. But a much greater heat source could cause a catastrophic detonation if a larger pile of coal dust is ever ignited. On a steam engine, if the firebox explodes, and the resulting flames should ever reach the coal car...

If your brains were dynamite, there wouldn't be enough stuffed up in there to even blow your nose. You'd best be RUNNING now instead of THINKING.

The sharpshooters opened fire, riddling the wooden case with bullets.

Winterhawk broke into a sprint, flinging the Hornbeam and quiver off the carriage as he ran. He was attempting to put as much distance between himself and the coal car before—

The remaining Ketchum grenades inside the box detonated, shooting out flames in every direction. Streams of fire rolled across the tracks as the heated air blanketed the steam engine and the overturned coal car.

Winterhawk was knocked forward by the concussive blast of the grenades. He tumbled onto the top of the dining car.

The compromised fire box inside the fallen steam engine reached critical temperature as the overworked plates finally gave way. Under the pressure of the grenade blasts, the boiler ignited as a second large explosion ripped through the air.

The front of the train was on its side when the fire tubes and the boiler each exploded, meaning that the monstrous expulsion of steam and the concussive force of the blast were forced straight downwards.

In a spectacular display of equilateral force, the concussive impact was massive enough to lift the steam engine totally off the ground.

Consumed with flames, the steam engine remained airborne for another two seconds, momentarily threatening to take the coupled coal and passenger cars up into the sky with it. Instead, the engine began to topple backwards.

Winterhawk had scrambled to his feet. He began to run wildly across the top of the dining car, arms pumping furiously.

Behind him, the flaming steam engine landed on top of the coal car with spectacular precision.

Winterhawk leaped off the edge of the carriage, body careening through the air.

With the highly combustible dust now totally blanketed by the fire from the steam engine, the coal car exploded. Like a volcano unloading magma into the sky, the blast sprayed flaming pieces of coal in all directions.

The burning shrapnel streaked through the air. One of the coal pieces lodged itself into the chest of a Zouave mercenary, boring deeply into his flesh. The burning coal torched his lungs, cooking him from the inside-out.

Winterhawk landed on the ground as the blast erupted behind him. He was shielded from the tremendous heat by the dining car itself, which was now totally enveloped with flame.

The dining car had taken the full brunt of the coal explosion. It had become uncoupled from the front half of the train. Then, it began rolling like a flaming desert tumbleweed.

Winterhawk was standing directly in the middle of the tracks. He couldn't outrun it, and there was nowhere for him to hide.

The lumbering carriage rolled along the ground like a skipped stone, the inertia momentarily bouncing it up into the air.

Winterhawk took a leaping dive towards it.

He began sliding between the tracks as the fiery dining car continued its brief airborne arc just a few terrifying feet above his head.

He felt the wave of flames move across his back, close enough to scorch his uniform before the dining car hit the ground again, bouncing noisily down the prairie.

Winterhawk rolled over between the heated rails, breath heaving in his lungs. He just needed a moment to think before--

Bullets buzzed inches above his head.

What's the matter? Did you forget all about your friends out there? They're just playing a little game of tag. But you'd better get ready, amigo. Because when those next shots ring out, looks like you're it.

Winterhawk squeezed his eyes shut, waiting for the next rifle shot, and the darkness that would swallow him whole.

CHAPTER 8

When the second pair of shots cracked through the air, the bullets impacted over twenty feet away from where Winterhawk was stretched out along the tracks.

He let out his breath with momentary relief.

The Zouave were shooting blind.

The sharpshooters could not yet pinpoint his exact position through all the billowing smoke. The Tiger Rifles knew he was somewhere along the tracks, they just didn't exactly know *where*. They were hoping the bullets would force him to give away his position so they could get in the kill shot.

These were relentless assassins, indeed.

Carefully pulling his head up from behind the tracks, Winterhawk scanned the prairie. He saw where the two men were crouched. They had taken cover behind the Parrott cannons.

He reached for the holstered Buffalo .44 caliber on his gun belt, inching it slowly from its holster.

"We only want the gold!" shouted the first Zouave sharpshooter.

Well, *that* was obvious. The question that *was not* so easily answered was if he was willing to die to protect it.

But there was another scenario left to consider: escape.

It would be easy enough for him to retreat from this battlefield. He could leave the ore to those mercenaries. And why not? He'd already put in his time. Now, he just wanted the life that he had been promised.

Promises. Your wife knows a little something about that, too. When you put on this uniform, you broke the wedding promises you'd already pledged to her. No longer were your souls eternally intertwined in a sacred marital union. Not anymore. As Chief Joseph's public relations tool, you also made Kaya recite another wedding vow: "In sickness, and in health, and until the United States Cavalry do you part."

Chief Joseph had been negotiating with the American government for years. He had been seeking lasting peace for the Nez Perce when he had offered ten of his best warriors to fight in the Civil War. In return for being one of those chosen men, Chief Joseph had promised Winterhawk's family a protected homestead.

The war itself had been easy enough to believe in. Abolishing slavery was a righteous cause, especially for his own people. The fear of the Nez Perce was that if the evils of slavery wasn't stopped with the Africans, then they would be subjugated to it themselves.

He would gladly die if it meant Kaya and Chenoa could live free.

Thus, saith Jolon Winterhawk. You might as well just close the page on this little sermon. Your too tightly wound to the past. Memories are what a starving heart feeds on. You know that better than most. Besides, you could have said no then; if you decide to run, you can still say no now.

Not a chance.

That was all wrong.

He was tasked with protecting the ore that was on this train. And if this was going to be his final mission, he would fight until the bloody end.

Another wild shot rang out.

This one was being used as cover fire, allowing the second Zouave sniper to climb to higher ground on the grassy hill behind the cannons.

Once that shooter reaches the top of that hill, you'll be more exposed down here on the tracks than a preacher's wife taking a Sunday morning bath in the baptismal tub.

Winterhawk thumbed the hammer back on the .44 Buffalo, preparing to make his move.

The second Zouave sharpshooter had taken his position atop the hill. He shouldered the Spenser, methodically tracking the rifle up and down the railroad tracks.

Still crouched behind the Parrott cannons at the base of the hill, the first Tiger Rifle tried his hand again at battlefield negotiations.

"Surrender! We won't harm you!"

Winterhawk decided to answer him.

Pointing the Buffalo .44 in the general direction of the shooters, he squeezed the trigger. The massive handgun barked loudly, the subsequent muzzle flash looking like a small bolt of lightning going off inside the dark plume of burning coal smoke.

The first Zouave mercenary reflectively jerked his body behind a Parrott cannon as the blast sounded off.

The second Zouave sniper swung the Spenser around. Zeroing in on the Buffalo's receding muzzle flash, he pulled the trigger.

Winterhawk somersaulted backwards between the railroad tracks, rolling to his feet. The impact from the rifle sprayed up gravel just a few inches away from his boots.

He stared at the three train carriages laying on their sides more than a hundred feet away from him: passenger car, boxcar, and caboose.

He needed to get to that boxcar.

Winterhawk launched himself forward across the tracks.

The first Zouave shooter had already reacted to the sudden movement and was shouldering his rifle from behind the Parrott. He centered the barrel onto his moving target and fired.

Winterhawk was just breaking into a full sprint as the first shooter's bullet tugged hard at the right shoulder of his uniform. The shot tore open the fabric above his arm, but didn't graze his skin.

The second Zouave sniper began methodically tracking his target.

Winterhawk could feel the man's rifle on him as he ran. He was now only three dozen feet from the boxcar. It might as well have been a mile.

Winterhawk gripped the Buffalo tightly in his right hand, body tensing in anticipation of the gunshot that would surely come streaking down on him in just mere seconds.

The Zouave perched on the hill had one eye squeezed shut as he aimed. He curled his finger around the trigger.

"Adieu..." the mercenary said, firing the Spenser.

As the shot rang out, Winterhawk shifted directions. Hopping over the rails, he began running directly *towards* the Tiger Rifles.

The bullet from the second shooter pinged against the tracks, striking the exact area where Winterhawk would have been just a split second later. The slug sparked as it ricocheted harmlessly through the air.

Winterhawk continued sprinting towards the two French mercenaries. His wild maneuver had taken the snipers by surprise. They had expected him to keep running away, not to make a beeline straight for them.

He could see both of the Zouave shooters quickly shifting their rifles. In the very next heartbeat, they would unload hellfire down upon him.

But incredibly, Winterhawk fired first.

While the Model 1858 New Army Buffalo .44 Caliber was a powerful single-shot revolver, it was not designed for taking down long-range targets. Not only was its intimidating 3-pound heft engineered for a shooter with amazing hand dexterity and upper arm strength, but the 141-grain round ball bullets produced 500 foot-pounds of muzzle-energy when fired.

That meant it delivered one hell of a kick for even a two-fisted shooter experienced with taking out a stationary target. But in this particular instance, it was not the target that was stubbornly refusing to remain stationary.

The shooter was the one who was in motion.

Winterhawk had sprinted off the tracks with the revolver raised up at shoulder level. The adjustable rear ramp sight had already been lifted, but the octagonal blue barrel was bouncing too much from the momentum to get a proper bead on his targets.

But even if Winterhawk had been able to fire off a perfectly aimed shot, there was still the factor of the target's distance to consider.

While dependent on both the conical bullet weight and the quality of the powder charge, the Buffalo's cartridge velocity averaged over 900-feet per second. The Model 1858 was also fitted with a standard 8-inch barrel length, with the loading lever doubling as a retainer for the six-shot cylinder axis pin.

The Buffalo .44 provided an effective shooting distance of no greater than 110 feet; however, the Zouave mercenaries were stationed nearly 200 feet away the moment Winterhawk had veered off the railroad tracks.

That meant that the first shot from the Buffalo had no chance of reaching them. But he was betting on the fact that the mercenaries wouldn't have time to ponder bullet velocity and distance accuracy. Instead, he had been banking on the two men reactively seeking cover as the .44 began unloading at them.

And that's precisely how things played out.

The two Zouave snipers jerked backwards as the massive boom from the .44 echoed across the prairie, their Spenser rifles momentarily pulled away from their prior firing positions.

The Model 1858 was a single-shot revolver, which meant that firing while running was made even more difficult because the Buffalo required the hammer to be cocked for each shot. He needed to not only hold the 3-pound weapon with his right hand and fire it, but he also needed his left hand to cock the hammer for another shot.

Only five seconds had passed since Winterhawk had left the tracks and turned towards them in a dead sprint. But a lot could happen in five seconds.

For the Tiger Rifles, the first several shots from the Buffalo had been nothing but a bluff tactic. They had reacted instinctively to being fired upon, quickly realizing that the range of the revolver wasn't a threat to them.

And that was their critical mistake.

In the span of five seconds, Winterhawk had now gotten within 100 feet of the mercenaries.

Close enough now to place him within perfect firing range.

Centering the rear ramp sight on the first Zouave shooter, he fired the Buffalo once again.

In his attempt to get a cleaner shot, the first Zouave sniper had moved from his original position. He was now standing between the row of cannons instead of shielding himself behind them.

He cried out as the 141-grain bullet from the Buffalo savagely tore into his left thigh. The impact of the bullet ripped out a palm-sized chunk of his upper leg, exposing the shockingly white femur bone underneath.

As the man staggered backwards from the force of the bullet's impact, he let loose with a high-pitch scream as the weight of his upper body was placed on the damaged leg.

Winterhawk fired again.

The man took the full force of the next shot in his face. In a spectacular explosion of dark crimson gore, the powerful .44 tore his chin completely off. The blast vaporized his entire face from the nose down, leaving nothing behind but a yawning flesh crater below two terrified eyes.

The man collapsed into a dead heap.

The second Zouave shooter had now centered the Spenser on his charging target, finger squeezing the trigger.

But once again, Winterhawk fired first.

The Buffalo roared in his hand, the muzzle flash licking the air like venom expelled from a metallic snake.

The mercenary cried out in frustration as the bullet tore into the Spenser. The impact splintered the oak stock, ripping the rifle from his hands, sending it spinning through the air.

Dropping the empty Buffalo, Winterhawk vaulted atop one of the nearest Parrott cannons, using it as a springboard to launch himself high into the air.

Reacting quickly, the Zouave unsheathed a 9-inch Bowie knife.

While in midflight, Winterhawk pulled out the 12-inch Girandoni that had been fastened against his left thigh. He landed a few feet in front of the mercenary, the razor-sharp whale bone on the war club glinting in the sunlight.

"Lutin..." the Zouave sneered.

You know that one pretty well, don't you, chief?

Lutin.

It was the French word for brownie. One of the many derogatory terms that Winterhawk had heard on the battlefield that had been used to denigrate Native Americans.

Brownies.

Brown-skinned.

Winterhawk shook his head in mock disappointment. "And to think, I was really hoping that we would become friends."

The man snarled, parrying with the Bowie, right arm thrusting with a quick jabbing motion.

Winterhawk had noticed that the Zouave had thrust with his right arm, but shifted all his balance onto his left leg. The man was feigning with the jab, expecting his opponent to step sideways, moving away from the slashing knife to protect himself.

The real attack would come just after that.

The man was planning to pivot fully on his left leg, bringing the Bowie sideways in a hacking motion that would have savagely opened up Winterhawk's ribcage.

It was an obvious first strike.

Winterhawk let the Zouave extend his right arm as he dutifully moved to the left, allowing the man to believe that he had just stepped right into his trap.

Still in motion, he placed the weight of his body completely on his heels, giving the impression that the thrusting blade had forced him into an unbalanced striking position.

Totally shifting his body weight onto his left leg, the mercenary swung hard with the Bowie.

As he rocked backwards on his heels, Winterhawk began to pivot, his left foot digging hard into the grass as he swung his right leg around. The move effectively twisted his entire body in the opposite direction of the slashing knife.

The Bowie flashed through the air, missing its flesh target by less than three inches. The Zouave had lunged hard during that maneuver, so impacting with nothing but air made him lose his footing for a brief second. He took one stumbling step forward as Winterhawk finished his pivot and was now standing directly behind the mercenary.

Lifting the Girandoni high above his shoulder, Winterhawk swung it down hard. The blunt edge of the war club caught the Zouave's extended knife arm, shattering the humerus bone upon impact.

Screaming shrilly, the man dropped the Bowie, staring helplessly down at the fractured bone now poking out from the flesh of his arm.

Winterhawk swung the Girandoni again, this time leading with the razor-sharp whale bone on the underside of the weapon.

The first blow from the club had destroyed the man's arm.

The second one removed his head.

. . .

WINTERHAWK SLOWLY MADE his way down the hill overlooking the Parrott cannons. He'd been enjoying the false tranquility of silence that had totally enveloped the prairie. It was a brief respite from the explosions and the gunshots and the—

Screaming.

Screams from the men he couldn't save from getting killed; screams from the men he couldn't stop from doing the killing.

He understood every soldier experienced war differently. It might be the same brain matter splattered across tree trunks, or the same coil of intestines lying in a steaming pile on the battlefield, but each man who sees these atrocities does so with a different pair of eyes.

That's the true curse of humanity. It isn't in what we see or what we do; it's all wrapped up in what we remember. In the end, memory is the war that every soldier eventually loses.

Seeing the Model 1858 laying in the grass, Winterhawk bent down and picked it up. While holstering it, something else in the field caught his eye.

He shook his head in mild disbelief.

Fire from the decimated coal car had continued to burn a wide swath of prairie grass more than a hundred feet away from the railroad tracks. But the Hornbeam bow had landed atop a cluster of rocks in the middle of all that grass, leaving it miraculously untouched by the flames.

Winterhawk made his way towards the bow and safely retrieved it from the fire.

Turning away from the field, he focused his attention onto the toppled boxcar. The loading door had sheared off during the crash, revealing dozens of straw bags stuffed with the unrefined ore.

There was over a million dollars' worth of pulverized rocks stashed inside those bags. When the *Goose* did not arrive at the White Salmon Blockhouse, the Army would send troops to scour the tracks until the train was located. It would take several days for them to find the *Goose*; perhaps even longer.

He needed to be prepared to wait things out. He would guard the gold from potential marauders until those reinforcements showed up.

And then he heard something that changed his mind.

It was coming from the direction of the woods behind the Parrott cannons. Several horses neighing. They sounded nervous; abandoned.

He understood what it meant.

Those horses must have belonged to the ambushers. After crippling the *Goose*, General Cornadez would have had a plan. He would have needed a way to escape.

The ambushers had arrived on horseback. They also would have needed several wagons to transport the cannons and the grenades. They must have been planning on using those same wagons to whisk away the stolen gold.

That gave Winterhawk an idea.

He had formulated a plan that would enable him to still complete the mission. It was as unorthodox as it was risky.

But it was all he had.

You're a rare breed, partner, soon to be made extinct. At least your father had enough sense to cut-and-run. But not you, amigo. You gotta play soldier instead of playing it smart.

Winterhawk began making his way towards the woods. He kept to a leisurely stride. There was no need to hurry. He had a huge task still ahead of him.

He sighed, feeling the ebb and ache of his muscles as his body began to unwind from the last few hours. He wanted to return to that hill and stretch out in the cool, soft grass. He desperately needed to rest.

Instead, he pushed himself forward into the tree line.

He thought once again of his plan.

It was going to be a very long night indeed.

CHAPTER 9

Nelscott Flume and Lumber Company
Buncombe, Oregon
1873

It would be a painful death.

Taking a satisfying step away from the heavy logging jack, Graham felt a hot flash of excitement blooming in the pit of his stomach. He had to press the back of his hand against his mouth to stifle a giggle.

Graham took a quick glance over his shoulder, peering through the pitch-black darkness to make sure that Holliger hadn't been standing behind him.

He saw nothing but the inky blackness of a night sky delicately offset by a nearly full moon. The silhouette of hundreds of trees crowding up against the hillside of the small timber community of Buncombe stretched out for miles around him.

But his oldest friend hadn't been standing there. For this, he let out a sigh of relief. If Holliger *had* been watching him, had heard his boyish giggles, Graham would have mumbled a half-assed apology about tipping back too much of the bottle earlier.

But Holliger hadn't been looming. He was probably still tampering with the Holbeer Steam Donkey and Grafton Crane. Ever since he had been fired from his job as a donkeyman last year, Holliger had been absolutely consumed with thoughts of revenge.

Graham returned his attention to the heavy logging jack, admiring the delicate act of sabotage he had just performed on it. The jack wouldn't collapse when hefting the first log, and probably wouldn't even buckle while hoisting up the second. But by the third, it would most definitely bend and break. And whomever was operating it would be crushed by a thousand pounds of timber.

At the thought of this, Graham felt another giggle welling up inside of him. This time, he didn't try to conceal it.

· · ·

IN THE OLD days, loggers would topple trees and use horse teams to drag the timber down from the mountains and into the rivers. This mode of transportation ended up being such a dangerous activity that a third of all American loggers ended up losing their lives in the process.

But help for the lumberjacks would soon be on the way.

With the advent of the steam engine and the mass introduction of the railroads into the western regions of the United States, the entire logging industry ended up taking a massive leap of innovation in the early part of the 19th century.

While it was the locomotive industry that was primarily responsible for the economic advancement of America during the 1800s, the single most profitable post-Civil War business enterprise was the saw mills.

For the majority of logging areas throughout the United States, the locomotive was crucial in its success because it allowed for safe transportation of enormous loads of timber to the waiting mills.

But in Oregon, most of the logging had been done in mountainous areas where railroad tracks had yet to be placed. With the largest mills often found near the Pacific Ocean, a new way to transport the logs from the harvest areas to the mills was needed.

The solution had been flumes.

Flumes were V-shaped wood structures that led from the logging area to the loading platforms. In most cases, flumes used a separate water source that buoyed the logs and pushed them down the structure. Once they had been deposited in the water staging area, it was up to the river rapids to finish guiding those logs to the mills.

The one operated by the Nelscott Lumber Company was the largest flume in the Cascade Mountains. Built 20-feet above the ground, it ran for an impressive half-mile before feeding into the loading platform built on the bank of the Rogue River. This particular flume was continually fed from a tall waterfall on the Nelscott property.

While it dramatically sped up the process of bringing fallen trees off the mountains and to the waterways, the biggest challenges the Nelscott loggers faced with the flume was how to load the logs safely onto them.

The answer would come through an innovative twist on the steam engine.

In the latter half of the 19th Century, the donkey steam engine was the next major technological application of the American industrial revolution. The invention of the steam-powered donkey engine made high-volume, mechanized logging possible, which ushered in the modern lumber era.

The pride and joy of the Nelscott Flume Company was the Holbeer Mini Steam Donkey. Standing fully upright at 20-feet and weighing over 5000 pounds, the machine was a twenty-horsepower rig. The Holbeer also had the capacity of extending 2,100 feet of rope, giving it the ability to pull heavy trunks up the steep mountain slope to the flume.

Mounted onto the side of the Holbeer was a steam-powered Grafton crane. Built upon a separate base with a simple wench control, the Grafton was capable of hoisting those massive tree trunks deposited by the steam donkey and lifting them up onto the flume. By utilizing the same type of steam shovel mechanism employed in so many of the cranes found in railroad lumber yards across the country, the Grafton could lift several thousand pounds of timber with relative ease.

Taken together, these were the technological marvels of their age.

. . .

IT HAD BEEN just over a year now since Holliger had been employed as a donkeyman. He had been operating this particular Holbeer while being brazenly intoxicated, which had resulted in a tragic accident. His actions had permanently crippled a lumberjack named Simon Pensley, a widower with a young daughter, Vickie.

Because of what he had done, Holliger had been fired. But if the company thought that would be the very last time they would see him, they were soon to discover that they were dead wrong.

Holliger glanced over at the long metal ladder fastened to the large dual rig. How many days and nights had he scampered up and down that ladder like a drunken primate? More times than he could count, and definitely more times than he'd like to remember.

He stared down at the large wrench he was holding, the slightest hint of a smile twitching across the corners of his mouth.

Both the steam donkey and the Grafton crane tended to break down under the strenuous demands of the logging industry.

In particular, the crane's pincer cable was widely known to snap in the field during a long stretch of log pulls. This was especially true if the cable had become loosened, which would put many lives at risk.

He grinned at the thought.

He felt no remorse for the act of sabotage he'd just committed.

Sometime soon, the cable attached to the Grafton would be unable to hold its load. Whomever was standing below the crane at the time would find themselves crushed by a thousand pounds of--

A sudden rush of wind brushed against his face.

Holliger turned his head sharply, eyes scanning the shadowy tree line flanking him. He squinted hard into the inky blackness, eyes boring into the shadows.

Graham. The dumb bastard had probably gotten lost. He must be stumbling drunkenly through the woods, searching for--

The surrounding air became thick with a revolting odor. Holliger's nostrils were filled with a darkly pungent aroma swirling around the platform.

After deeply inhaling the sickening smell, he felt immediately nauseated. The pungent odor wafting through the air was animalistic, savage...

Primal.

The wrench dropped from his grasp as he instinctively reached for the holstered Colt Peacemaker strapped to his waist. His fingers tugged at the handle as he tried to dissect every looming shadow of the forest.

Without warning, one of the trees *moved*.

Holliger sensed it even before his eyes could register what he had seen. Something absolutely massive had been crouching in the forest, its formidable shape blended against a tree trunk.

But now, it had shifted position.

It was moving towards him.

Fast.

Holliger felt abject terror consume him as he realized that the massive shadow was actually some sort of wild creature. He caught a flash of crimson eyes and twin rows of horrible teeth, but his mind was trying to make sense of something else.

Whatever the animal was, it was coming at him on two legs.

And it was *running*.

"Oh, dear God..."

Holliger finally pulled the Colt from its holster, feeling the weight of the handgun in his trembling hand. He raised the weapon at the rushing blackness.

He had no time to fire.

The impact felt like he had just been clipped by a locomotive. The air was torn from his lungs, the Colt flying from his grasp. His right shoulder was painfully dislocated as he felt his arm being yanked forcefully over his head.

He had a sudden, sickening realization.

When the massive shape had barreled directly into him, it had its trunk-like arms outstretched. It hadn't wanted to knock him off his feet. The impact had been a calculated attack.

It had wanted to grab him.

The creature now had a secure grip on his arm and was dragging him through the forest with remarkable speed. Holliger began kicking his legs wildly against the ground as he was pulled headlong into the blackness of the woods.

Through the disorientating madness of the last few seconds, he understood something else about what was yanking him across the ground.

What was holding onto his arm wasn't a claw.

It was more like a giant hand.

The creature squeezed him tighter. The hairy palm emanated an incredible heat as its long fingers curled around his skin like a vice.

Holliger felt himself being forcefully pulled away from the forest and yanked into an overgrown thicket of bushes. Then, he was falling into darkness as a large hole hidden in the muddy ground opened up to swallow him alive.

Holliger let out a shrill scream that faded into oblivion as he tumbled down into utter blackness.

. . .

GRAHAM WASN'T AFRAID because he had just heard a scream. What chilled him to his very core was he knew that the scream belonged to Holliger.

In the midst of sabotaging a second timber jack, he pulled himself away from the task, cocking his head up towards the dark shape of the steam donkey looming a hundred feet away.

"Holliger?!"

He heard another scream, but this one seemed even more distant; muffled.

Graham bolted fast towards the elevated platform of the Grafton crane, his heart hammering. He heard his own boots crunching loudly against the leaves, breath hitched in his throat as he ran.

Graham bounded beneath the platform, head whipping around, eyes peering up into the darkness.

There was no sign of Holliger.

Anywhere.

"Holliger? Where are--? "

Something caught his attention on the ground near the platform ladder. It glinted beneath the full moonlight.

Holliger's revolver.

The Colt had been left behind, unfired.

Graham felt icicles of fear trickle through his veins. He stumbled away from beneath the large crane, cupping his hands over his mouth, yelling into the dark expanse of forest crowding all around him.

"Holliger! Holliger!"

He was answered with another scream.

Graham whipped his head around towards the sound. It had come from somewhere from the east of the flume. Only a few hundred feet away.

He bent down and retrieved the fallen Colt. "Holliger! Hold on! I'm coming!"

Gripping onto the handgun, Graham began running towards the direction of the last scream. The chilled night air on his face exacerbated the growing coldness of fear that was seeping out through his skin.

He was trying to make sense of what danger awaited him out in the darkness. Had Holliger been attacked by a bear? Or stalked by a mountain lion? He had heard horrifying stories of loggers who had disturbed animal lairs and had paid for it with their lives.

He imagined his friend huddled somewhere in the dark woods up ahead; body savagely mauled, slowly bleeding out from a fatal attack wound.

His thoughts were so consumed with these frightening possibilities that he didn't take notice of where his feet were landing while he was running. He didn't see the deep grooves in the ground that had been made from Holliger's body being dragged across the dirt.

Even with the moonlight illuminating enough of the forest so that he could successfully navigate his way between the trees without tripping on exposed roots, Graham didn't see the opening in the ground that awaited him behind a large cluster of bushes.

One moment he was crunching loudly across solid ground, and the next, there was no more soil beneath his feet.

Graham fell into a gaping hole in the forest terrain, the Colt flying from his grasp, arms pinwheeling wildly.

The fall itself seemed like an eternity; in reality, it was only a three second tumble through space.

He landed face down onto an unforgiving stone floor, the sudden impact clicking his mouth shut with jarring force. His teeth clamped down hard onto his tongue, completely severing it in half.

Opening his mouth to scream with pain, Graham felt the wet remains of his tongue plop sickly down onto the ground beneath his bleeding face. It glistened wetly like a large slug.

Graham wretched at the sight, vomiting blood. He felt excruciating pain, like the inside of his mouth had been doused with kerosene and lit on fire.

With one hand over his mouth to stymie the steady flow of blood, he pushed himself up off the ground until he had regained his wobbly footing.

Graham realized he was standing at the end of a large cavern. The dark maw of a tunnel stretched out behind him, vanishing at the edge of the moonlight. He could hear the distinctive roar of the flume's waterfall echoing somewhere off in the distance.

"Graham..."

He whirled towards the voice. It had come from Holliger.

He saw the crumpled form of his friend wedged up against one of the cavern walls. His head was lolled over against his right shoulder, the jagged tip of his broken collarbone protruding from his skin. His right arm was missing, strips of ragged flesh dangling over the hole where it had been ripped from his body.

"...eating me..."

Graham stared at him in horror.

Eating?

And suddenly, Graham heard it.

The sickening sound of crunching bone became louder than the roar of the distant waterfall. This was followed by a grotesque chewing noise, as if large chunks of flesh were being ravenously consumed.

This was followed by a deafening silence.

Then, an object was tossed carelessly at his feet.

He looked down, eyes going wide with terror. It was Holliger's severed arm, the flesh nearly picked clean from the bone.

A dark shape was making its way towards him. It was massive, covered in thick hair, standing over eight feet tall. It let loose a ferocious growl, flashing a row of needle-like teeth in his direction.

It looked like a monster.

The creature pounced at Holliger, moving with startling speed. Burrowing its fingers deep into his chest, he cracked open Holliger's sternum and began pulling out giant handfuls of flesh.

Graham heard loud screaming before he realized it was his own.

He turned away from the horrific sight of the monster feeding, his mind reeling. There was a tunnel somewhere behind him. The roaring sound of the flume's waterfall wasn't too far away. If he could somehow reach it, he could escape.

He took a step forward, then stopped.

He smelled a pungent odor emanating from out of the blackness of the tunnel. He could hear a low growl and the unmistakable sound of heavy, lumbering footfalls. Whatever it was, it was coming in his direction.

His stomach clenched with fear.

There was now a second monster prowling inside the cave.

Graham saw the crimson eyes first.

Then he saw the teeth.

And a moment later, he saw nothing at all.

CHAPTER 10

Malheur Indian Reservation
Eastern Oregon
1872

Jolon Winterhawk crouched low behind the massive shape of a fallen Douglas fir, eyes scanning the thick underbrush. He cocked his head, muscles tensed with anticipation. His body was primed to bolt from the cover of the tree at the slightest hint of danger.

He waited for a strong gust of wind to push its way through the forest. He used the loud rustle of branches to mask the sound of his own heavy footfalls as he stepped away from behind the fallen tree.

He needed to seek higher ground. It would provide him a better line of sight through the dense foliage that—

Winterhawk stopped moving.

He felt that he was no longer alone in the woods.

Head cocked, he heard the distinct snap of a low-hanging tree branch crumpling beneath the weight of something far too heavy to support it. The sound had come from ten yards southwest of his position.

Digging the heels of his boots into the soil, he spun around, dipping his body down into a crouch, attempting to throw off the aim of his attacker.

He was a half-second too late.

Winterhawk heard the incoming *whoosh* of air hurtling towards him from the tree line a moment before he felt the stinging impact.

It was a direct hit into the dead center mass of his chest.

He knew it was all over...

He dipped his head down, solemnly watching as the large pinecone dropped to the ground between his feet.

Smiling, he looked up towards the tree line. "That was a very lucky shot, Chenoa. I guess our pinecone war is over."

"You can't talk!" Chenoa scolded him from her hiding place in the forest. "You're dead!"

He smiled again, making a show of brushing off the dirt the pinecone had made on his shirt. "How did you find me so fast? I had a fifteen-minute head start."

"It wasn't hard, Papa. You were trampling through the woods like an expecting *ya-ka*."

Winterhawk threw his head back and laughed. "Are you calling me a pregnant bear?"

Chenoa giggled as she scrambled down from her tree perch, tightly clutching the slingshot that had just been used to bullseye her father. A bandolier was slung sash-style over her small shoulders, the leather pouches filled with pinecones.

"No," she replied, dropping to the ground. "You actually sounded more like a raccoon trapped inside a rolling tumbleweed."

Winterhawk grinned again, running a hand across his sweaty forehead. "How old are you now, Chenoa?"

His daughter let her mouth drop in faux shock. "I'm six; almost seven!" She placed both hands on her hips, firing him a look of totally righteous indignation. "As. If. You. Didn't. Know."

Winterhawk could see his wife reflected in that stance. He had faced the same mannerisms from Kaya many times. Seeing his wife now so perfectly mirrored in their daughter made his heart ache.

Chenoa cast him a quizzical look, brow scrunched with confusion. "Why did you want to know my age, anyway?"

"Because I was planning on making you a deal."

"Really?" She responded excitedly; single eyebrow arched with obvious mistrust. "What kind of a deal?"

"If you ever want to see that seventh birthday, you might let me win at pinecone wars next time."

Chenoa shook her head, sliding the slingshot into a makeshift holster strapped to her belt. "You know something, Papa? The Creator should have made you into a mountain."

"Why's that?"

"Because you're hill-arious!"

Winterhawk groaned at her horrible quip, but broke into deep laughter. Chenoa tried her hardest not to smile, but soon she was lost in the throes of a contagious giggle. Their combined laughter echoed across the forest for several long minutes.

It was a moment that he wished could have lasted forever.

Glancing down at his daughter, he felt the laughter drain from his face. It was the realization that all of this *wouldn't* last that finally stole the moment from him.

Winterhawk grimaced when he imagined saying a tearful goodbye to his wife and daughter all over again. This 30-day furlough from his Cavalry duties was all too brief.

The last time, Chenoa was too young to remember; this time, she was old enough to never forget.

Chenoa let her giggle fade into silence. Her large eyes took in her father's troubled features. "What's wrong, Papa?"

He cast his sad gaze down upon her. "I'm just hungry," he answered. "We'd better go home and get some breakfast."

His daughter nodded dutifully as they began walking together back through the forest. The dense canopy of foliage offered relief from the beating sun, while a cool breeze mopped the sweat from their faces.

They walked in silence for a few minutes, but Winterhawk knew his daughter was only momentarily lost in her own thoughts. Chenoa kept glancing up at him, acting as if there were a thousand questions running through her mind. In the end, she settled on asking only one.

"Papa, do you like it here?"

He unconsciously bristled at the question.

Here.

The word itself hung heavy in the air like a hovering boulder.

Even a six-year-old could sense that the Malheur Indian Reservation wasn't their home. For thousands of people in the Northern Paiute and Nez Perce tribes, it had become their corral.

By the end of 1871, President Grant had negotiated a treaty with Chief Weahwewa and Chief Joseph and sectioned off nearly three thousand square miles of federally protected land in Southeastern Oregon to induce hundreds of displaced Native Americans to settle there. It was the hope of President Grant that it would reduce the conflicts that had been building between those tribes and the hundreds of settlers whose ranches continued to encroach onto their territory.

The Malheur Indian Reservation was 1,462,400 acres of beautiful Oregon forest and sprawling farmland. The combined majesty of the Snake River and the Columbia River provided a bountiful migration of salmon, while ten thousand head of bison still roamed the vast prairies.

Yes, the Malheur Reservation was certainly many things.

But it wasn't home.

Chenoa was right. It was just...*here*.

"It doesn't quite feel like home yet, but I think Chief Joseph wants us to make the best of it."

Chenoa frowned. "He expects a lot."

"He's doing everything he can to keep our people safe. We have to continue to trust him, Chenoa."

Chenoa glanced up at him, eyes flashing briefly with anger.

"I heard the elders talking with momma a few weeks ago. They asked me to leave so they could talk with her alone, but they were whispering loud enough that a deaf groundhog could have heard them."

Winterhawk felt a knot of anger beginning to balloon in the pit of his stomach.

Why would Kaya have taken a private meeting with the elders? Those men knew better than to involve her with any tribal concerns. Leaving his family in peace was part of the arrangement he had made with Tuekakas when he had first enlisted in the Army. The elder Joseph had given him his solemn promise that Kaya and Chenoa would be shielded from that sort of harassment.

"Really, Chenoa? What were the elders discussing with your mother?"

"You, Papa; they were talking about *you*."

He felt the white-hot stab of rage explode behind his eyes. His fists involuntarily clenched. Somewhere high above him in the trees, several jays squawked loudly and took flight, as if somehow sensing his rage.

Chenoa noticed it, too. She soaked in his hard features, lips pursed into white slits. "I'm sorry."

Winterhawk took in a deep breath. When he could no longer feel his heartbeat throbbing in his temples, he glanced down at her, offering a reassuring smile.

"You did nothing wrong in telling me. I promise you that. Now, do you remember exactly what those men were talking about with your mother?"

"You mean, what they were saying about you?"

"Yes."

Chenoa scrunched her nose as she dredged up the memory.

"Well, they were talking about how long you've been away from home. Momma told 'em it didn't bother her none, that she was proud of everything you were doing for the Nez Perce people by 'listing in the Cavalry."

Chenoa began fidgeting nervously with the pinecone bandolier. Both cheeks flushed red as the next memory unceremoniously dropped back into the rotation of her thoughts. Whatever had transpired next, it was painfully obvious that his daughter didn't want to tell him.

But he had to know.

"Go on. It's alright."

His daughter nodded. She kept her eyes focused on the winding forest trail ahead, and away from his piercing gaze.

"I didn't hear every single word everyone was sayin' in there, Papa, but I *did* hear what they said that made momma throw 'em all out. You shoulda *seen* how mad she was. After she started cussing and hollering, those elders got out of our tipi so fast you might have thought they had trampled into a bee hive."

Winterhawk had no difficulty imagining how this scenario had played out. He had been on the receiving end of his wife's fiery temper on many occasions.

Chenoa returned her gaze to the forest trail. They could see thin wisps of campfire smoke snaking towards the sky. "Almost home!" Chenoa exclaimed, noticeably quickening her pace.

He shifted rationales around in his mind until what might have been wrong a few minutes before now looked right. He decided he could hate himself later for it. But right now, he just *had* to know.

"I bet you can't even remember what those men said to get momma all riled up like that. You were probably too busy chasing butterflies."

Chenoa spun around, returning to the hands-on-hips stance she had so aptly displayed earlier. She began flinging words at him like a barrage of stones skipped across the river.

"They called you a fruit, Papa! If you *really* must know! Those stupid men said you were play-acting as a soldier. They thought you shouldn't be fighting in the white man's Army. They called you an apple!"

"The elders called me an apple--?"

"Yes! Momma got so angry. Chased those men right out of our tipi like they were stink bugs!"

Winterhawk felt another flush of anger course through him.

Those sanctimonious bastards didn't know the first thing about the sacrifices he'd made. They didn't understand everything he had done. Only his wife understood. And in the end, her support was the only thing that mattered.

Winterhawk reached down and scooped up Chenoa around the waist, hugging her tightly against him. He pulled her close and kissed her on the cheek. "I love you so much, Chenoa. Never forget that."

"I love you, too," she replied, kissing his own cheek in return.

"Let's race home," Winterhawk said, gently setting her down. "The loser has to finish all the morning chores—blindfolded!"

Chenoa giggled. "Deal!"

Winterhawk's smile evaporated as he heard a sound emanating from somewhere on the eastern side of the forest. It was unmistakable.

Howls.

He felt a strange pulling sensation coming from inside of him, almost as if his body was tugging at his subconscious, telling it that time was up.

He wanted to fight against it, but he knew he couldn't.

The reality was already fading into memory.

The howls intensified.

Scrunching her nose at the noise, Chenoa turned towards the trees. "Papa, that sounds like--"

CHAPTER 11

CloudTrail Railway Pass
Cascade Mountain Range
1873

"...wolves!"

Winterhawk awoke with his daughter's voice still echoing through his head. He could feel Chenoa standing close to him through the hazy fog of dreams.

He was momentarily disorientated; his pulsating heartbeat pounding hard against his temples like war drums. It was like all of it was still happening right now, not some fragmented recollection from last year.

The haze of sleep dissipated from his vision. The dream had vanished. And once again, Chenoa was gone.

But the howling of the wolves remained.

Winterhawk scrambled to his feet, boots sinking low into the lush prairie grass. The morning sun was already mercilessly battering down against his skin; sweat beads thickly collecting on the back of his neck like insects.

He cursed himself for sleeping through the sunrise.

Go easy on yourself, amigo. Not even John Henry himself could have unloaded fifty bags of ore from that boxcar without taking himself a little nap afterwards. Besides, it ain't like you could have asked for help; what, with everyone being dead and all.

While the intense carriage fires from the *Golden Goose* had nearly abated by the following morning after the attack, the flames had provided him more than enough illumination throughout the night for the arduous task of removing the bags of gold from the boxcar.

After confiscating one of Cornadez's supply wagons and two horses from the woods, Winterhawk had loaded half of the ore bags into the covered wagon.

He had decided that the remaining twenty-five bags were to remain hidden right here on the prairie. This was done in case he was ambushed while taking half the ore to the White Salmon Blockhouse. If that happened, at least the attackers wouldn't get their hands on all the gold that the soldiers had died protecting.

That's the sage and noble answer. Now, between us old friends, what's the real one? Why did you hide half of the loot?

Security.

There was the possibility that those bootlickers at White Salmon would not think kindly upon the fact that the sole survivor of this military massacre was an Indian. Knowing the location of the rest of the gold might go a long way towards--

Blackmailing?

--influencing them not to renege on that promise of discharge that would be sending him home.

More howls sounded across the prairie.

The wolves were definitely getting closer.

He reached for the Spenser rifle propped up against a nearby boulder. He had taken it from one of the Zouave corpses before utter exhaustion had forced him to rest. He remembered promising himself just a few hours of sleep before he had drifted into unconsciousness.

He had obviously broken that promise.

Hefting the rifle, he felt the throbbing ache of his shoulders. His body was apparently displeased with the previous night's exertions.

He could hear the nervous neighing coming from the two horses. They were both tied to a pair of Parrott mountain cannons. The gold-laden supply wagon had been parked nearby.

More howls. Much closer than the ones before. That meant the pack leader was getting closer.

Although wolves are typically nocturnal hunters, the influx of white settlers into their land had disrupted those instincts. Disruption had made them unpredictable.

And wolves weren't the only species who'd adapted.

Circling high above the train wreckage was a trio of bald eagles, their high-pitch squawks echoing across the landscape. While he had never known them to attack a human, he'd once witnessed two eagles take down a mountain lion as they fought over the remains of an elk carcass.

Another long howl.

The pack leader was ringing the dinner bell for the rest of the pack.

Winterhawk looked at the corpses scattered around the landscape. He didn't care if those wolves wanted to gnaw the bones of the ambushers, but they would not strip any flesh from the dead soldiers. And they sure as hell would not desecrate the corpse of Colonel Smythe. Not on his watch.

Winterhawk moved swiftly towards the twisted remains of the coal car.

He considered it luck that the wind was pushing the thick smoke to the southwest, directly towards the area of the forest where the howls were emanating from. By moving into a position behind the simmering coal fire, he was hoping the black smoke would mask his scent.

Taking a knee, Winterhawk shouldered the Spenser. He swung the barrel around, sighting it on the wooded area behind the horses.

His pulse suddenly raced as he felt the proximity of the wolf.

Movement.

Speed.

Hunger.

The pack leader had edged out of the forest clearing and had found his way onto the grassy hill overlooking the Parrot cannons. The wolf was enormous, his body flanking the wagon, eyes locked onto the two horses, muscular body poised to attack.

Winterhawk felt ice course through his veins, realizing that he had been fast asleep near that same hill just a few minutes ago. Had he not woken from that dream exactly when he did...

Winterhawk quickly shifted the rifle.

The wolf unleashed a savage growl, body propelling forward. His head immediately vanished in a shocking spray of crimson vapor as the report from the Spenser sounded loudly.

The dead wolf tumbled down the hill, coming to rest against one of the Parrot cannons.

Agitated howls crept out from the forest.

Winterhawk lowered the rifle and regained his footing.

He was confident that the rest of the pack wouldn't venture into the prairie until well after nightfall. By then, he should already be several hours into the wagon-bound journey.

Winterhawk calculated he was 100 miles away from the White Salmon Blockhouse. Given the fact the horses would be pulling a heavily laden supply wagon through rugged wilderness terrain, he would be lucky to cover 20 miles each day.

Those Army boys won't just be standing around scratching their prairie oysters when that train doesn't arrive. They are going to look pretty hard for the gold, and even harder when it comes for someone to blame.

Winterhawk understood the protocol.

When the *Goose* did not reach White Salmon within a day of its expected arrival, the Army would dispatch various search parties to find it.

If he just holed up here, they would probably locate him in less than three days.

But that presented its own set of risks.

There were marauders canvassing the land for treasure like ants swarming for crumbs beneath a picnic table. The black coal smoke burning off the corpse of the *Goose* was a stark reminder of how just a handful of dangerous men had derailed a military train and slaughter everyone on board.

While he had fended off the ambushers, there was certainly the danger of a second attack being sprung against him. He figured it wouldn't take much for a gang of thieves to notice the coal smoke and follow it to its source. If he stayed behind to guard all the gold, there was the possibility of finding himself outmanned and outgunned.

No, it was much more dangerous to stay. And besides, his final mission had been to escort the gold.

He was a soldier. He had been given his orders.

So, he had formulated a plan fraught with risks and dangers, but he thought that this was his best chance of completing the mission.

Besides, the gold he was leaving behind was stashed in a safe place.

Only the birds of the air could locate it now.

And that reminded him of something.

Winterhawk cupped his hands over his eyes, shielding his vision from the direct sun as he looked up at the sky. There were now five large eagles soaring high above the train wreckage. They were squawking loudly, eager to feed.

He needed to get moving.

But there was one final task left to do.

He turned towards the shredded wreckage of the passenger car; mouth set in a hard frown.

He had always hated funerals.

·   ·   ·

WINTERHAWK DIDN'T KNOW how long it took him to pull all the corpses out of the passenger car. While some of the men had been reduced to nothing more than a kaleidoscope of torn limbs, he had labored to carry whatever pieces of them he could get off the train.

He felt he owed those soldiers at least that much.

Just before embarking on that gruesome task, he had collected a large pile of branches and doused them with gunpowder taken from one of the cannons. The branch pile would soon act as a funeral pyre.

As Winterhawk placed the remains of the soldiers onto the branches, he felt their blood sticking against his uniform. It was almost like the soldiers were still clinging tightly onto him.

In the southwestern corners of the United States, tribes like the Apache and the Navajo feared the recently deceased because they believed that some of the dead returned as vengeful ghosts. They thought ghosts came back from the dead because they resented the living.

Winterhawk had once considered those beliefs to be incredibly primitive. But after he tasted combat during the Battle of Cold Harbor, he came to believe in a lot of things that he had dismissed in his youth.

Even ghosts.

In his own Nez Perce culture, the face of the recently deceased would be painted red before being buried. The paint would later come to be representative of Christ's atoning blood sacrifice, a nod to the Presbyterian teachings that the Elder Chief Joseph had willingly introduced to his people. But the tradition actually began many centuries earlier. The red markings were a way to symbolize that peace had been achieved in death.

It was something he truly wanted to believe. But in his own experiences on the battlefield, blood wasn't symbolic of anything but sacrifice. And it was in those same moments that the dead will take it upon themselves to haunt the living.

Winterhawk now understood that the Apache and the Navajo weren't all that wrong about ghosts. What they had misunderstood is that the dead didn't haunt them because they resented the living. In the trenches of that bloodbath in Mechanicsville, he had finally realized what other soldiers had already understood for centuries: ghosts represent the guilt of still being alive.

That was the true horror of what was now lying on top of those broken branches. It's what propelled him to move away from the accusatory gazes staring up at him from the pile of bodies. It's what made his stomach roll when he had first looked inside the demolished hull of the burned-out dining car.

It was the realization that the circle of life was a noose.

Death rarely travelled far. It didn't have to.

What's the matter, chief? Get up on the wrong side of the wigwam this morning? With you, the glass is never half-full or half-empty. There's simply no damn glass at all.

Winterhawk traversed the prairie at a light sprint until he came upon the body of Colonel Smythe. The wolf had come to its final resting place less than a foot away from his corpse. Winterhawk stretched out his right leg and gave it a rough push. The blood from the wolf splashed against his boot as the carcass rolled away in the high grass.

He placed his hands on Smythe's face. He carefully dragged his fingers across his cold, dead skin. There was enough of the other soldier's blood still left on his hands to paint his whole face red.

It is the belief of the Nez Perce that a fallen warrior may return from the other side in order to guide the path of the living. Many have sworn to have heard voices of deceased warriors guiding them during impossible battles and near-death experiences.

He prayed that wouldn't be the case here. If anyone deserved peace in death, it was Colonel Smythe. The man had given his life to save him.

He hoisted Smythe off the ground, slinging him across his shoulder with as much gentleness as he could muster. The dead weight was almost crushing, but he forced himself to carry him across the rails and back to the resting place of the other soldiers.

He heaved Colonel Smythe atop the other bodies, wincing as branches snapped beneath the additional weight.

Winterhawk felt the blaring sun cooking against every inch of his exposed skin. It was getting harder to ignore the sharp jab of thirst scratching against the inside of his throat. And the constant rumble in his stomach was another harsh reminder that he had nothing to eat since the assault on the train's dining car the morning before.

If he could only rest for a moment...

His back straightened with a jolt.

No.

He needed to put as much distance between himself and the *Goose* before he could even think about resting. Besides, Cornadez had stocked that stolen Army supply wagon with enough provisions to last at least a month. He'd be feasting on salted venison and consuming jugs of warm water soon enough.

At present, there was still one gruesome task left to accomplish.

Winterhawk reached into his left pant pocket and pulled out a small tin box of matches. He struck a match against the side of the box, tossing it towards the bottom of the wood pile. The small flame sparked against the gunpowder, igniting it with a distinct pop. Within minutes, the wood pile had transformed into a raging funeral pyre.

Satisfied that it was going to continue burning, he shoved the tin box back into his pocket. Then, he raised his right arm and saluted.

"Amid the din of battle, nobly you should fall," Winterhawk said. He was reciting the lyrics of Charles Sawyer's *Weeping, Sad and Lonely*. It was a song so many Union troops had bellowed to one another as they marched into battle.

"Far away from those who love you, none to hear your call," he continued, "when this cruel war is over, praying that we meet again."

Overcome with grief, Winterhawk abruptly turned his back on the pyre and began making his way to the wagon.

After untethering the two horses from the Parrott cannons, he ran through a checklist of what he had already packed inside the wagon.

The Hornbeam bow, the Girandoni war club, and the Buffalo .44 were already stashed on the floorboard. In the back, twenty-five bags of unrefined gold ore jostled for space with enough stored provisions to see him through the journey.

Winterhawk flicked open the locket on his wrist. He took a long gaze at the portrait of Kaya and Chenoa.

One last mission.

Deliver the gold.

Then, he would return home to them.

He snapped the locket closed and walked up to the supply wagon.

"When this cruel war is over," he said, pulling himself up onto the jockey seat, "praying that we meet again."

He pulled hard on the reins as the wagon lurched forward.

The pyre was still raging behind him. He took great pains not to look back at it. Not because of the burned corpses, but because of the fire itself. He was afraid he would see a reflection of his own face caught in the flames. That would be frightening enough, but what *terrified* him was that he somehow wouldn't recognize his own face staring back out at him.

So, instead of glancing behind him, he raised one hand above his shoulder. It was a farewell gesture to those men he was leaving behind. He realized that he was also bidding goodbye to a part of himself, too.

Soon, the thick woods swallowed him whole.

PART II
The Final Flight of the Balloon Corps

CHAPTER 12

Bitker Springs Fire Lookout Tree
Buncombe, Oregon
Cascade Mountain Range

He had seen better days; hell, he had seen better *years*.

While Jim Sweet had read somewhere that the things that don't kill you just make you stronger, he had *also* read that the Good Lord won't give you more than you can rightfully handle.

Both concepts sounded like a pile of dung to him.

It was a temptation that had nearly destroyed his life after the Great Rebellion. The lure of fast money had darkened his soul, ultimately twisting his conscious into a poisonous snake that kept biting itself.

He had traded life as an iron foundry worker in Atlanta for a chance to join up with a motley group of tumbleweed bandits preying on family ranches left undefended after the end of the Civil War. But when innocent blood had been shed, the good days hadn't lasted very long. He had then fled the law across multiple states until he found himself hiding out in Oregon.

Becoming a cattle poacher hadn't killed him, but the consequences of his actions had certainly murdered all the dreams he had ever had. He was now nothing but a fugitive, a man sentenced to live out the rest of his life on borrowed time.

But right now, his life was all about going out on a limb.

Literally.

A strong gust of wind kicked up, forcing Sweet to put a steadying hand on one of the large branches crowding up against the lookout platform. He could feel the massive Douglas fir swaying beneath him.

This panoramic glimpse of the Cascade Mountains might appear to be a God's-eye view from his unstable perch, but he knew there wouldn't be any resurrection should he take a 200-foot tumble down to the forest floor. He had worn out all hope for miracles years ago; now, he just prayed for a steady hand.

The wind finally subsided, and Sweet let out the breath he hadn't realized that he had been holding. *That* had been close.

He widened his stance, which would provide better balance if another unexpected wind gust tried to remove him from the tree like a dead leaf. He frowned hard at the unsettling creak of plywood shifting beneath his boots.

Of all the many dangerous situations he had survived throughout his life, Sweet never would have thought that something has innocuous as manning a lookout tree would be the one that would finally end him.

But that's the unfortunate thing about luck--eventually it runs out.

Shaking his head, Sweet mulled over the recent history which had brought him here.

While toiling at the Buncombe Lumber Mill for the better part of two years, he had learned about an unusual job opening at the Nelscott Flume Company.

After a lightning storm had sparked a fire that had nearly taken the lives of fifty men before they were safely evacuated, it was decided that a lookout needed to be built in order to warn the lumbermen of approaching danger.

The Bitker Springs Lookout Tree was ultimately chosen to be the solution. Situated five miles outside of Buncombe, the fire lookout was constructed on top of a 200-foot Douglas fir that provided an unobstructed view of the forest in all directions.

A large ladder had been fastened to the base of the tree for the first 50-feet of the climb. From there, the lookout person needed to use the branches as footholds until he reached a second ladder that had been hung just beneath the platform.

The only thing harder than scrambling up to the platform was the treacherous trip down. This was nearly an impossible task even under the best conditions, but something never attempted during inclement weather or nightfall.

Or any other damn time.

Sweet took a quick glance over the platform's edge, staring down at the long drop to the forest floor. He knew the fall would probably kill him, but he had heard stories about men who had survived these types of accidents.

Survived?

Yes, that *was* stretching the truth.

While there had been lumbermen who had lived after falling from enormous heights, they certainly hadn't survived that first harsh winter laid up with a broken back. Even the luckiest among them didn't even make it after the first spring thaw.

That was solid proof that sometimes living was worse than dying. As if more proof of that was actually needed.

Carefully steadying himself on the platform, Sweet took a second glance down, casting his gaze at the structure that had been his home for the last year.

Built parallel to the Douglas fir was a small cabin--a glorified shanty, really--that offered just enough shelter for Sweet and his lookout partner, Benson, to spend their evenings.

Sweet heard the rumble emanating loudly from his stomach. It was yet another reminder that their provisions had run out nearly a day ago.

Benson had left this morning before dawn with the horse and wagon for a trip to Buncombe. He was late returning with the supplies. He should have been back hours ago.

Sweet checked the sun's position on the horizon, estimating that dusk would be approaching soon.

And then he saw something else.

There were tendrils of dark smoke curling up into the sky above the southwest tree line.

The smoke appeared to be coming from a fire source that was at least 30-miles away. That was the same direction where he and Benson had thought they'd heard the sounds of several large explosions yesterday. They both thought the blasts had come from one of the many mines throughout the Cascades. Now, he wasn't so sure.

He wondered if it had been some large-scale attack deep in the mountains, perhaps against one of the numerous supply trains.

"Sweet!"

The scream came from somewhere deep in the forest.

It was absolutely bloodcurdling.

He reached behind him for an 1863 Sharps Carbine rifle. He picked it up, palms sweaty, fingers clumsily touching the trigger.

His heart hammered relentlessly against his chest.

The voice itself was unmistakable.

"Sweet!" Benson screamed out again, the terrified echo landing much closer this time. "They came from the trees!"

Sweet felt ice coursing through his veins.

They?

Benson was a man of resolute calmness. Not once had Sweet ever seen him in a state of panic. Not even when that mountain lion had attacked them last spring.

They came from the trees...

A thundering noise took him by surprise.

Gripping onto the carbine, he swung his body around in the sound's direction. He balanced the rifle on his shoulder as he tried to make sense of the commotion.

It sounded like a small bison stampede, but he shook the thought away. Impossible.

But whatever the hell it was, it was definitely coming from the area of the woods flanking the western edge of the platform.

And it was coming fast.

Just then, a horse bolted from out of the tree line, galloping at a ferocious speed. Even from his high vantage point, Sweet could see the horse's bulging, panicked eyes; could hear the rapid snort of fear as it forcefully sucked in air.

Although the horse was dragging the neck yoke and wooden tongue behind it, there was nothing fastened to the end of it. There was no trace of the supply wagon.

"Sweet! Get away from here! Run!"

Benson was riding the horse bareback, arms wrapped tightly around its neck as he struggled to hold on. He kept snapping his head back, looking behind him with abject terror into the woods.

Looking for himself, Sweet saw nothing but looming shadows and deep darkness in the trees.

"Benson! What in the hell--?"

The rest of the words dropped from his mouth.

He was immediately silenced.

One of the largest shadows in the tree line had suddenly begun moving.

It was an enormous shape, moving at an extraordinary speed.

The horse had sensed the incoming danger. It seemed confused; powerful legs shifting as it attempted to veer sideways, hooves kicking up huge plumes of soil.

The creature emerged from the forest directly parallel to the horse, becoming nearly a blur as it streaked across the ground.

Sweet recoiled at the sight of it, mind reeling as he tried to comprehend what he was witnessing. He estimated the creature stood at least 8-feet off the ground. It was covered in matted black fur. Its muscular girth would dwarf even the largest grizzly. He had seen nothing like it outside of nightmares.

The thing charging out of the woods was most definitely an animal, but it moved just like a man.

But it *wasn't* a man.

It could only be described as a monster.

Sweet felt his gorge rise as sheer terror enveloped him.

The monster was *running*.

Sensing his impending demise, Benson tilted his head back, eyes going wide with horror. He screamed as the creature charged straight at him.

The monster let loose a guttural roar as it dipped its right shoulder, colliding against the horse at full speed.

Even from his perch high above the forest floor, Sweet could hear the sickening *crunch* of the impact. The horse was killed instantly, its broken neck flopping down like a lifeless doll.

The horse was driven onto the ground, catapulting Benson off its back as he began flipping end-over-end through the air. He landed twenty feet away, bouncing hard against the soil, limbs akimbo as he rolled across the ground.

Sweet kept his eyes on the creature, staring with utter incredulity as it lumbered on for another dozen yards before circling around in a wide arc.

It was now running directly towards Benson.

Hands shaking with fear, Sweet pressed the stock of the rifle tightly against his shoulder. He tracked the monster, barrel wavering, left eye squeezed shut as he aimed.

"Shoot it, Sweet!" Benson climbed to his feet and stumbled forward across the ground. "Shoot the ugly fucker!"

Sweet squeezed the trigger.

The blast from the Sharps pulled wide, kicking up a small plot of dirt behind the charging creature.

Although he was over three hundred yards away, Sweet could distinctly hear Benson's anguished cry of frustration as his feet tangled up beneath him. With arms flailing against the air, he tumbled forward, crashing facedown to the ground.

The monster reached him a second later.

It stomped down hard onto the back of Benson's legs, both femur bones shattering under the incredible weight. Benson writhed in agony, his high-pitched scream reaching an unbearable pitch.

Reaching down, the creature plunged both massive hands against Benson's waist. Its fingers dug deep into his flesh before pulling upwards against the ribcage, ripping his floundering prey completely in half.

With a victorious roar, the monster picked up the twitching lower half of Benson, sinking its gaping maw into the quivering mass of intestines.

Blocking out the horrifying feeding sounds, Sweet centered the rifle on the impossibly broad back of the creature, attempting to get in a kill shot before--

His head snapped back in shock.

While the shot from the rifle had done nothing to deter the path of the creature that had been chasing Benson, the echoing blast managed to get the attention of something *else*.

It had been lurking in the shadows of the tree line opposite the lookout cabin. Alerted by the rifle blast, the gigantic shape had stepped out of the forest, completely revealing itself beneath the harsh sunlight.

It was a second monster. And unlike the other creature, it wasn't at all interested in Benson. Its attention was entirely fixated on the lookout platform.

Its crimson eyes were staring up at Sweet. It unleashed a savage roar, teeth flashing hungrily. Then, it began running.

It was coming for him now.

Sweet knew he wouldn't stand a chance of scaling down the Douglas fir before the second monster reached him.

That left him only two choices.

Jump.

Or fight.

The decision was easy.

Sweet sunk to one knee, carefully aiming the Sharp at the oncoming monster. He would probably only get a single chance.

"Ain't life a bitch..." he muttered, pulling the trigger.

The bullet streaked towards its target with a marksmen's precision. The shot tore into the creature's left shoulder, a small geyser of blood erupting through the matted fur.

It did absolutely nothing to slow it down.

The monster had reached the Douglas fir with astonishing speed. It bounded onto the top of the cabin in a single leap, scaling the roof with all the dexterity of a cougar. The thick beams cracked beneath its immense weight, the snapping wood sounding off like rapid gunfire.

Sweet staggered backwards on the platform, eyes locked onto the horrifying sight two hundred feet below him.

"There's no way you're able to climb up here, amigo!" Sweet rapidly chambered another round into the rifle. "No! Fucking! Way!"

The monster paused briefly on the cabin roof, red eyes hungrily staring up at him. And then, it jumped. Its massive hands grabbed onto the thick lower branches of the Douglas fir as its body thumped hard against the trunk.

The monster began scrambling up the tree like a scurrying spider.

Sweet skittered backwards on the platform. Sinking down again onto one knee, he leveled the rifle in front of him.

Waiting.

If that big bastard wanted to climb all the way up here, then he would get a headshot at close range the second he showed his ugly face on the platform.

The thundering cacophony of the monster clamoring up the branches was almost deafening.

But there was another sound that was even worse.

Silence.

Maybe the monster had lost its grip--

The whole platform shook beneath his feet, throwing him off-balance. Sweet cried out in surprise, the rifle dropping from his grasp as his entire world began to tilt sharply.

Directly below him, the creature was pressing upwards against the platform, completely yanking it off the tree. The planks were momentarily balanced midair between both of its massive hands before the entire platform was turned upside down.

Sweet felt himself plummeting to the ground, arms flailing wildly before he landed dead center on the roof of the cabin. There was a jolt of excruciating pain as one of the snapped wooden beams punctured his lower abdomen, brutally impaling him.

He wanted to scream, but his lungs had already filled with blood. He was left writhing helplessly on the broken piece of timber.

Moments later, a pungent odor filled his nostrils.

The monster was now beside him.

Sweet prayed for a fast death as the monster began stripping off his flesh. But like every other prayer he'd said throughout his whole miserable life, this final one remained unanswered.

CHAPTER 13

CloudTrail Railway Pass
Cascade Mountain Range

Major Ambrose Toomey absently brushed soot from the shoulder of his uniform. It took him a moment to realize that the thick ash slowly raining down around him was actually human remains.

"Holy Cleopatra," Toomey said, his gravelly voice sounding as warm as a cry for help. He pulled his gaze away from the smoldering bonfire of Cavalry corpses, taking in the spectacular wreckage of the *Golden Goose* spread out behind him. "Looks to me like somebody had some fun."

The hulking soldier standing behind him obviously didn't share that particular sentiment. While Captain Thomas Isbell was adorned with the type of hardened facial expression that was standard military regulation, he could not match the unpleasant coldness of Toomey's grin.

For the enlisted men who knew Major Toomey only by reputation, he was best described as being eccentric.

Eccentric.

Isbell thought that eccentricity was a rather generous summation of his brash leader. For those soldiers whom had fought right alongside Toomey in the trenches of warfare, those men had a vastly different assessment of his sordid qualities.

To those who knew him best, Major Toomey was considered to be blatantly--

Psychotic?

No.

But he *was* passionate.

Committed.

Remorseless.

And--

Soulless.

A large shadow swept ominously over them.

Glancing up, Isbell watched the *Intrepid* military balloon drifting overhead, its oval shape sweeping across the prairie landscape like some type of prehistoric bird.

The two aeronauts onboard the *U.S.S. Intrepid* raised their hands in acknowledgement as the balloon floated high above. The soldiers manning the *Intrepid* were Captain Tucker and Captain Walker. They were hardened veterans, men trusted to always have his back.

He raised his own hand in acknowledgement as they passed overhead.

Isbell had flown to the crash site earlier in the *U.S.S. Excelsior*, which Toomey had expertly landed on the small hilltop overlooking the train massacre.

Both the *Intrepid* and the *Excelsior* had been stationed out of the White Salmon Blockhouse, which contained the last remaining Army aeronaut outpost on the entire west coast.

Created for long-range reconnaissance operations, the United States Balloon Corps was a special division of the Army. At its peak of service during the Civil War, the Army had operated two dozen hydrogen-fueled balloons that had flown over one-hundred combat missions for the Union.

But immediately after the war had ended, the Army had almost entirely disbanded the Balloon Corps. Nearly a decade after the Civil War, only a handful of aeronauts remained in active service. By 1873, there were just four active military balloons still in operation across the entire United States.

Two of those balloons happened to be stationed in Oregon.

Looking at the train wreckage, Isbell couldn't help but wallow in the irony of the Army turning its back on the Balloon Corps in favor of the reliability and stability of the railroad industry.

Major Toomey motioned towards the pile of corpses. "I reckon those railroad boys are going to have a heart attack when they see this mess, wouldn't you say, Captain?"

"I wouldn't say, sir," Isbell answered.

"What do you think happened here?" Toomey asked, gesturing at the wreckage strewn all around them.

"Ambush. The train route was compromised. Our boys rolled into some sort of trap. The gold was stolen. Things went south. Everyone died."

Toomey arched an eyebrow. "*Everyone*, Captain Isbell?"

"It looks that way to me."

"Then look harder," Toomey said.

Isbell stared at him for a long moment. Not for the first time, he wondered if Toomey was keeping something from him about this mission.

After the USMRR LV-426 had failed to arrive at White Salmon, the Army had dispatched two different search teams to investigate. While a separate mounted horseback unit had already been sent to canvass the first fifty miles of track leading its way up to White Salmon, the Balloon Corp had been ordered to survey the entire original route by air.

Major Toomey had informed the aeronauts under his command that the Army had feared a terrible disaster had occurred. They had been ordered to look for survivors.

Isbell finally realized that's what had been bothering him.

Survivors?

He didn't believe there was enough intel to make that sort of unilateral assumption yet. The way the brass at White Salmon had reacted to the train not arriving on schedule was definitely indicative of something else.

Suspicion.

His mouth twitched into a frown of understanding.

"We aren't looking for survivors, are we, Major Toomey? We're looking for a traitor."

Major Toomey brushed more ash from his uniform, striding purposefully away from the bonfire. Isbell followed closely beside him.

"Are you familiar with intrauterine fratricide, Captain Isbell?"

"No, sir."

"When the Good Lord created baby animals," Toomey said, "He made them irresistibly adorable. But the harsh reality is that far too many of them are nothing but calculating killers. The runts in wolf litters are pushed aside by larger siblings and left to go hungry; egret chicks will kick the weakest out of the nest to certain doom; baby eagles will snack on their smaller brothers and sisters while their mother proudly looks on."

"Fascinating. But how does any of that--?"

"Perhaps most disturbing of all," Toomey interrupted, "is the plight of baby sharks. Those little devils set an entirely new precedent. They practice a form of fratricide called intrauterine cannibalization."

"Thank you for the biology lesson," Isbell said. He absently swept a hand across his wet brow, flicking the collected beads of sweat off his fingers with distaste.

Toomey shot him a glance. "Would you believe that those hungry sharks end up eating their own brothers while still in the womb? It's sibling cannibalism, Captain."

The men had reached the battered remnants of the boxcar. The cargo door had been sheared open; its innards picked clean.

"That's precisely what we're dealing with here," Toomey continued, gesturing towards the empty boxcar with a dramatic flourish. "Intrauterine fratricide writ large."

Isbell nodded. "You're saying that there was a traitor on board this train who ate his own."

"Exactly."

Isbell stepped away from the boxcar. "It was definitely an ambush. Those cannons weren't placed here by happenstance. Taking down this train took planning, precision, and skill."

Toomey nodded enthusiastically. "I agree. The assault was extremely well-orchestrated. But as you surmised, it wasn't done by happenstance. The train route was a closely guarded secret; yet, the ambushers knew exactly when and where to strike."

Isbell felt a hot flash of rage. "Somebody on the train sold us out."

Toomey shrugged indifferently. "Somebody had to."

In the distance, the *Intrepid* had finished with its reconnoiter. Tucker and Walker were now maneuvering their balloon around in a slow arc, making their way back to the crash site.

Isbell closed his eyes for a long moment, thinking about what had happened to those soldiers. "Even if it *was* one of ours who was responsible, there's no way to know if this person even survived. After the ambush started, he could just as well have been one of the many casualties."

"It was a U.S. Cavalry soldier who survived this, Captain. I guarantee you that."

"How can you be so certain?"

Toomey pointed to the pile of burned corpses. "Somebody moved those dead soldiers, then burned the bodies. I'll wager that same somebody slaughtered all of those men laying out there in the prairie before absconding with the gold."

Isbell mulled it over. It was certainly a plausible explanation.

The traitor must have brought in some hired guns, giving them the false pretense of splitting the gold when it was over. He let those mercenaries and his fellow soldiers shoot it out until there were no survivors. Then, he made a clean getaway with the ore.

But where exactly did this traitor go? The bastard had at least a two-day head start on them. And in these woods, a man could hide and stay hidden.

He noticed Toomey was staring at him. "You look like someone just played hopscotch on your balls, Captain. It isn't as dire as all of that. The traitor left us a trail of crumbs to follow."

Isbell furrowed his brow. "Really? Where?"

Major Toomey placed a hand on his arm, gently escorting him towards the grassy prairie. "I saw it from the air."

Isbell was confused. He had been the first to see the crash site from the *Excelsior*. He'd spotted the cannons, had been the one to point out the dozens of dead bodies spread out along the blood-splattered ground.

What exactly had he missed?

Toomey stopped walking, letting go of his arm. "Here we are, Captain."

Isbell craned his neck, scanning all around him in confusion. "What exactly am I supposed to be seeing? Where is this trail of crumbs?"

"Right at your feet."

Isbell glanced down.

He took a sudden intake of breath.

His eyes bulged with surprise.

They were standing in a pair of deep indentations in the grass.

Wagon tracks.

Toomey squatted down, placing his hand into the dirt. "You can tell from how deep these marks are that the wagon was fully loaded; probably *overloaded* with all of our missing gold."

Isbell had been too distracted with the train carnage to have noticed the obvious. He had missed this vital detail from the air. He glanced over at Toomey with renewed admiration.

Toomey pointed to the wheel marks that led into the thick forest beyond. "The bread crumbs lead to the southeast. My guess is that he plans on heading all the way to Buncombe with the loot."

Isbell thought that over. It made perfect sense.

Buncombe was the next largest town, probably less than a three-day journey on horseback from their present location. It was a huge timber community. The perfect place to hide in plain sight.

"Buncombe. Alright. What do we do now, Major?"

Toomey motioned at the approaching balloon. "Signal to Tucker and Walker to ground the *Intrepid*. We have to tell them all about this land shark we're now hunting."

Isbell summoned up a grin.

There was blood in the water now. All they had to do was find their thrashing prey. And then, they would tear the poor bastard to pieces.

CHAPTER 14

Van Duzer Forest
Buncombe, Oregon
Cascade Mountain Range

Her granddad had once remarked that a man walked no finer line between bravery and stupidity than when he was going about the business of having to put food on the table.

Shivering in the midnight cold, shaking hands gripping onto a battered hunting rifle, Vickie Pensley thought her granddad might have somehow missed a third observation.

It was also suicide.

That's certainly how it felt to her tonight.

But what other choice did she have?

Granddad was already long dead. And unless Vickie brought back some meat to the cabin, her crippled father would probably breathe his last before the first snowfall. After that, Vickie knew she wouldn't be too far behind him.

Over the last several months, perishing from starvation had moved from a nightmare to a waking reality.

That's enough pressure to debilitate the decision-making process of even the most hardened individual, much less that of a 12-year-old girl forced to be her own father's caregiver.

After the accident with the Holbeer steam donkey had cost him the use of his legs, her father, Simon, had been confined to a wheelchair. While her father's mobility was now limited, his determination certainly was not.

He and Vickie's mother had travelled to Oregon during the Great Migration from the Midwest, hoping to build a better future for their family. Those hopes had been decidedly stripped away when Vickie had turned eight. That was the year that her mother had been taken by pneumonia.

"Suffering in this life, peace in the next." Those were her mother's final words.

After burying her mother that night, Vickie's father had pulled her close, allowing her to weep against him as he had gently stroked her hair. "Life isn't fair," he had told her. "It just *is*."

For the next several years, they had both pushed on together; struggling, but surviving. Until the horrible accident last year.

Vickie had been told that if that man Holliger hadn't been drinking, he wouldn't have passed out over the controls of the steam donkey. She had also been told that it was purely an act of God that her father hadn't been standing any closer to the logging jack when it had swung backwards.

"Any closer to that infernal machine, and I would have been laying out there in the ground right next to your mother instead of sitting here beside you," her father had remarked at the supper table one evening.

Vickie was ashamed to admit that she had stayed awake in bed many nights wishing that he *had* been standing closer to the steam donkey when the accident occurred.

It would have put her father out of his misery. It would have done something else, too. It would have freed her from the life she was now confined to by the chains of obligation.

Her father's death would have changed many things.

There would have been no stubborn refusal to abandon their cabin, no headstrong insistence in not accepting charity, no more suffocating moments of panic whenever her father tumbled from his wheelchair, and no more shameful memories of helping him bathe.

But over time, all of her hopes of freedom from those very things had vanished. All that remained for her now was resolve and strength.

And hunger.

The truth was they were both very close to starving.

The traps she had set outside the cabin hadn't yielded any meat. Their stockpile of provisions had slowly diminished into nothing. They had run out of money long ago.

Every day, she watched her father grow weaker. The accident at the Nelscott Flume had killed him; he just didn't know it yet. Vickie just couldn't watch him slowly die anymore. She had to do something.

Which is why, earlier tonight, she had waited patiently for him to fall into a deep sleep. Then, she had taken his rifle and snuck out of the cabin. She was desperate to bring back something that could nourish them. After her father was feeling stronger, she would convince him to let her go into Buncombe and beg someone for help.

She would plead for mercy to whomever would listen.

It was the only way.

But until then...

"Suffering in this life," Vickie said, teeth chattering in the cold, "peace in the next."

As she moved deeper into the woods, Vickie began praying that a lone deer would materialize from out of the blackness, presenting itself like some kind of sacrificial atonement.

The striking of a match caused her to cry out in surprise. It was raked against the bark of a tree five feet away from her. The igniting flame sounded as loud as a dynamite blast in the dead silence of the night.

"Haven't been to Africa yet," a gravelly voice said, "but a stampede of elephants would probably be a lot quieter than you." The stranger moved the match towards his mouth, touching it against the crooked cheroot dangling from his lips.

Vickie felt her heart hammering in her chest as the glowing tip of the cigarette cast an eerie red hue over the man. The lit match totally illuminated him before he snuffed it out with a flick of his wrist.

The man looked to be as tall as a Redwood, with shoulders broad enough to support the weight of a caboose. He was clean shaven, but had a thick mass of greasy blonde hair that spilled down the middle of his back.

With a shotgun nestled under the crook of one arm, he was casually leaning against the tree like he was waiting patiently for a ride.

His eyes glinted in the cheroot's light. "The name's Templeton. Don't think I caught yours."

"Victoria Pensley."

"The cripple's kid?"

Vickie bristled at the remark, feeling a hot flush of anger spread over her face. "My father had an accident."

Templeton took a long drag from the cheroot. "It was a damn shame what happened to Simon. With him being a widower and all, I guess that leaves you as the woman of the house."

She felt sharp daggers of fear stab into her stomach. She needed to get as far away from this man as possible.

Tightly gripping the hunting rifle, she took a careful step away from him. "I need to get back. My father is expecting me home any minute."

Templeton scoffed. "Expecting you to do what, darling? Wipe his ass? If your daddy wastes away any further, he'll probably be asking you to chew his food for him next."

Vickie felt like she was in the presence of a wild animal. Templeton represented the very worst of men. Her impulse was to raise the rifle and command him to leave her alone. But the moment she did, he would easily swat the rifle away like it was some annoying insect.

She realized how incredibly foolish her idea had been. Sneaking out under the cover of night, not telling a single soul about what she had been planning. Nobody would even know where to look if she went missing.

She had to get back home.

But first, she had to get away from this man.

Templeton lightly clucked his tongue demonstratively. "Darling, I think you'd best put those half-cocked ideas of yours to bed. You ain't gonna shoot me, and I certainly ain't gonna shoot you. I only want to be your friend."

Vickie took another step away from him. "What are *you* doing out here?" she asked, struggling to keep her voice calm.

"Same as you: hunting. Only difference is that my daddy, rest his pitch-black soul, wouldn't have sent a girl to do a man's job."

Vickie couldn't control the anger that coursed through her. "He didn't send me! He doesn't even know--"

She snapped her mouth shut, realizing too late what she had just foolishly shared with him.

"What doesn't he know, girlie?"

Vickie shook her head, not answering him.

Templeton grinned. "Doesn't know you stole his rifle? Doesn't know you've snuck out? He certainly doesn't know about this cockamamie plan of yours to go skipping around the woods under the moonlight."

Vickie felt tears rolling down her cheeks. It made her feel weak; ashamed. "Please let me go."

Templeton spread out his hands. "There's no reason to be so frightened. I ain't gonna be putting no hurtin' on you."

"I want to go home now."

"You *will* be going home. And you'll be bringing some fresh meat home to your daddy. I scored myself an elk today. Too much carcass for me to haul around. By taking some of it off my hands, you'll be doing me a favor. Consider it a fair trade."

Vickie felt the hot sting of bile in her mouth. "I have nothing to trade."

Templeton dropped the cheroot, forcefully grinding it into the ground. "Yes, you do."

At that, Vickie bolted. He might be bigger, but she was faster. She was counting on that advantage in order to--

Templeton reached her in just a few quick strides.

She felt one massive hand grab onto her shoulder, his fingers clamping down painfully. The other hand wrapped around the back of her neck.

Vickie cried out as the rifle dropped from her grasp. She raised both of her arms, small hands clawing uselessly against his much larger ones.

"I hear the young ones wriggle like a fish," Templeton panted excitedly into her ear.

"Hook *this*, asshole!" She clamped her teeth down onto Templeton's exposed index finger on her shoulder. She felt the satisfying crunch of bone echo inside her mouth; tasted copper as blood spurted across her tongue.

Templeton threw his head back, screaming shrilly. Twisting her head, Vickie ripped his index finger completely off. She spit out the severed digit, hearing it hit the ground with a satisfying thump.

Templeton stumbled backwards, the mixture of shock and pain causing him to lose his grip on her.

Taking advantage of the split-second opportunity, Vickie began running. But she was crashing through the woods blindly, with absolutely no sense of direction. She desperately needed to find somewhere in the woods to hide.

Vickie heard the ripping of fabric. Templeton had just torn off a piece of his shirt to use as a tourniquet on his bleeding hand.

Then she heard something else. The sound was absolutely chilling.

It was laughter.

"Well, well; ain't you a feisty one. Go ahead and run, Victoria. I'll find your sweet little ass soon enough."

Vickie felt a second wave of fear cascade over her. It pumped more adrenaline through her body as she crashed through the forest.

She could hear the man coming after her again. Despair washed over her. She hadn't been able to put enough distance between them. Templeton was gaining on her too fast.

Vickie pushed her way through a thick clump of bushes, finding herself entering a wide clearing in the forest. She was out in the open; totally exposed. There was nowhere she could hide.

But she had other problems now.

There was something else wrong. A savage smell wafted through the air in the clearing. There were thick masses of unidentifiable clumps all over the ground. Whatever they were, they glistened wetly in the moonlight.

She also glimpsed something else. At the edge of the clearing. Two very large shapes. They looked almost like haystacks, only these appeared to be alive; moving, breathing and--

Still running, Vickie suddenly lost her footing. She knew she hadn't stumbled over some fallen tree limb or an exposed trunk root. In fact, she hadn't tripped at all.

She'd slipped.

The ground beneath her feet was sopping wet, almost like there had been a torrential downpour earlier.

But it hadn't rained for several days.

This was something else.

As she slid across the ground, rolling hard, she felt her face plunge into a small puddle, getting a mouthful of thick liquid that she recognized was—

"Blood!" Templeton shouted out from behind her.

His prey was momentarily forgotten. He was clutching onto the shotgun with his wounded hand, wide eyes transfixed on the scattered clumps in the near distance. He kept lifting his boots, the noise sounding like thick mud pulling up against the leather.

Vickie wanted to get up, knew that she needed to start running, but a heavy sense of dread had caused a momentary paralysis in her limbs.

Templeton struck a match with his good hand. He swept his arm around, the flickering light illuminating a large swath of the clearing.

And for the second time that night, Vickie screamed.

The match had provided just enough light for her to see what the glistening clumps were: dead bodies. Six Army soldiers that had been savagely torn limb-from-limb.

There were also two military wagons encroaching at the very edge of the match's light, the eviscerated bodies of several horses laid out beside them.

"They're all dead," Templeton gasped. "What in the hell could have done that to 'em?"

They both heard the growling.

It was a guttural noise; primal.

Looking up towards the sound, Vickie stared at the haystack shapes. She realized now that she had been looking at a pair of massive shadows. Now, those two gigantic shapes were standing.

They looked like monstrous apes.

Templeton's match extinguished, plunging them back into darkness.

The growling of the creatures stopped, quickly replaced by the sound of lumbering footfalls.

"Scratch my balls with a hacksaw," Templeton spat, raising the shotgun, "those hairy bastards are running right for us!"

Vickie felt the anchor of fear dissipate as her survival instincts took over. She scrambled to her feet, panic consuming her.

The shotgun blast reverberated across the clearing.

Running with wild abandon, Vickie threw herself into a thicket of bushes. There was the sound of a second shotgun blast. And then, a terrible, high-pitched wail filled the air.

"They're eating me!" Templeton screamed. "They're! Eating! Me!"

She heard wet flesh being stripped from the bone as the two monsters tore him to pieces. The creatures were now consumed with satiating their limitless hunger, intently gorging on his body, forgetting all about her in their blood lust.

Vickie continued to run through the woods until Templeton's tortured screams were only an echo inside her head.

CHAPTER 15

Van Duzer Forest
Buncombe, Oregon
Cascade Mountain Range

It was just after dawn on the second day into his trip to the White Salmon Brickhouse when Jolon Winterhawk came to the understanding that he was a dead man.

An hour ago, he had decided to stop driving the wagon and tether both horses to a Douglas fir inside a large clearing. The horses neighed at him disapprovingly, hooves stomping nervously against the ground.

I hate to break the bad news to you, but those horses aren't the bait—YOU are.

Winterhawk was in a prone position atop the transport wagon, the Buffalo .44 clutched in his right hand. His eyes scanned the edges of the forest, ears attuned for even the slightest noise. Although he hadn't heard the wolves howling for a long while now, he knew they were still out there.

The pack had been tracking him ever since he left the CloudTrail Railway Pass. He had killed their leader, but that hadn't scared them off. It had just incited more bloodlust. It was uncommon behavior, but not altogether rare. He'd once heard a story from the tribal elders about a particular wolf traveling one-hundred miles to avenge a slain mate.

One wolf, sure, but a whole pack of them hunting a human for revenge sounds more like a scary story told over the campfire to a litter of squeamish squaws.

Wolf howls were a ubiquitous sound in the Cascade Mountains. But what had troubled him wasn't the howling itself; rather, it was where the noises were coming from. Not from a fixed location like cries from a pack would typically sound. The howls he had heard had been coming from multiple directions.

It was then that Winterhawk finally understood that he was no longer just being hunted. He was being surrounded.

Nobody told you to kick that dead wolf after you shot it; to get its bloody scent smeared all over your boot. That made it easy for them to track you. You aren't exactly the tallest pole on the teepee, are you?

Winterhawk glanced down at his boot with a grimace. He could still see dried splotches of the pack leader's blood on the leather.

At least it's only those wolves who've tracked you down from that crash site. You're also still covered in the blood of those soldiers. Now, just imagine seeing all of those burned corpses lumbering through the woods after you...

Winterhawk didn't have to imagine it, all he needed to do was close his eyes. Sleep had already brought those men back to him in nightmares. He reckoned it probably always would.

The air became still.

Winterhawk felt sudden movement coming from his left, barely catching the streak of fur in his peripheral vision. He jerked his body sideways, swinging the massive handgun towards—

Nothing.

The area to the left of the wagon was clear.

His heart was hammering, pulse throbbing in his temples.

The horses neighed loudly, bucking hard against the tethered rope.

Winterhawk sensed a blur of motion.

Danger coming in fast from two different directions.

A pair of wolves exploded from out of the forest, their powerful bodies streaking towards the wagon. One was coming directly at him, the other was attacking from the right side.

Winterhawk pulled himself to a sitting position, aiming the Buffalo at the predator charging towards him. After he made the kill shot, he would count on the gun blast to frighten away the second wolf. This would afford him precious seconds, more than enough time for him to—

He suddenly heard the third wolf.

It had been methodically hunting him from behind, stealthily climbing on top of the covered wagon while the other two had distracted him.

He could smell its rancid breath, sensed that its muscles were coiled to pounce. There would be no time to face his attacker. He would be torn apart within the next heartbeat.

The wolf let loose a savage roar behind him. Its body sprang forward, mouth outstretched, jaws reaching for the back of his neck.

Winterhawk fired the Buffalo .44

But he hadn't aimed the massive firearm at the onrushing predator. Instead, he had fired downwards, directly into the wagon's canopy. The 141-grain round ball bullet shredded the cloth beneath him, dropping Winterhawk from view.

He landed atop the pile of gold bags as the wolf soared inches above his head. He heard its frustrated cry as it landed on the ground beside the wagon.

He knew he wouldn't get that lucky again.

Winterhawk began pulling the bags of gold ore forward, attempting to use them as a makeshift barrier. If he could put even the slightest shield between himself and those wolves, those additional few minutes would allow him the chance to defend himself.

Three clean shots and it would all be over.

He never got the chance.

He felt tremendous pressure clamping down on his right boot. Before he could even react, he was roughly yanked forward by one of the wolves. The Buffalo dropped from his grasp as he instinctively reached out for a handle hold, fingernails scraping futilely against the wood.

Winterhawk felt panic as the wolf finished dragging him from out of the back of the wagon. Still gripping his boot in its jaws, the wolf continued pulling him along the dirt for another ten feet. Finally letting loose, it ran in a wide circle, coming to a stop behind him.

Winterhawk scrambled to his feet, hands balled into fists.

All three wolves were now facing him. They had their fangs bared, bodies crouched low, eyes hungry for the kill that had so far eluded them.

Winterhawk was defenseless. There was nowhere to run, nowhere to hide. There was no time for prayers, no time for pleading. All that was left now was for those ravenous wolves to tear him to pieces.

He brought up his fists in a show of defiance. If he had to take each of them down with his bare hands, then that's exactly what he would do.

The heavily muscled haunches of the three wolves began to uncoil, their eyes boring into him.

They were preparing to pounce.

The air suddenly came shockingly alive with the deafening sound of gunfire that began streaking down from somewhere in the sky. The hail of bullets snapped through branches, punched large holes into nearby tree bark, and gruesomely eviscerated the three wolves.

Winterhawk looked up at the sky in astonishment.

A large shape was drifting down through the clouds.

His eyes narrowed as he recognized what it was.

And then he remembered something that Colonel Smythe had told him in the dining car right before the ambush.

Sometimes the Devil answers prayers, too.

CHAPTER 16

The *U.S.S. Excelsior* was hovering just over the top of the tree line, large spurts of hydrogen gas fanning the intense flame that kept the military balloon airborne.

Major Ambrose Toomey grinned down at him from his perch inside the basket. He was holding onto a pair of Colts, the smoke from both barrels nearly obliterating his features.

Captain Thomas Isbell was standing beside him, aiming with a Henry repeating rifle.

Winterhawk stared up at the *Excelsior* with absolute incredulity.

During his time stationed in Mechanicsville, he'd heard many perilous accounts of the Army Balloon Corps' involvement during the Civil War.

Originated by presidential appointee Thaddeus Lowe, a renowned inventor who had pioneered the use of hydrogen gas for flight, the Balloon Corps had engaged in a hundred reconnaissance missions during the war.

Beyond those endeavors, the Army aeronauts had also taken part in dozens of decisive battlefield victories. The soldiers involved in those skirmishes had assassinated high-ranking Union officers from the air, while also dropping explosive ordinances onto unsuspecting artillery bunkers and troop outposts. But mostly, the balloons had just provided target practice for the Confederates.

Winterhawk thought the Army had officially disbanded the entire unit back in 1863. But if that was the case, what were aeronauts doing still flying around out here in middle of the Oregon wilderness?

Are you getting the drift of things yet, amigo? If you steal a few coins from a stagecoach, they might let you waltz off into the sunset without too much of a fuss. But when a military gold train is ambushed, the brass will make damn sure no rock is left unturned as they search high-and-low for the stolen loot. You just happen to be the cute little bug that scurried out from underneath the stone.

Winterhawk felt a knot of fear slowly tightening in his stomach.

What exactly did these men think happened on that train?

Major Toomey reached for the fulcrum handle located inside the basket and pulled it, lessening the subsequent flame by venting hydrogen from the balloon envelope. After a minute, the *Excelsior* set down safely in the clearing, landing close to the transport wagon.

Isbell clamored out of the basket first, the Henry repeating rifle never wavering even a millimeter off its target. "Name and rank, soldier!"

Winterhawk felt himself bristle at the man's aggressive demeanor. He had experienced commanding officers resenting having to associate with someone from the tribal lands in a military uniform, but this seemed like something else entirely. Angry, yes; but this one came across as much more spiteful. The man sounded hateful.

"Lieutenant Jolon Winterhawk," he answered. "United States Cavalry, 9th Division."

Following Isbell out of the basket, Toomey shook his head. "I'm sure that you won't be offended when I say that I've never heard of you before, Lieutenant Summerhawk--"

"Winterhawk."

Toomey dismissed him with a quick wave of his hand. "Winterhawk. Summerhawk. All you Indians have such colorful names. Who can honestly keep track of them all?"

Winterhawk felt the throbbing of his pulse begin to tap against the side of his temples. "Who are you?"

"My name is Major Ambrose Toomey. And this formidable looking gentleman standing beside me is Captain Thomas Isbell. We're aeronauts with the Army's illustrious Balloon Corps."

Isbell's unwavering stare was colder than the barrel of his rifle. "Were you assigned to protect the LV-426?"

"That's right."

"I probably wouldn't list that soiled accomplishment on your military resume," Toomey remarked. "Bit of a blemish there, I'd say."

"It looked like a real shit show to me," Isbell said. "Do you mind explaining to us exactly what happened, Lieutenant?"

"Things got bad."

"And?"

Winterhawk steeled his eyes. "Then they got worse."

Isbell jerked his head towards the transport wagon. "What's the load you're carrying back there, soldier?"

Winterhawk didn't like where this conversation was headed.

He thought briefly of the Hornbeam bow and the Girandoni war club he'd stashed beneath a blanket in the back of the wagon. He wished he had made them more accessible. If he could just get close enough to grab them...

And if a bunny had wings, it wouldn't bump its ass a-hopping. You really think those basket boys are going to let you get anywhere near those weapons?

There was a dangerous flicker behind Isbell's eyes. "I believe I asked you a question."

"Twenty-five bags of gold ore," Winterhawk answered.

Toomey nodded. He strolled over to the wagon, peering into the back. His gaze was transfixed on the bags. Something flashed briefly across his features. It was a dangerous look.

"And just how did you come into possession of this gold?" Toomey asked.

"After the ambush, I unloaded the bags from the boxcar into the wagon. I was taking it to White Salmon."

"Ambushed?" Toomey asked. "By whom, exactly?"

"General Ramón Cornadez," Winterhawk replied. "He brought a militia with him, along with field artillery and Zouave sharpshooters."

"And an informant," Toomey asked.

Winterhawk narrowed his eyes.

Are you missing those wolves yet, chief? At least they had been predictable. These two characters? They're operating on animal instincts of an entirely different *kind.*

"I never saw an informant on the train," Winterhawk replied.

"Our Lord observed not being able to see the wind," Toomey said, stepping away from the wagon, "but He instructed us to believe that it still exists. The same thing can be said about this informant. You claim you didn't see him on the train; yet, I assure you, the man was most definitely there."

Are you getting the big picture yet, boy-o?

"There's been some type of misunderstanding," Winterhawk said. He cast his eyes between the two men. "It's not at all what you think."

"You know what I think, soldier?" Isbell took a menacing step forward. "I *think* I want to see your hands in the air. Right now!"

"Listen to me. I'm not the informer. I'm not a traitor. I didn't kill those men. I wasn't stealing the gold."

"We believe you," Toomey said. "Let's just all try to keep a cool head about this, shall we?"

Winterhawk held out both of his palms in a show of peaceful solidarity. "First, you'd better tell your ape to lower his rifle."

Toomey opened his mouth to respond, but was momentarily distracted. He was staring intently at Winterhawk's left hand. His eyes were fixated on the battered silver locket fastened to his wrist.

Realizing what he was staring at, Winterhawk jerked the locket away, hiding it within one of his fists.

"What have you got there?" Toomey asked.

"Nothing."

Isbell snorted. "How about I break your goddamn wrist? Then we can all get a peek at that little nothin'."

Winterhawk steeled his eyes. "Do you remember the advice that your wife gave you on your wedding night?"

"I don't rightfully recall," Isbell answered. "What advice was that?"

"Go fuck yourself."

Eyes flashing angrily, Isbell's finger began to shake against the trigger.

Toomey clucked his tongue disapprovingly. "Now, now. I thought your people were hospitable by nature, Lieutenant. There's no need for that kind of crass barbarism."

Toomey reached out his hand. "Hand it over."

Winterhawk didn't move.

Isbell shoved the rifle flush against his forehead, pushing the barrel hard into his skin.

The air grew eerily silent. Winterhawk felt a lone trickle of sweat rolling down his back as he stared down the long barrel of the rifle.

If he pressed slightly forward, the motion would be just startling enough that Isbell probably wouldn't automatically pull the trigger. If anything, the man would anticipate him to want to reach up and defiantly pull the rifle away from his face; perhaps even to jerk his body sideways and gain a few feet of distance between them.

Isbell would be expecting anything *except* for Winterhawk to move towards him. He could probably wrestle the rifle away before the man could even get a shot off.

Winterhawk thought he could move fast enough to bring down Isbell with his own rifle, but having to take out Toomey next would be another matter. Still, it was an option he needed to consider.

That type of grandstanding maneuver would be plain suicide. Think really hard about what happens next, chief. The best strategy right now is to live long enough to die another day.

Winterhawk slowly opened his left hand, revealing the locket to the aeronauts. Toomey reached out and yanked it off his wrist. He snapped open the locket, staring at the picture of Kaya and Chenoa. "Is this your family?"

Winterhawk held out his open hand. "I want the locket back."

Toomey stared hard at him. "And *I* would like to know how you were planning on getting away with the gold."

Winterhawk felt a cold knot of fear bloom inside of his stomach. "I took the ore that had been on the train, but not for any of the reasons you think."

"What was your plan, Lieutenant Winterhawk? You made a deal with General Cornadez? You provided him with the train route in exchange for half of the money?"

"No! That's not what happened. We were ambushed."

"I would guess that you jumped off the train when the attack started," Toomey remarked. "Tried keeping yourself hidden until all the shooting was over. But our soldiers resisted a lot harder than anyone expected. The ambushers took considerable casualties during the fighting, which allowed you to pick off the rest of them without too much difficulty."

"None of that is true—!"

A shouting voice came from the direction of the sky. "Major Toomey! That Indian! He must have killed them all!"

Winterhawk jerked his head up. He saw Captain Tucker and Captain Walker riding together in the *U.S.S. Intrepid*.

"Captain Walker, whom did our Indian kill this time?"

Walker began gesturing frantically behind him as the balloon floated closer. "The search party, Major! Massacred! We just found their bodies in a clearing not too far from here."

Winterhawk forcefully shook his head. "What search party? I don't know what they're talking about!"

"You're better than a fish bowl," Toomey said. "There's something interesting to watch every damn second."

CHAPTER 17

Even as he felt the noose tightening around his throat, Jolon Winterhawk stared with disbelief at the large footprint stomped into the ground beneath him.

He estimated it to be at least 12-inches wide and nearly two feet long. It had a singularly large indentation in the rear of the print that indicated something with an extremely large body mass.

Would you kindly explain to me what kind of animal leaves footprints when it walks, chief?

Bears.

Grizzlies often reared onto their hind legs to establish dominance during threatening encounters. He had also seen black bears walking on their back legs while foraging for food.

Those aren't bear tracks, amigo. And you damn well know it.

He took another hard look at the footprint.

No, it definitely didn't come from a bear. But whatever *had* made it, that creature would have to be enormous, much bigger than anything he had ever encountered.

The size of the footprint would indicate something of almost mythical proportions. It would reveal the existence of the fabled Nu'numic.

Winterhawk remembered the frightening stories he had heard from the elders when he was a young boy at Chompuunish.

The legend had been told among his people for centuries. Tales of a wild-haired, flesh-eating monster roaming the woods. A fierce and savage protector of the forests.

The Nez Perce elders had named it the Nu'numic. The Chinook and Shasta tribes referred to it as the Wendigo. The Makah and Snoqualmie people called it the Sasquatch.

After the Yupik and the Inupiaq had settled along the northern coasts of Alaska and Canada centuries ago, those tribes had been the first to describe the existence of the Ancient Ones. These indigenous forest creatures were fabled to have originally migrated from the east before the Big Flood had separated all of the land masses of the earth.

When the earliest missionaries had met the Spokane and Cayuse tribes, they spoke about a catastrophic flood that had once come upon the earth. They were informed by Chief Spokane Garry that mankind had provoked the Creator with their evil ways, but a good man named Nanabozho had been spared after he had received word from the Land Above that a big water was to cover the earth. In the fable, Nanabozho had built a raft and rescued enough animals and people to restore the balance of nature once the wrath of the Creator had been satisfied.

Eventually, the flood waters had receded. But according to the beliefs of the Inupiaq tribe, the Ancient Ones had remained.

He shook away the thought. That was impossible.

If a creature like the Nu'numic truly existed, it would represent the literal incarnation of ancient folklore, and the physical manifestation of tribal legends.

Winterhawk continued to stare down at the massive footprint.

He thought of something else.

The Nu'numic also had an English translation.

Teeth of the Forest.

Your ability to multi-task during a crisis is admirable, but don't you think you have got more pressing concerns to ponder than the existence of mythical monsters? Like the fact that there's a noose around your neck?

As if sensing the perilous situation its rider was in, Winterhawk felt the unsettling shifting of the horse he was straddling. It took a nervous step forward, the rope around his neck pulling taught.

Winterhawk squeezed his legs gently against the horse. "Calm yourself," he whispered soothingly. The horse snorted loudly in response, advising him to mind his own business.

Winterhawk looked up at the thick branch that the noose was fastened around. He knew it was strong enough to hold his weight when the hanging begun.

Not that he was able to do anything about it.

His hands had been tied tightly behind his back, barely affording him the room to flex his fingers and keep the circulation flowing. He wasn't going anywhere.

The four Army aeronauts were huddled off in the distance, their heated conversation muffled.

This is a real fine mess you've gotten yourself into, chief. Arguably your worst one yet; but who wants to argue?

When the aeronauts had first arrived, everything had moved fast.

While Tucker and Walker had landed the *Intrepid* in a large clearing a quarter-mile to the north, Winterhawk had been escorted by gunpoint to the area by Toomey. Following them, Captain Isbell had driven over the gold-laden supply wagon.

What they had discovered next had been horrifying.

The corpses of six soldiers from the White Salmon search party. What was left of their bodies was strewn across the ground, ghastly and unrecognizable. Their horses had met with a similar grisly fate.

Huge swarms of carrion birds had taken flight immediately upon the group's arrival. They now circled high above, impatiently waiting for the opportunity to continue feeding.

"Looks like every beak in the sky has taken a nibble down here," Major Toomey had remarked, taking in the full scope of the carnage spread out around them. "Those wolves must have had themselves a heyday after you killed these boys."

Winterhawk knew it hadn't been wolves that had torn these soldiers to pieces. And he wasn't the one who had killed them.

Something *else* had. Something with enough speed and force to wipe out an entire squad of armed horsemen.

He took another quick glance at the massive footprint.

The Ancient Ones.

Bad luck just seems to follow you around like a thirsty mosquito, doesn't it?

To believe in luck was to embrace a worldview that was far too simplistic. If he was going to have any chance of surviving this, he needed to look at circumstances beyond himself; circumstances beyond the present moment.

In a war, survival came down to nothing but perspective.

Perspective nothing. You let your guard down and it cost you. Truthfully, the only reason that you aren't already dead is because you are still valuable to them.

He felt the noose scratching against his throat. He had the urge to swallow, but his saliva was like a clump of sand wedged against the back of his mouth.

Winterhawk stared over at the huddled aeronauts.

There was a reason Toomey had not ordered his execution yet. He was still alive because he had something they needed. What Toomey must be doing now was convincing the other soldiers that doing the wrong thing really meant doing the right thing.

You're tailor-made to take the fall for this whole thing, you know. Toomey had you sized up for a pine box the moment he slapped his greedy eyes on you.

But Toomey couldn't possibly get away with it. Between the train wreck and the slaughter out here in the field, there were too many loose ends. Besides, the Army brass would never believe that all the gold ore had not been found.

Why wouldn't they believe it, hombre? With you taking a dirt nap, those aeronauts will be free to make up any story they choose. They'll be celebrated as heroes because they killed the Indian traitor. Nobody will question their bedtime story about the missing ore. And in a few years from now, after all the dust from this has settled, those boys will dig up the gold they'll be burying today. They'll live out the rest of their lives like kings.

If that was the case, then he had one last card to play. It was time to give these men something they didn't even know they wanted. He needed to tell them about the hidden gold.

"Toomey!" His parched voice cracked under the strain of yelling. "You need to know something important about the gold."

The group of aeronauts stopped talking, turning towards him. "What is it, Lieutenant?" Toomey asked. "Don't leave us hanging."

"Before I left the ambush site," Winterhawk explained, "I loaded twenty-five bags of ore into the wagon."

Situational realization dawned on Toomey's face. "But not *all* the gold from the train made it onto the wagon, did it?"

Isbell shook his head violently. "Bullshit! You saw the inside of that boxcar, Major. It was empty. There was nothing there."

Tucker and Walker glanced at each other, sharing a look of disbelief. "That's right," Walker stated. "Tucker and I canvassed the crash site from the air. We didn't see any gold bags, just dead bodies."

Winterhawk felt the noose constricting tightly against his Adam's apple. "That's because I hid them."

"Then we might have some business to discuss," Toomey said.

Isbell whipped around angrily to face him. "You're not serious, Major! The man's lying! He would tell you he knew how to piss diamonds if he thought it would save his own neck."

"Lieutenant Winterhawk *is* attempting to save his own neck, but I don't think he's lying."

Captain Tucker absently rubbed the stubble on his chin, casting an uneasy glance between the other aeronauts. "Well, if the injun ain't fibbing, then what do you reckon we should do now?"

Toomey stared at him with a cold gaze. "The plan remains unchanged. It's just the scope of everything that's been altered."

"Why don't you just be a smart boy," Walker said, slowly licking his lips, "and tell us exactly where you hid those bags?"

"Cut me down first," Winterhawk answered.

Walker reached for his belt and unsheathed a large Bowie knife. "Why don't I cut you *up* first?"

That's the trouble with playing blind man's bluff. Eventually, you gotta rip that smelly old blindfold off and see exactly where you wound up. If you're lucky, you'll find yourself standing flat-footed on a nice bed of soft, green grass. But if you're unlucky, you might just look down and see that you've already got several toes wiggling over a high cliff. In this little game you've been playing, where do you think you stand now?

Winterhawk felt the horse tremble uneasily beneath him. He squeezed his thighs gently against the animal's flank, praying that it wouldn't get spooked and—

Bolt.

The sun glinted against Walker's Bowie knife, the glaring reflection cast directly into the horse's eyes. Whinnying with a sudden jolt of fear, it sprang forward, hooves digging into the ground.

Winterhawk felt his stomach lurch as the horse careened out from beneath him. He futilely began pulling against the binds that secured his hands behind his back. He could feel each agonizing second of his life slipping away as his legs slid off the animal's back.

The horse broke into a full gallop.

And then...

He was plummeting to his death.

CHAPTER 18

The sound of the rope snapping taught cracked as loud as a bullwhip.

Winterhawk's legs jerked involuntarily, his body swinging like a pendulum. The noose constricted around his throat; blackness swarmed across his vision.

Then, he was hitting the ground. The pressure of the noose against his windpipe was mercifully gone. He began taking in huge lungfuls of air. He barely registered the sound of the reverberating gunfire.

His life had just been spared, and he knew by whom.

Seconds earlier, Major Toomey had drawn both of his holstered Colts, firing off a succession of shots that had severed the rope from the branch.

Toomey was now pointing those guns squarely at Winterhawk. "This is the second time today that I've saved your life."

Winterhawk climbed to his knees, breath still heaving in his lungs. "If I wasn't already married, I'd crawl over there and give you a sloppy kiss."

Isbell was on him with lightning speed.

He lashed out with his right foot, the heavy boot impacting against his midsection. Winterhawk cried out as the blow drove him back down to the ground. Pulling back his leg, Isbell struck again, this time landing the blow against the middle of his back. A third vicious kick crunched loudly against his ribcage.

"That's enough," Toomey cautioned.

Isbell reluctantly stepped away from Winterhawk's prone body. "I could beat him like a dog all day!"

Just then, a very unexpected sound could be heard. It was so startling that all four aeronauts could do nothing but stare at one another in astonishment.

It was the sound of laughter.

"There are many different dogs," Winterhawk continued to laugh, rolling over onto his back. He placed both feet flat against the ground, knees tented sharply, his hands still bound behind his back.

"You beat some and all they do is beg you to stop hurting them. I've even seen a few lick their own blood off a man's boots after being whipped."

Winterhawk locked his eyes on Isbell. "I've also seen others take the same kind of beating. But these ones are different. They're the kind just waiting to turn around--"

Winterhawk rocked forward with explosive force, the momentum carrying him onto his feet until he was standing nose-to-nose with Isbell.

"--and show you their bite!"

Even with Winterhawk an inch away from him, Isbell hadn't budged a single millimeter. "I guess there's still some juice left in this one," he remarked.

Toomey motioned with his pistols. "Unless you want to start to whistle when you walk, I recommend you take a step back."

Winterhawk waited for a beat, then slowly backed away from Isbell.

"It looks like we might have underestimated you," Toomey said.

"Enough with the chit-chat," Tucker sighed. "Let's just *make him* tell us where he hid the rest of that damn gold."

"He won't talk," Isbell answered. "Not even if we peeled every inch of flesh off his bones."

"I agree with your assessment, Captain," Toomey replied. "But there are *other* methods at our disposal."

He tossed something at him through the air.

Isbell caught it in mid-flight.

Winterhawk didn't even need to look. He already knew what the man was now holding. It was the locket.

Walker frowned with confusion. "What's the big deal about that cheap trinket?"

"That," Toomey motioned towards the locket, "is a priceless key that will soon lead us to the location of the gold."

Winterhawk tugged uselessly against the binds fastened around his hands. He wanted to bargain with these men, to try somehow to reason with them, but he knew it would lead nowhere. The only way you could truly satiate a predator was to indulge its hunger for gluttony.

And that's *exactly* what he was going to do.

"Here's the plan," Toomey continued, "Isbell and Tucker will remain here and guard the bags already in the wagon. Walker and I will fly Lieutenant Winterhawk back to the *Golden Goose*. Once there, he'll show us where he hid the gold."

Tucker snorted. "I'm sure he'll be falling all over himself to show you what hole it's hidden in."

"He'll be very cooperative," Toomey answered.

"Why so sure?" Walker asked.

"Because of the second part of the plan. If you and I don't return with any evidence of the gold, or if we simply don't come back at all, then Isbell and Tucker will pay a visit to the two women whose picture can be found inside that locket."

Winterhawk felt white-hot rage building up inside of him. He thought of Kaya and Chenoa being abducted, and how much these men would make them suffer—

Those thoughts lead nowhere. Let these animals threaten your family all they want. They're hungry for that gold. And once they get it, they'll kill you and forget all about this little sightseeing trip to the Malheur Indian Reservation. What you have to do right now is survive, and make sure they *don't. That's the game now, amigo; play it.*

"I'll take you to the gold," Winterhawk said with resignation. "Just promise that you won't hurt my family."

"That will depend entirely on you," Toomey answered.

Isbell flicked open the locket, gazing down at the picture. "That's a pair of juicy-looking girls there," he said. Beads of perspiration were quivering above his upper lip.

Winterhawk could feel the thump of his heartbeat pulsating behind his temples. His hands curled into tight fists behind his back.

You make a dumb move now and you will *be the one responsible for what happens to your family. Captain Isbell is nothing but hot air. Remember, hombre, an asshole farts just so it can hear itself talk.*

Winterhawk fixed his tough gaze on Isbell. "After I've finished with them, I'll be coming back here. And when I do, I'm going to kill you."

Isbell raised the locket up to his lips, giving it a grotesque kiss. "I'll be waiting, brownie."

Toomey threw a hard glance at Captain Walker. "We're done wasting time. Escort Lieutenant Winterhawk to the *Excelsior*. Then pump as much hydrogen out of the *Intrepid* as possible. We need the extra fuel."

Walker motioned at Winterhawk with his pistol. "You heard what the man said. Move your ass."

Looking down, Winterhawk realized something. He had been standing in one of the massive footprints of the Nu'numic.

Ironic imagery. We might find ourselves standing in the footprints of the monsters that walked before us, but we have a choice where we take our next steps.

He moved across the field towards the waiting balloon.

He knew it wouldn't be a long journey back to the ambush site.

Death rarely traveled far. It didn't have to.

CHAPTER 19

"They say you can see the entire world from up here," Major Toomey bellowed proudly from his perch inside the rope basket of the *Excelsior*.

Winterhawk was not inclined to disagree.

Taking in the breathtaking view of the Cascade Mountain Range, it was easy to be lulled into a false sense of idyllic tranquility.

He couldn't help but marvel at the fact that the same journey that had taken him two days in the horse-drawn wagon was now being accomplished by the *Excelsior* in only a few hours.

A massive wind gust rocked the balloon, forcing Winterhawk to reach out with both hands to steady himself on the edge of the basket. It was his third near-tumble in less than an hour.

Captain Walker looked down at Winterhawk's unbound hands with a disapproving glance.

Although he was stationed behind the barometric contractor box located dead-center in the basket, Walker still had his pistol drawn. He needed to have his hands ready to engage the automatic altitude control device, which would lower the hydrogen flame and allow them to land quickly. Knowing Winterhawk was no longer tied up simply brought him too much anxiety.

Holding onto the gun made him feel a lot safer about cutting off any bright ideas their prisoner might have had about escaping.

At first, Walker had vehemently disagreed with the order to cut off those rope cuffs. But after seeing Winterhawk stumbling around in the basket, he now better understood Major Toomey's concerns.

"He needs to hold on to the basket in case the winds pick up," Toomey had explained earlier. "We can't have our valuable guest tumbling to his death prematurely. Besides, we're several hundred feet off the ground. Where could he possibly run off to?"

When Toomey had decided to cast off in the late hours of the morning, he did it with the full understanding that the wind was at its most unpredictable during that part of the day. Typically, balloon missions were launched at either sunrise or sunset. Those were the times that wind speeds were at their lowest.

Unlike now.

While the current gusts were propelling the *Excelsior* at an incredible rate of speed, it was doing so at a tremendous risk to their safety.

But even in wartime, personal safety was never at the forefront of Major Toomey's thinking. From the very beginning, he'd always been more concerned with strategy, and objectives, and—

"Legacy!" Toomey boomed thunderously. "History books will describe everything we've accomplished in this generation as being what propelled America into the next industrial age."

Apart from extended moments of libation, Walker had rarely seen him this fiercely animated. He was halfway expecting Toomey to launch into a Sunday sermon next.

Winterhawk cocked his head, rubbing his jaw in contemplation. "I didn't realize you held such a high opinion of robbery, Major."

Ignoring the remark, Toomey turned and clasped a strong hand onto his shoulder. "You should consider yourself fortunate to be alive during such a time as this."

"I'm definitely grateful to be alive," Winterhawk replied, "especially when so many thousands of my own people have been denied the privilege."

Walker couldn't help but throw him an appreciative glance. Winterhawk definitely had balls as large as church bells. He respected that.

A flicker of disappointment crossed Toomey's face. "It's a political world. You're either the one following the elephant with a shovel, or you're the poor fellow who stepped right into the dung heap."

Winterhawk felt the tendrils of hot bile tickle the back of his throat. His urge was to spit it out onto the man's face; instead, he swallowed hard. "I've never had forced colonialism explained so eloquently."

Toomey waved him off. "You hint of dishonor and betrayal against your people; yet, here you are, standing right before me as a member of the United States military. Your allegiance to us came at a great personal cost to your tribal reputation, did it not?"

Winterhawk narrowed his eyes. "Let's just say the verdict is still out."

He returned his gaze to the distant horizon. He figured they had less than two miles left until they reached the site of the wreckage. That meant that he only had a few nuggets of valuable time left to formulate a plan once they landed.

No matter what else might transpire, Winterhawk knew that both men riding with him in the balloon would die today. Then, he would somehow make his way back to Isbell and pry the locket from out of his dead hands.

. . .

NOT FOR THE first time since he had run afoul of their captive, Walker had trouble imagining what exactly had driven this proud Indian warrior to behave so treacherously against his fellow soldiers.

The man was guilty of high treason. Divulging the top-secret train route to those ambushers was the only explanation for the massacre they had discovered.

He also believed that the ambush had been entirely orchestrated by Winterhawk to abscond with the loot. The where's and how's of his devious plan had become mere window dressing at this point.

So, why did it truly matter, anyway?

It mattered because the aeronauts had decided to confiscate the gold for themselves. They'd earned it. The treasure would be, as Major Toomey was so apt to say, their legacy.

But the decision for grand larceny hadn't been made today. The seeds of betrayal had first been sown back in 1863 after the Army had officially disbanded the Balloon Corps.

Although the aeronauts had engaged in dozens of successful missions during the Civil War, they had been grounded. The once-proud military unit was almost totally dismantled; today, there were just a handful of aircraft still operating in the United States.

Recently, things had gotten even worse.

Toomey had informed them that the search for the whereabouts of the *Goose* would mark the final flight of the Balloon Corps. Soon, their accomplishments would fizzle out into the cold darkness of historical oblivion.

The selection of this final mission was the highest irony. After being punted aside because of the dominance of the steam engine, the once-novel Balloon Corps had been dispatched to locate a missing train.

And so, they had.

They'd also discovered the man behind the treachery that cost the lives of all those soldiers. It would be a shame that this traitor would never stand before a military tribunal for his crimes. It had already been decided that Winterhawk was going to be unfortunately killed while attempting to elude capture.

But there was an even greater tragedy ready to unfold.

In a spectacular turn of bad luck, none of the gold ore had been recovered. It was assumed to have been destroyed, burned into oblivion during the ambush.

It would be quite coincidental that these same disbanded aeronauts would strike it rich a few years from now. They would innocently stumble upon a hidden stash of gold mysteriously buried deep in the Cascade Mountains.

And with no living witnesses to contradict their version of events, they would be free to tell any story they chose.

That was the plan that Major Toomey had put into place.

It's what all four men had agreed to.

Right now, all that stood between them and their legacy was this traitorous Nez Perce warrior riding alongside him in the *Excelsior*.

The Indian was dangerous, and had already caused them far too much trouble. Once Winterhawk led them to where he'd hidden the rest of the gold, Walker would gladly put a bullet in his brain.

Afterwards, Isbell would undoubtedly make good on his promise to pay his respects to the man's family. What would ultimately happen to the Indian's wife and young daughter would be a fate worse than death itself.

To that, Captain Walker could only shrug with indifference.

Fuck 'em.

. . .

WINTERHAWK WAS ASTONISHED that the wreckage of the *Golden Goose* looked as devastating from a hundred feet in the air as it had appeared from the ground.

He felt Captain Walker shifting uneasily behind him. Somewhere along the line, he and the other aeronauts had gotten too complacent with observing the carnage of war from afar. Distance had poisoned their well of reality.

But isn't that the way it usually was? It was too easy to dismiss something unless you had actually experienced it firsthand. Proximity was oftentimes the only harbinger of understanding.

Winterhawk thought briefly about the tumultuous spiritual upbringing that he'd experienced growing up in his Oregon tribal home of Chompuunish.

Chief Joseph's father, Old Joseph, had been one of famed missionary Henry Spalding's first Presbyterian Indian converts in the mid-1800s. In later years, Joseph had attempted to convince the Nez Perce to accept the Holy Scripture alongside his people's long-held religious beliefs of the Seven Drum.

This had led to many fiery debates among the tribal elders. "We may sometimes quarrel with each other about things on this earth," Chief Joseph had once remarked, "but we should never quarrel about God."

Seeing how much strife existed between the Catholics and the Protestants with whom he had spent so much time around, Joseph had eschewed bringing a formal church building onto his land. Instead, he preferred to feel the Spirit as it coursed through the wilderness, not contained between four walls that man had constructed.

"It is when the wind ruffles our hair," Joseph had told him, "that we know the Great Spirit has felt our suffering."

Winterhawk understood immediately what he had meant.

Christianity had been built upon the foundational belief that God had become flesh and walked the earth. The mortal presence of Christ was indicative of His passion, as well as His commitment to suffer on the Cross. Mankind wanted to believe that their pain was not only felt, but truly understood by God.

Great sermon, chief. But do I have to stare at a pencil if I wanna see the point?

The point was, that as a species, we would forever seek the meaning behind the wind that ruffled through our hair. Winterhawk further believed that it was that disassociation that had brought them here. The destruction of the train below them was merely a moral construct of removing something precious from the sacred land in order to use it for further subjugation of an entire race of people.

And not just *his* people, either.

Wealth in this burgeoning nation was not being used to fortify people, it was being used to classify them. The Pilgrims might have fled to this country because of religious persecution, but their descendants were being crushed to rubble beneath the onslaught of the Industrial Revolution.

I hate to break the sad news to you, amigo, but the rich just get richer. That's been the law of the land since King Ramses II went skinny dipping in the Red Sea with his golden chariot.

Yes...

The Promised Land.

That's what this whole ordeal was about. The security of knowing that, when this was all finally over, Kaya and Chenoa would be given their own piece of the promised land.

He absently touched the crumpled discharge papers that were still nested in his pocket. Even if he didn't make it home, he believed that Chief Joseph would honor the commitment given to his family.

And just why don't you think you'll make it out of this in one piece, Geronimo? Because you're stuck in this floating handmaid's basket with two bloodthirsty lunatics? Or is it knowing that you'll be fitted for a pine overcoat once you lead those degenerate saddle humpers to the gold?

The faintest trace of a smile touched his lips. When those men got their hands on those hidden bags of ore, they were in for a surprise of a lifetime.

Winterhawk felt Toomey's calculating eyes studying him. "You are a man who obviously feels the full weight of the world. I can't say that I've ever met anyone quite like you, Lieutenant."

"It would probably be hard to tell if you had," Winterhawk said, "because that would mean occasionally looking down and seeing who you've been stepping on."

Toomey dropped his hand onto the butt of his Colt, fingers drumming against the worn stock. "I'm getting real sick of your mouth."

"That's funny," Winterhawk replied, "but I'm guessing your wife says the same thing."

There was a momentary muscle spasm in Toomey's left cheek as his face flushed with anger. Walker nervously cleared his throat. "We're within landing range now, sir."

"Then take us down, Captain Walker. Our legacy awaits."

The vast destruction littered across a quarter-mile of railroad track grew larger as the *Excelsior* began its quick descent.

Taking in the horrific imagery of twisted steel and dead bodies, Toomey shook his head with disgust.

"Do you know why I am going to kill you, Lieutenant Winterhawk? It's not because I believe you're the sole progenitor behind this massacre of American soldiers. I could have just as easily fed you to the hungry lions of the military tribunal if that was the only reason.

"I am going to kill you because you think I'm stupid.

"You were trying so desperately to have me believe that you single-handedly repelled an attack from ambushers armed to the teeth with a plethora of stolen Army field artillery.

"After being caught red-handed with the gold you took from the train, you further regaled me with wild tales of being consumed with patriotic fervor. You weren't stealing that gold; rather, you were merely escorting it because of some half-assed code of honor. You must think I am very stupid, indeed."

Winterhawk scratched the stubble on his cheek. "The only thing I'm guilty of is being unlucky enough be at the wrong place at the wrong time."

Toomey lashed out, backhanding Winterhawk forcefully.

"Idiot! Look at the devastation down there. Do you know what it would take for a person to survive something like that?"

"Sure," Winterhawk answered, letting the fresh blood drip off his broken lip. "I think it would probably take somebody just like me. And Major Toomey, there is *nobody* like me."

CHAPTER 20

Interestingly enough, for all his psychotic personality faults, Captain Walker turned out be an expert balloon pilot. Even with more unexpected wind gusts, he landed the *Excelsior* with absolute precision on the grassy hill overlooking the row of Parrott mountain cannons.

From their vantage point on the hill, Winterhawk could clearly see the funeral pyre that he had left burning just two days ago. Mercifully, that fire had completely burned itself out. All that was left was blackened hunks of wood, tattered strips of uniforms, and a large, haphazard pile of...

Bones.

Winterhawk felt the hard, insistent jab of a gun barrel probing against the small of his back. It was Walker, impatiently prompting him with his pistol. He glanced over at Toomey, noticing that he had both hands resting firmly on the grips of his guns. "Think of the locket in the possession of Captain Isbell. What happens to your wife and daughter is *your* responsibility now."

Toomey grabbed the balloon's mooring line and cast it down the hill. He climbed out of the *Excelsior* and made his way to the Parrott cannons, choosing one of the barrels to tie the mooring line onto.

When the balloon was secure, Toomey glanced back up at Captain Walker and nodded.

Winterhawk once again felt the prodding of the gun against his back.

"Hope your memory is as long as my willy," Walker said. "I would hate for you to forget where you buried things out here."

Winterhawk nodded. "It's close, Walker. We're not far." He gingerly raised both his arms, carefully stepping over the balloon basket and onto the hill.

He noticed the bodies of the Zouave mercenaries. They were definitely more like carcasses now; meat nearly stripped to the bone, with large tufts of hair still attached to their skulls.

"Lead the way, soldier!" Toomey barked.

Winterhawk began to stride purposefully down the hill, making sure that his movements were measured and controlled. He didn't want to give either man an excuse to put a bullet in his leg.

After two full days of baking beneath the sun, the *Goose* now looked like a battlefield antique. It was broken in three distinct halves, its metal shell completely sheared from the multiple explosions and the heat.

Winterhawk walked a path that was parallel with the tracks, taking his armed escorts passed the yawning open door of the empty boxcar.

He forced himself not to look at the passenger car as they passed it. He could make out the blood-splashed interior in his peripheral vision, while his nose could still barely detect the horrific stench of burned flesh and hair.

"How much further?" Walker asked. His voice cracked a little. The horrific imagery of what he just glimpsed must have gotten to him.

Winterhawk set his jaw.

Good.

"Not far now." He threw a brief glance back over his shoulder, feigning a look of wide-eyed helplessness at his two captors. "Once you get your hands on the gold, you promise that my wife and daughter...now, they really won't be harmed?"

He could hear the wind whistle briefly between Toomey's teeth before he answered. The bastard must have been trying to conceal his grin. "You have my word."

Winterhawk hunched his shoulders as he walked, looking like he was trying unsuccessfully to hide a growing sense of defeat. "I don't care what happens to me, only to them. They're my world."

Careful there, amigo. You'd better save that type of syrup for flapjacks. You keep going on like this, and they'll see right through your little stage act here.

"If you really believe that," Toomey said, "then you'll lead us straight to the gold. No tricks."

They passed the caboose next, which was the only part of the *Goose* that appeared to not have received even the slightest blemish during the ambush.

Amazing, really. There were certainly people like that, too. They endured the worst that life had to throw at them; yet, unlike others around them, they came through unscathed.

That was because being the one leading out front is where you encounter the greatest risks. It was true in the military, but it was just as true in civilian life.

But what *else* was true was that those with enough courage to make the footprints for others to follow typically reaped the greatest rewards.

You honestly believe that? I think you'd better take another long look down these tracks. You'll notice that the caboose, however symbolic of a deficit of courage it might indeed represent, was still *the only part of this train to survive. That's a lesson just by itself, ain't it? If you value breathing, sometimes the best strategy is hanging back and letting some other poor bastard take that first bullet.*

A dozen paces behind the caboose, Winterhawk moved away from the tracks and down a slight gravel embankment. He then began leading Toomey and Walker across the grassy prairie and towards a thick cluster of trees that had pushed their way closest to the railroad tracks.

It was here that Winterhawk planted his feet.

"Why are we stopping, soldier?"

"Why do you think?"

"It's an odd place to stash a half-million dollars in gold," Toomey answered. His eyes searched the tree line for any hint of where the treasure was located.

"Sometimes," Winterhawk stated, "the best hiding spots are the ones that are right out in the open."

"Major!" Walker exclaimed, his voice pitched an octave higher with excitement. "I see where those bags are!" He began pointing at a spot ten feet away, towards a very large, hollowed-out stump nearly hidden within the clump of trees facing them.

Once part of a massive oak that had apparently been taken down during a fierce lightning storm, the stump itself was a mini-tree in its own right. It stood a good six-feet in height, with a total circumference of at least three times that. An unusually large hollow was at the base of the stump. And wedged inside that hollow was the distinctive shape of a cloth sack.

"You stuffed all twenty-five bags in there?" Toomey asked.

"Seemed as good a place as any," Winterhawk answered. "The bugs hollowed out that stump. It's like nature's safety deposit box now."

Toomey unholstered one of the Colts, thumbing back the hammer. "You Indians sure are clever. When it comes to living off the land, you boys never miss a trick."

"I think we should just shoot him now," Walker said. "We know where the gold is."

"Do we? Let's make damn sure that he isn't lying before we do anything rash, shall we?"

Toomey stepped up behind Winterhawk, pressing the Colt against the base of his neck. "Here's what I want you to do now, soldier. Slowly, and I mean *slowly*, I want you to grab that bag from out of the hollow and show us its contents."

Winterhawk made a display of swallowing hard, nervously clenching and unclenching his hands. He stood his ground, not moving.

Toomey pressed harder with the gun, twisting the barrel into his skin like a corkscrew. "That wasn't a request, Lieutenant. Do what I asked. NOW."

Winterhawk took several steps towards the tree stump. He felt the eyes of the two aeronauts boring into his back, watching his every move; mistrustful. It's exactly the response he had wanted.

Approaching the hollow, he bent at the waist, reaching out with his right arm, fingers touching the protruding bag—

"Stop!" Toomey unholstered the second Colt. "Hands in the air! Turn around, step back!"

Winterhawk did precisely as he was told.

Walker looked confused. "Major? What's wrong?"

"A smart man might have a weapon hidden in there," Toomey answered. "I'm not taking any chances, Walker. I want *you* to pull out that bag."

Winterhawk raised his hands, taking several steps away from the stump. "It seems like you trust me as much as I trust you."

"In a moment, Lieutenant, none of this will matter anymore," Toomey replied. "At least, not for *one* of us."

Still holding onto the gun with his right hand, Walker bent down to the hollow and grabbed the cloth sack with his left. He tugged at it for a moment, but it wouldn't budge.

"Damn thing's heavy," he grunted. "Some of the other bags jammed up in there are stacked right on top of it."

"Then start using some elbow grease!" Toomey barked impatiently.

Walker took a tighter grip onto the sack and pulled hard. He stumbled backwards, nearly losing his footing. The bag was now dangling in his hand, freed from inside the hollow.

Winterhawk took another careful step away. He was now standing in the middle of both men, his back to the stump.

Walker dropped the cloth sack to the ground, stomping hard on it with the heel of his boot. The bag split apart, a trickle of unrefined gold ore spilling out onto the dirt. "Ladies and gentlemen, we have ourselves a winner!"

Toomey grinned. "I think it's time that we retire our traitor."

Without hesitation. Walker raised his pistol and aimed it squarely at Winterhawk's face.

CHAPTER 21

Winterhawk stared down the barrel of the gun pointed directly at him.

"Say goodnight, ass wipe!" Walker shouted, finger closing around the trigger. He suddenly paused.

A low thumping sound was emanating from behind him.

Seeking the location of the noise, Toomey turned his gaze to the stump. His eyes snapped wide open with shock.

Walker jerked his head around, staring backwards with a look of dumb disbelief.

A Ketchum grenade could now be seen laying on the ground just inside the hollow of the stump. It had been effectively hidden underneath the cloth bag of gold ore that Walker had removed.

A large piece of bark had been placed behind the grenade, carved in such a way that it resembled a chute. The thumping noise was coming from that chute. More precisely, the sound itself was actually a large stone that was now rolling down it.

It was an old-fashioned rabbit trap.

Two days earlier, Winterhawk had almost considered *not* constructing such an elaborate counter-measure to safeguard the hidden gold. But uncovering an unused Ketchum grenade among an ammunition pile left inside the supply wagon had given him an idea.

After carefully stacking the cloth bags inside the stump, Winterhawk had used the razor-sharp whale bone on the Girandoni to carve a long chute from a piece of splintered bark. After setting the single bag of ore onto the grenade as bait, he had placed the chute against the cloth and balanced a stone on a bag near the top. Pulling hard on the bag would jostle the chute, and set the stone into motion.

Which is exactly what had happened.

Walker jerked his body away from the hollow, face aghast with horror, mouth twitching as his eyes locked briefly onto Winterhawk.

"Goodnight, ass wipe," Winterhawk echoed.

Behind them, the stone tumbled off the chute and landed onto the grenade.

The explosion was instantaneous.

The loud double-thump from the initial blast was concussive, sending a low wave of flame and shrapnel sweeping out from the hollow.

Winterhawk reacted by pulling his body down into a crouch, placing both hands flat against the dirt.

Crying out, Toomey flung himself to the ground, rolling as flames scraped against his uniform.

Walker threw back both his arms, puffing out his chest as a shrill scream escaped his throat. He had been standing less than five feet from the epicenter of the blast when it had gone off, his lower body taking the full force of the initial explosion.

The back of Walker's torso was immediately peppered with grenade shrapnel and burning fragments of the ore. Ragged flesh chunks flapped in every direction a half-second before the explosive force of the grenade sawed off both of his legs below the knees.

Walker screamed in agony. His legless torso toppled forward, the pistol spinning into the air.

Winterhawk moved with explosive force, pushing himself up from the deep crouch and leaping upwards.

With one of his coat arms still on fire from the explosion, Toomey rolled into a kneeling position, swinging both Colts around.

Winterhawk grabbed the falling pistol while he was still airborne. Slamming his left foot down hard onto Walker's dropping body, he used the man's shoulders as a springboard, further propelling himself through the air.

He twisted his body while in mid-flight, now facing backwards, unloading with the pistol.

Toomey staggered sideways as the bullets tore into the ground at his feet. He frantically began waving his right arm, attempting to douse the flame that was still crawling over his uniform. He screamed as the flames burned their way through the fabric and touched the flesh of his arm. Dropping the pistols, he used both hands to bat out the fire.

Behind him, Winterhawk had crashed hard against the stump, groaning with pain as he dropped to the ground.

There was a merciful moment of silence.

Before—

A sizzling noise.

Black smoke wafted across his face.

It took a brief second for Winterhawk to realize what had happened.

The fire...

The residual blaze from the grenade had just ignited the stump like it was a pile of kindling.

Winterhawk felt panic suddenly envelope him.

That *other* sound.

He knew where it was coming from.

The cloth bags stacked inside the stump. They were also burning. And the hundreds of pounds of ore were acting like a fuse. When the temperature inside that stump became hot enough...

Toomey was already in motion. He was sprinting hard towards the tracks. He was making a run for the *Excelsior*.

Winterhawk scrambled to his feet, feeling the intense heat as he staggered away from the burning stump. Looking over his shoulder at the flames, he stumbled over Walker's corpse, nearly falling.

Seconds...

That's all the time he had left.

The unrefined ore contained in those bags was highly combustible. When a volatile substance is divided into smaller particles, the surface area available for a chemical reaction will increase. When that area expands during a large fire, a collision occurs between the oxygen molecules. In the presence of a flame, those molecules become highly combustible. The presence of heat forces a rapid release of the gases being formed, creating a tremendous shock wave. Whenever that happens, even the smallest particles floating around can cause a massive explosion. And with several hundred pounds of ore cooking inside that stump...

Winterhawk launched into a dead sprint.

In the distance, he could see that Toomey had already gained a lot of ground as he made his way towards the *Excelsior*. He couldn't allow the Major to launch that balloon and return to Isbell. Because if that happened, he knew neither one of those men would rest until Kaya and Chenoa were dead.

He then saw the caboose. If he could somehow reach it, he might be protected from the force of the blast.

His arms were pumping furiously as he coaxed the maximum amount of speed from his exhausted legs.

The caboose loomed ahead.

He charged up the slight incline leading towards the tracks.

Ten feet away.

The roar of the fire behind him escalated in volume.

Five feet.

He was close enough now that he could see his charging reflection against one of the windows.

The ore detonated inside the stump with a loud thunderclap.

Winterhawk flung himself into the air.

The concussive blast was enormous, gouging a meteor-sized crater in the ground. The surrounding trees were covered in a shroud of fire as flaming pieces of the ore showered out in every direction.

. . .

CHARGING UP THE grassy hill to the *Excelsior*, Toomey winced as the deafening blast swept across the prairie floor. He glanced back at the explosion, seeing the tongue of fire curl its way past the railroad tracks. The force of the explosion had hit the caboose with enough force to roll it over.

He thought of the half-million dollars in gold ore that Winterhawk had just been vaporized with. "That's an expensive funeral," Toomey muttered disgustedly.

He scrambled inside the *Excelsior*. Unsheathing his Bowie knife, he cut the mooring line tied to one of the Parrott cannons.

He felt the balloon begin its slow ascent. Gripping onto the side of the rope basket, he took a final look at the burning fortune that he was leaving behind.

His eyes went wide.

There was movement coming from inside the dark layers of smoke blanketing the caboose.

No! It was impossible.

And yet, he saw something emerging from the smoke that he thought he would never see again.

It was Winterhawk, running with all the speed of a cannon blast.

Toomey sneered.

The fool was too late. By the time he even reached the crest of the hill, the *Excelsior* would be well beyond his reach.

Actually, Toomey thought it was better this way. Winterhawk would be close enough to look in to the eyes of the man who would murder his family, but far enough away to not do a damn thing about it. It would be a memory that would bring a lifetime of anguish.

Toomey cast him with a final salute before turning to the automatic altitude control device, raising both the hydrogen flame and the speed of the balloon's ascent.

CHAPTER 22

Winterhawk had crashed headfirst through the window of the caboose a half-second after the detonation. He hit the floor, rolling hard against the wall as the force of the explosion rocked the outside of the car.

There was a horrible screeching sound as the caboose was pushed off the rails, tipping dangerously forward.

Winterhawk cried out, feeling himself helplessly sliding up the wall as the caboose rolled over onto its side, crashing to the ground with a wallop.

And kept going!

Incredibly, the inertia of the blast caused the caboose to flip over a second time. The car came to a full stop after it rolled upside down. Its wheelset was now pointing up at the sky, the frame assembly sheared halfway off, hanging limply in the air.

Winterhawk was stretched out on the floor. It was with a groggy realization that he understood it was now actually the ceiling.

And then he saw something else.

Through the broken caboose window and the coils of black smoke, he saw Major Toomey had already climbed into the *Excelsior*.

He felt the fangs of despair coiling deep within his stomach.

NO.

It wasn't over yet. He had to do something.

Winterhawk pushed himself unsteadily to his feet, his battered and bruised body screaming in harsh protest.

He staggered towards the shattered caboose window.

And stopped in his tracks.

Something on the ground had caught his attention. An object laying near his boots. It was a mail hook.

In the earliest days of the railroad, trains would make frequent stops at postal annexes strategically placed along certain routes. The mail would be loaded onto the train and delivered to the next annex for delivery. Although this method allowed for a much more efficient postal delivery system, passengers soon grew weary of how much these mail stops were adding to their overall travel time.

The mail hook system was devised as a way to still grab the mail from those postal annexes without having to slow or stop the train. With this method, railway workers would fasten a rawhide strap around their wrist that was attached to the four-foot metal hook. As the train approached the postal annex, they would lean out and grab the mail bags off an elevated platform built beside the tracks.

Every train in America had a mail hook as part of its essential supplies, even the military ones.

Winterhawk snatched the hook up from off the floor, sliding the sweat-stained rawhide strap tightly around his right wrist.

Outside the caboose, he could see that the *Excelsior* had just risen off the ground. By the time he reached the top of that hill, he feared it would be at least fifteen feet in the air.

Winterhawk launched himself through one of the broken windows, flinging his body to the ground. Rolling to his feet, he hurtled forward, breaking free from the dark clutches of the smoke in a savage sprint, arms pumping wildly.

Even from this distance, he could clearly make out Toomey's look of astonishment. He was obviously stunned to see that his adversary was still alive, but that moment of hesitation didn't last very long.

Saluting him, Toomey turned to the automatic altitude control device, increasing the volume of the hydrogen flame, quickening the balloon's ascent.

Crying out with exertion, Winterhawk attempted to coax as much speed from his legs as possible.

But that was the problem.

His entire body was bruised and battered from the horrific events he'd endured over the last several days. No soldier had ever survived what he just had.

You might be right about that. But do you wanna hear some hard truth now? You ain't fighting as a soldier anymore. Those men threatened to harm your daughter; they promised to kill your wife. Soldiers, they give up the fight when the battle's been lost. But a father, he's never gonna give up the fight for his family. That's who you are now; hell, that's who you've always been. So, if you need to find some more strength to press on, then by God, you find it.

Winterhawk felt a jolt of adrenaline surge through his body as he weaved his way around the rows of Parrott cannons and onto the hill.

The balloon had now risen over ten feet above the ground.

"Don't worry about your wife," Toomey sneered, "we'll give her a second honeymoon for you!"

Reaching the top of the hill, Winterhawk launched himself upwards. With his left hand reaching high above his head, he pinwheeled his right arm around, swinging the mail hook through the air.

While airborne, Winterhawk followed through with the arc on the hook, feeling his right deltoid pop with the ferocious exertion.

With only two inches left to spare between the zenith of his arm's extended reach and the bottom of the balloon, the mail hook attached itself firmly against the basket.

Winterhawk grunted as he felt the rawhide strap tighten around his wrist, his body twisting beneath the *Excelsior* as it continued its ascent.

Toomey's face appeared at the edge of the basket, lips contorting with shock as he stared down at his unwanted passenger. He began to slash savagely downwards with the knife, but his target was just out of arm's reach.

The balloon was battered by a sudden wind gust. It momentarily tipped the basket, causing Toomey to use both hands to stop himself from toppling overboard.

As the balloon shifted at a thirty-degree angle, Winterhawk completely lost his grip on the hook. His palm slid down the iron until he felt the sharp pain of the strap digging into his wrist.

He now found himself twisting helplessly beneath the balloon, legs kicking through the air as he stared up at the leather strap.

The *Excelsior* had already reached a height of over a hundred feet. It was still being hit by random wind gusts, jerking the basket in various directions. Toomey was hunched over the altitude control device, shifting the balloon's path from a southeastern direction to a southwestern one.

Now, the *Excelsior* was moving rapidly towards a wide row of Douglas firs.

Winterhawk watched the line of trees loom closer.

Toomey was planning on skimming directly above the treetops, dragging him straight through the dense foliage. He would either be dislodged from the hook and plummet a hundred feet to the ground, or the thick tree branches would flay the flesh straight off his bones.

Either way, Winterhawk knew he was a dead man.

He began to twist frantically beneath the balloon, attempting to secure a handhold on the basket before it was too late.

He lunged up, the fingers of his left hand grabbing onto the side of the basket, but his grip just wasn't secure enough. With a yell of frustration, he sunk back down to his original hanging position beneath the balloon.

There wasn't any more time left.

They were right on top of the trees now.

Praying that the mail hook wouldn't become dislodged from the basket, he tightened his grip on the rawhide strap.

Things were about to get rough.

CHAPTER 23

Winterhawk's body collided with the first Douglas fir, the hard impact twisting him around like a Kansas weathervane. He grunted in pain as several of the larger branches snapped against his lower body.

Gasping for breath, he tried to prepare for impact with the second tree that was approaching fast. It had a massive cone. He tried to raise his legs to avoid hitting it, but it was a futile gesture. He cried out as one of the massive tree limbs slammed into his abdomen, knocking the air out of his lungs.

Winterhawk still hadn't regained his breath by the time the *Excelsior* had reached the third tree. He felt himself helplessly dropping into the thick cluster of upper branches. He squeezed his eyes shut as the jagged limbs began scratching along his face. The branches were hitting all over his body now, acting like wooden fingers as they attempted to pull him down.

For one terrifying moment it felt like his right shoulder was going to be pulled out of its socket. The rawhide strip was biting deeply into his flesh, drawing blood. The surrounding darkness was punctuated by brief slashes of light through the thick branches crowding in all around him.

The whole ordeal felt like it lasted for an eternity.

And then the *Excelsior* was mercifully free, floating into open air and away from this grouping of large trees.

Toomey poked his head over the edge of the basket. "I'm glad that you're still with us!" He disappeared from view. A moment later, the *Excelsior* had once again shifted directions.

It was now heading towards another large cluster of trees.

You'd better think of something fast, Jolon. I don't think you'll survive another pass through those treetops.

Winterhawk looked up at the balloon, feeling the stinging wind caressing the dozens of scratches on his face. He caught small glimpses of Toomey through the gaps between the woven ropes of the basket.

He then stared at the mail hook suspended on the end of his right arm. He had an idea.

Wrapping his hand around the rawhide strap, he dipped his body beneath the basket, feeling the agonizing pull against his bruised deltoid.

He squeezed his eyes shut.

When he was younger, his father had taught him a valuable fishing lesson. While others would walk away from the rivers empty-handed, his father had always returned to the camp with a plentiful bounty of fresh steelhead.

"It's what you put on the end of your line, Jolon," he had once offered by way of an explanation.

And do you remember exactly what *was always on the end of his rod?*

Winterhawk snapped his eyes open.

Fresh bait.

With an enormous burst of upper body strength, he swung up towards the balloon. Reaching out, he wrapped his left hand around the basket, his fingers now curled around the gap between the ropes.

With his right arm, he pushed upwards against the mail hook, effectively dislodging it from the basket. He painfully slid his wrist out from beneath the rawhide strap, letting the hook hang beneath him as he gripped it tightly.

He was now hanging unsecured by his left hand a hundred feet off the ground while the *Excelsior* was moments away from dragging him into another row of trees. If his body so much as brushed against one of those branches, he would fall to his death.

"Toomey!" Winterhawk's booming voice carried above the cacophony of the intermittent blasts coming from the balloon's flaming hydrogen tank.

Hearing him, Toomey whirled around. His gaze immediately locked onto Winterhawk's hand wrapped around one of the crisscrossing ropes of the basket. He grinned as he saw the exposed fingers move reflexively, clawing for better traction.

Brandishing the Bowie knife, Toomey lunged forward. Spittle hung from his upper lip as his mouth quivered with excitement.

"Any final acts of heroism, Lieutenant?" Toomey asked. He had the Bowie in an overhand grip, preparing to sever Winterhawk's fingers, which would send him plummeting to his death.

"Sure," Winterhawk growled, swinging his right arm, bringing the mail hook around like a pickaxe, "how does this grab you?"

He imbedded the hook into Toomey's left shoulder. It sunk deeply into the thick flesh of the trapezius, just inches away from his neck. Toomey yelled in agony, staggering backwards, his knife dropping to the floor of the basket.

Seeing the massive shape of the approaching Douglas fir filling his peripheral vision, Winterhawk forcefully lunged upwards. His right hand curled around the edge of the basket, allowing him enough leverage to hoist his body safely inside the balloon.

A split second later the *Excelsior* had reached the tree line, skimming several feet above the row of Douglas firs.

Winterhawk landed in the basket, breath heaving in his lungs, heart hammering. His hands were numb, nerve sensors tingling from the exertion of holding onto the balloon for his very life.

Crying out with pain, Toomey pulled the hook out of his flesh, casting it over the side. A small geyser of blood splashed against the side of his face as the jagged wound was fully exposed. His left shoulder was hunched to the side, the corresponding arm dangling uselessly.

Toomey reached down with his good right arm and picked up the Bowie. His face was quickly draining of color as the effects of shock took over his body.

Winterhawk climbed unsteadily to his feet. He tore the tattered Cavalry uniform off his body. His exposed chest and back revealed a roadmap of cuts and bruises.

"It doesn't have to end this way," he said, wrapping the shirt around his right arm, wincing as the fabric grazed the bleeding gash on his wrist. "You and your men can take the rest of that gold. I only want the locket back."

The balloon jostled dangerously with a fresh gust of wind.

The wide expanse of the Cascade Mountains and the dense wilderness of the Van Duzer Forest could now be seen off in the distance.

Even with the high-altitude wind buffeting the basket, droplets of sweat had already pooled on Toomey's face. He shifted his position slightly, moving away from the flaming hydrogen so that he could look into Winterhawk's eyes.

It was apparent that this sick and twisted monster of a man would not give up without a fight to the death.

That's the power of gold, amigo. Greed does that to a man. The most dangerous flag a person will ever swear allegiance to is the one they hoist in the name of their own self-interests.

Winterhawk had finished wrapping the uniform around his arm. At best, it would deflect one solid parry against that Bowie before the blade sliced it into useless tatters.

Toomey shook his head, holding the knife at an angle across his chest. "Am I to understand that you are offering to spare my life if I let you go?"

Winterhawk nodded resolutely. "It's your last chance."

Toomey laughed. "In my experience, whenever a man brings his fists to a knife fight, it's usually the one who's swinging his knuckles that meets the undertaker first."

There was five feet of distance between the two combatants.

Winterhawk braced himself on the unsteady floor of the basket, slightly bending his knees for balance. He turned his body, left hand down near his waist, right arm raised in a defensive posture.

Toomey sunk into a crouched position. He shifted the Bowie slightly, making sure that the tip of the blade was pointing squarely at Winterhawk's midsection.

While an amateur might go for the quick strike and use an overhanded grip in a downward swinging motion, that left too much of the assailant's upper body open for a potential defensive counterstrike.

Lunging at an upward angle was a more effective option during a close-quarter attack. Not only did it allow for additional strength because of the powerful thrust of the legs as the attacker swung his body weight, but the arc of the blade itself traversed a pattern from the groin through the sternum.

If you were punctured in either of those vital areas with a knife, your time on this earth was done.

That was the stance that Toomey had just taken.

By shifting the Bowie down across his hip, he was preparing for an upward thrust. He knew Winterhawk wouldn't be able to move backwards from such a strike because of his placement in the basket. Slashing vertically, it would force Winterhawk to shift sideways to evade the blow.

From there, the next question to ponder would be which direction would Winterhawk shift to escape the knife. If he moved to the right, it would place him too close to his attacker, while a move to the left would put him closer to the burning hydrogen. Going towards the flame would allow the possibility of being quick enough to circle around the basket, placing him in a position to move behind his attacker.

It would then be a reasonable assumption for Toomey to signal that he would thrust upwards with the knife, only to lunge sideways as Winterhawk shifted to the left. The blow would plunge into his ribcage and puncture his lungs like a hot knife through butter.

At least, that was what he *wanted* Winterhawk to think.

There was a third option to consider.

It was the technique Winterhawk would use himself if he was the one attempting a close-quarters attack with the Bowie.

Jabbing.

Using the blade as if engaged in a fencing tournament, the attacker would make quick jabbing motions against their target. While none of the strikes would immediately prove fatal, the rapid-fire jabs would cause multiple flesh wounds around the arms, chest, and legs. The target would soon experience enough massive blood loss that he could no longer defend himself, leading to the inevitability of a fatal finishing strike.

Toomey would probably begin with an upwards lunge with the knife, shifting to rapid-fire jabs with the blade. By the time Winterhawk had figured out this strategy, Toomey would have effectively delivered a half-dozen deep puncture wounds.

And by then, it would be too late.

Of the three options for a knife attack, Toomey would utilize the jabbing technique. Winterhawk was all but certain of it.

He flicked his eyes down to the Bowie, giving the intimation that he was planning a defensive strategy. He needed to make him confident enough to—

Move.

Toomey lunged upwards with the knife.

Winterhawk feigned a shifting of his upper body to the left, but kept his feet planted on the floor of the basket. Midway through the upward arc, Toomey jabbed with the knife, the blade whistling forward with deadly accuracy.

Winterhawk brought his right hand down across his body, the knife puncturing the uniform wrapped around his arm. He could feel the pressure of the blade ripping through the fabric, the tip barely pressing against his skin.

Toomey had already pulled his arm back, going in for another fast jab. As he did, Winterhawk threw his body backwards, limbs splayed out as his full weight crashed against the basket.

The balloon tilted dangerously, throwing Toomey off-balance. The angle of the Bowie arced sharply, connecting with nothing but air.

Toomey staggered forward with a surprised grunt, slashing futilely with the knife. Winterhawk lashed out with his leg, his boot impacting against Toomey's left knee with bone-shattering force.

Toomey took a haphazard step forward, screaming with pain as he inadvertently placed his full weight down on his shattered kneecap. His good arm flailing wildly, he lost balance, body careening backwards. The Bowie spun from his grasp as he fell, flying end-over-end as it sailed over the lip of the basket.

Winterhawk moved over Toomey's writhing body.

"Please don't kill me!" Toomey whimpered. "I'll do anything you want! I swear to God..."

Bending down, Winterhawk yanked Toomey back onto his feet. Spinning him around, he jammed his knee into the small of his back, roughly shoving him face-first into the flaming hydrogen.

Toomey emanated a high-pitch scream as the flames wrapped around his head. His hair immediately caught fire while he frantically attempted to push his body away from the hydrogen.

Winterhawk released his hold and stepped back.

Shrieking with agony, Toomey slithered away from the flames. The skin on his face was already blackened, the flesh beneath his eyes drooping off the cheekbones. Both of his lips had been seared off, giving the impression of a perpetual death grin.

"You've been discharged, Major."

Reaching down, Winterhawk hefted his squirming bulk up onto his shoulder. And without hesitation, tossed him over the side like a bag of garbage. The echo of Toomey's screams ended abruptly a few seconds later as he impacted against the ground.

Winterhawk moved to the balloon's automatic altitude control device, recalling how Captain Walker had operated it on their flight back to the wreckage of the *Goose*.

He took a quick glance at the position of the sun and the location of the Cascade Mountains before being satisfied that he was heading in the right direction. Given the wind currently at his back, he figured that the return flight back to Captain Isbell would not take long at all.

Death rarely traveled far. It didn't have to.

PART III
The Heart of the Monster

CHAPTER 24

Captain Thomas Isbell was growing increasingly impatient with all the waiting. It had seemed to him that the *Excelsior* should have returned hours ago. He knew that Major Toomey wouldn't have been able to transport back any of that gold in the balloon, but at least he would know by now where it was all hidden.

He was now afraid that something had gone terribly wrong. But that was irrational; more so, it was absolutely impossible.

Lieutenant Winterhawk had been taken as a prisoner. His family had been threatened if he didn't cooperate. He would have been summarily executed after leading them to the exact location of the gold ore.

It should have all gone according to plan. And yet, somehow it wasn't.

Several hours ago, Isbell had moved the supply wagon away from the grotesque field massacre and return to the location where they had first found Winterhawk.

Captain Tucker had voiced concerns over leaving the *Intrepid* behind, but Isbell had waved him off with irritation. The Army balloon was tethered and secured. It wasn't like one of those corpses was suddenly going to reanimate and take it up for a ride.

But there were *other* considerations.

For one, Isbell had to get away from the stench of that field. The rancid smell of rotting flesh cooking under the sun for the last several days was almost unbearable. It made him seethe with anger thinking about how

Winterhawk had cut those men down, leaving their bodies to be picked clean by predators.

And there was another reason he had wanted to leave the killing field. Isbell had wanted to get away from the eerie sensation that they were being watched. He knew how irrational that sounded. But there was a pervasive sense of foreboding looming over the forest. Trepidation hung thick in the air like a dense fog creeping stealthily into the subconscious.

Plus, there had been the massive tracks.

He didn't know how they had missed seeing them before. The aeronauts had obviously been too distracted with the horrific sight of the butchered men to take notice of the ground the corpses had been strewn down upon.

It had been Tucker who had seen the gigantic footprints first. He'd happened upon it shortly after the *Excelsior* had lifted off for its return trip back to the site of the train derailment.

"Captain Isbell?" he had said, finger absently scratching the unkempt stubble on one side of his face. "If these poor boys got themselves tore up by the wolves you and Toomey shot down, then what do you reckon *this* is doing here?"

It was an excellent question.

Upon first inspection, Isbell had assumed that the print had come from a bear. But given the diameter and sheer girth of the track pressed deep into the blood-soaked ground, it would indicate a bear of considerable size.

While he heard wild campfire tales surrounding grizzly bears reaching dizzying heights of ten feet or more, Isbell had never encountered one of that size out in the wilderness. He doubted many ever had.

But *something* had made that print. Whatever animal it was, the thing had obviously gorged itself on human flesh.

And it would undoubtedly be hungry for more.

Convinced it had come from a grizzly, Tucker had been rather nonplussed about the footprints. "Bears are scavengers," he had remarked. "Probably came running out of the bushes after Winterhawk killed those men. The grizzly would have scared off those wolves, too."

"Perhaps," Isbell had answered.

But he wasn't so sure anymore.

He knew Tucker couldn't find his own dick with both hands and a map, so he had taken it upon himself to investigate the killing field in greater detail. He had uncovered more of those gigantic footprints, but not a single wolf track.

That had been unsettling, but that hadn't been the worst of it. That moment came a few minutes later, when he had felt *something* watching him from the woods. There had also been a pungent, animalistic odor in the air.

The whole thing had spooked him immediately. He didn't know exactly why, but he felt strongly that staying in that place for even a minute longer wasn't safe.

They had to move.

When he had first ordered Tucker to assist him with driving the wagon back to the area where they had killed those wolves, he had been met with some fierce resistance.

"Major Toomey will expect us—"

"To do whatever we can to keep the gold secure. No more questions. Just do what I say."

And so, they had returned to that area in the forest where Winterhawk had been attempting to make his last stand before the aeronauts had come to his rescue.

We should have just let the bastard die, Isbell had thought for the hundredth time that day.

Tucker was mulling around the trio of dead wolves, absently kicking at them with his boot. "You know," he said, arching an eyebrow up at Isbell, "that Indian might have been telling the truth. Things on that train might have gone down exactly as he said they did. Have you even considered that?"

Isbell unsheathed his Bowie knife, motioning with it. "Have you considered what it would be like living the rest of your life without a tongue?"

Tucker held up both of his hands in defense. "I'm not sayin' he *is* telling the truth. Damn. I was just asking if you thought it *might* be possible."

"An Indian telling the truth? No, that's *not* possible."

Isbell returned the knife to its sheath. He felt a cold, distant rage thumping in the back of his head. "There's just one thing Indians are good at," Isbell continued, "and that's butchering all of us. Trust me, Tucker. I know all too well."

His nostrils flared as he inhaled the acrid smell of burned flesh. It took him a moment to realize that what he was smelling wasn't coming from anything around him. It was his senses drudging up memories.

Less than a decade ago now.

The Snake War had begun in 1864 after the Shoshoni Indians had revolted against settlers moving into their tribal lands along the Snake River. Those settlers had wanted to stake their claim on a series of recently discovered silver mines, which set off a vicious war with the various tribes who had been living on that very land.

Although the Snake War had originated in Idaho, the uprising eventually spread to Oregon, California, and Nevada. It was ended after four years when the U.S. Army finally quelled the unrest after engaging in hundreds of deadly skirmishes. All told, there were 1,762 documented casualties on either side of the Snake War.

Two of the dead had been Isbell's own wife and infant son.

Slaughtered by a band of bloodthirsty warriors from the Shoshoni tribe during a nighttime raid while he had been off serving his country.

He hadn't been there to save them. He hadn't been there to hear their tormented screams. He hadn't forgotten the hate that drove him to avenge their deaths.

It would be pleasurable for him to inflict that same level of pain and suffering onto the wife and daughter of Lieutenant Winterhawk. He understood that nothing he did could ever bring back the dead, but he would certainly have a lot of fun trying.

The distant chugging of a powerful steam engine roaring to life could be heard echoing throughout the valley.

Tucker jerked his head towards the sound, brow furrowed. "What the hell is that?"

Isbell motioned with his head towards the eastern edge of the Cascade Mountains, pointing towards the tall silhouette of the Nelscott flume that had been cut into the forest.

"It's those lumber boys down from Buncombe. Somebody must have just fired up the steam donkey. Those bastards sure make one helluva racket."

"Are we that close to Buncombe?" Tucker asked.

"Less than five miles."

"Are we going to hide out there, you think?"

Isbell shrugged indifferently. "Maybe. Probably. I don't really know, Tucker. Haven't really thought that far ahead yet."

Tucker nodded at the supply wagon. "That old bucket is going to stand out like a sore thumb. If we wheel it into Buncombe, those townsfolk will likely think—"

"Whatever we tell them to think," Isbell said with an exasperated sigh. "They'll take one look at our pretty uniforms and not think twice about the tall tale that goes with it. Understand something, Tucker. People are genuinely stupid. That's what makes it all so easy."

"Do you ever think that *we* just might be the stupid ones?"

"Just how do you figure?" Isbell asked, casting him with an irritated glance.

"My father served in the Army," Tucker continued. "My granddaddy before him. In fact, the long line of men in my family are all soldiers. Fighting against the French, fighting against the British, and fighting against the South. I guess we don't know any other way of providing for our families."

Isbell could feel a dull throbbing behind his eyes. He very much wanted Tucker to just stop talking. The blathering idiot needed to shut his mouth before something bad happened to him.

"I'm sure your family tree is really very interesting," Isbell remarked calmly, "but let's pretend I'm an outhouse so you can remind me why I should give a shit?"

"It's just this thing that we're doing," Tucker said. "Doesn't feel like something that my own sons would be very proud of."

"You're sounding like a man who is having second thoughts about a few things. Is that what's going on here, Tucker?"

"It's a bit more complicated than that," Tucker replied. "What we've already done, it can't very well be undone. But what we're planning on doing next; well, sir, it doesn't have to happen. There's still time to make another choice. We don't have to live our whole lives knowing that we didn't even try."

Isbell stared at him for a long moment. "Captain Tucker, do you know what generational wealth sounds like? No? Well, I'll make it easy for you, then. Let's begin by going over what it *doesn't* sound like.

"Generational wealth doesn't sound like that steam donkey snorting off in the distance. It doesn't sound like the crash of a coal mine coming down on top of your head. And it doesn't sound like hundreds of cannons hurling destruction across whatever blood-soaked trench you might find yourself cowering in. For your children and great-grandchildren, generational wealth will ensure that they will *never* have to hear the sounds of struggle that you and I have had to endure for our entire lives. We owe that type of life to them, Tucker. And we damn well owe it to ourselves."

"But the gold on that train isn't ours to take," Tucker answered.

"It isn't anyone's! Someone took it off a mountain; then, the Army took it from them. Now, *we're* taking it for us."

Tucker slowly ran a hand beneath his stubbled chin. "They'll believe us about what happened to the gold? That the ore was burned up on the train? They won't suspect that we hid it all somewhere?"

"What did I tell you before?" Isbell sighed. "People are stupid."

He was certainly testing that particular theory right now.

Of course, neither Toomey or himself had any intention of sharing even an ounce of that ore with those two buffoons from the *Intrepid*. Walker and Tucker were needed solely for collaboration on a uniquely fanciful story they would concoct for the military tribunal board at the White Salmon Brickhouse.

The board would believe that Lieutenant Winterhawk was the lone traitor who tipped off General Cornadez to the exact whereabouts of the *Golden Goose*. They would also believe that the gold ore was tragically destroyed along with the train during the bloody skirmish.

With his plan foiled, Winterhawk had tried to escape the scene of his crime, but was ultimately captured and executed by the last four remaining aeronauts of the United States Balloon Corps. The Army might even decide to throw them a parade to express their sincere and heartfelt gratitude for taking down such a vile traitor.

Afterwards, the gold ore would be buried, hidden for years until they felt it was safe enough to dig up and make a life-changing discovery. But well before that, Walker and Tucker would both meet with unfortunate accidents. Those two decorated war heroes would be tragically taken from this world way too soon, leaving Toomey and Isbell as the last two survivors of the Balloon Corps.

They would also be the only two men alive who knew the hidden location of a million dollars of unrefined gold ore. But until that moment when they would claim all of that gold for themselves, Isbell needed to wait patiently.

But how would he ever pass the time?

Grinning, he pulled the battered silver locket out of his pocket. Clicking it open, he stared hungrily down at the picture of Winterhawk's daughter. While he was on the reservation, he would undoubtedly find many different forms of entertainment that would fancy him.

"Captain Isbell!"

Tucker's voice was frantic and high-pitched. He had an arm extended towards the southwestern edge of the Cascade Mountains, pointing excitedly towards the clouds.

Isbell narrowed his eyes.

And then he saw it, too.

Skimming low over the tree line.

It was the *Excelsior*.

CHAPTER 25

Captain Tucker raised a hand over his brow, shielding his eyes from the glaring overhead sun as he stared intently at the incoming *Excelsior*.

"What the hell is Walker thinking?" he asked. "Piloting the balloon so close to the treetops like that is plain stupid. The slightest downdraft would bring the *Excelsior* down like it was a damn clay pigeon. He knows better than that."

"Yes," Isbell frowned. "He most certainly does."

The unusual flight pattern of the balloon itself was troublesome, but there was something else that bothered him even more.

Army regulations. More specifically, the total *absence* of it.

It was standard protocol within the United States Balloon Corps that every approach procedure be heralded by a series of arm gestures that would inform the soldiers on the ground as to intent.

If the aeronaut returns from a mission and has both arms raised above his head, it indicates a neutral landing with no expectation that a visible threat was seen.

If that aeronaut has both arms raised and pointed to the starboard direction of the balloon, it translates that a potential threat was seen, but that the enemy was not close enough to pose an immediate danger.

If the aeronaut has both extended arms gesturing to the port side of the balloon, it translates into taking action against a threat that is within close striking distance.

There should have been two men standing inside that basket. One piloting the balloon, and the other following those established landing protocols.

But from his vantage point on the ground, the *Excelsior* looked like it was totally unmanned. In fact, it appeared almost as if it was a ghost craft drifting aimlessly in the wind.

Isbell felt a cold coil of fear nest in the pit of his stomach.

The death stench of the wolves spread around them overwhelmed his senses. It was as if the slaughtered animals had become a grim harbinger of his own pending fate.

He felt a prickling at the back of his neck.

They were too exposed out in this field.

"Get in the wagon," he barked at Tucker. His voice was cracked and hoarse. "Take the reins and drive us out of here. We don't have much time."

Tucker turned and stared at him. "What the hell are you talking about? The *Excelsior* will be landing in just a few minutes. Toomey and Walker—"

"They're dead, you asshole!" Isbell shouted. "I don't know how, but the Indian killed 'em both; now, he's piloting that fucking balloon. Don't you get it? Winterhawk's come back for us."

The color drained out of Tucker's face until his skin resembled the splotchy color of dirty bathwater. "Oh, shit," he muttered.

"Get your stupid ass onto the wagon! Now!"

Both men bolted across the field and climbed into the driver's seat of the wagon. The two horses hitched to it whinnied anxiously at the commotion.

As Tucker grabbed tightly onto the reins, Isbell scooped up the Henry repeater that had been placed on the seat.

He looked back at the *Excelsior*. The balloon was less than a mile from them now. And it was gaining ground quickly.

"Where do we go now?" Tucker asked breathlessly. "Do we head back to the *Intrepid* and fly the fuck out of here?"

"We're not leaving all of this gold behind," Isbell answered. He busied himself by chambering rounds into the Henry. "And besides, Toomey ordered most of the hydrogen to be syphoned from the *Intrepid* before they took off in the *Excelsior*. We wouldn't get very far."

Tucker's eyes nervously flicked down to the rifle. "Are you thinking about making some kind of half-assed last stand out here? In case you haven't been keeping up with everything, it would seem that indestructible Indian just bought himself a one-way ticket up your stinkhole."

"I have a plan for dealing with him."

"I have a plan, too." Tucker replied. "Let's just leave all the gold behind in the wagon, drop that damn locket, and ride away like crazy bastards."

"The only thing that we'll be dropping," Isbell growled, "will be your balls after I cut 'em off and leave them for the field mice to nibble on. Are we clear on that, soldier?"

"Clear as mud," Tucker answered. He angrily turned his gaze up front to the horses, hands balling into fists as he gripped the reins.

Isbell shifted in the carriage, pulling the Henry repeater up to his shoulder. "I want you to drive straight up to that lumber camp. Take us right to the edge of the flume. Go as fast as you possibly can; then, go even faster."

"What are you going to do?"

Isbell narrowed his eyes as he stared up at the *Excelsior*. "I'm going to avenge the Major. Now, go! Go!"

Tucker snapped hard against the reins, shouting at the horses as they lunged forward. The overloaded supply wagon dragged its wheels sluggishly against the grass, the frame shifting dangerously sideways. Both men could hear the loud creaking of wood as the bags of gold ore tumbled hard against the paneling.

Isbell cursed under his breath. They were burning valuable seconds here. If this rolling heap didn't pick up speed soon, then Winterhawk would be on them in just a few minutes.

Tucker was right. Winterhawk *was* seemingly indestructible. He had survived a coordinated train ambush, a wolf attack, and a military execution. Not only had he taken out Toomey and Walker, but he also commandeered an Army balloon.

It was all so absurd, but reality oftentimes was. In the end, life is just a series of poor choices that we attempt to justify as fate. We might attempt to live our lives by continually looking forwards, but that becomes the wool we've successfully pulled over our eyes.

Life is lived backwards.

Isbell could feel the weight of the locket scraping up against the fabric of his pants. It felt heavy and burdensome, the way that the worst decisions often do.

A short time ago, the four remaining aeronauts had all agreed on a plan for their future. Now, his closest friends were dead. He knew with absolute certainty that Winterhawk wouldn't rest for a single moment until he was dead, too.

He squeezed his eyes shut. They should have let him go; or maybe they should have let just let him hang. But things had gotten too out of control.

He was living life backwards with this fresh regret, but not remorse. Winterhawk had certainly done his part to make this happen. He was the traitor who had betrayed his own men. He could have decided to flee and not come back.

But he didn't.

Because of the threats made against his family.

Isbell knew he was the one primarily responsible for those threats. He had provoked this wild animal, and now it was time to put it down.

The wagon found the traction it needed and bolted unencumbered across the field. Navigating forcefully with the reins, Tucker guided the horses towards the direction of the lumber camp.

Isbell looked at the looming silhouette of the flume and back towards the fast-approaching shape of the *Excelsior*.

They would make it, but it was going to be close. Better yet, the balloon was now finally within firing range.

Isbell centered the Henry repeater on the frame of the basket. He didn't have an exact target yet, but he knew Winterhawk was crouched somewhere behind the dense coils of rope; hiding and probably unarmed.

It was time to pray for some luck.

He fired off a single shot.

One of the basket ropes frayed sharply from the bullet's impact.

Tucker glanced over at him; his lips were curled into a sneer. "Do you even know what you're aiming at?"

"I'm just making sure that he's still awake up there," Isbell answered.

The supply wagon rattled noisily atop a cluster of stones, wheels sliding haphazardly for a moment before once again finding traction on the dirt.

They were now close enough to the Nelscott camp to see the shapes of the various lumberjacks milling around the area. Framed behind them, the hulking Grafton crane rose high above one section of the flume like a monstrous steel insect.

"Why are we going into the lumber camp, anyway?" Tucker asked, shouting to be heard above the ruckus of the horses.

"Reinforcements!"

Tucker glanced over at him. "What are you talking about? What reinforcements?"

Isbell fired a second shot up at the balloon. "Once those lumberjacks find out that we're being pursued by an Indian who has slaughtered United States soldiers, Winterhawk will find himself surrounded by a dozen new enemies."

Tucker grinned. "Shit, boss. Once those men hear something like that, they'll be tripping all over their axes trying to cut him to pieces."

Isbell nodded. "And while they do our dirty work for us, we'll use that distraction to escape with the gold."

Eyes flashing with excitement, Tucker snapped the reins with a renewed fervor, coaxing even more speed from the charging horses.

Isbell was totally confident that his idea would work.

The lumberjacks would probably be no match for the savage killing machine they would soon be facing, but their blood sacrifice wouldn't be in vain. He would gladly trade their meaningless lives for his own. And he would do so without a shred of remorse about it.

Isbell looked up again at the balloon. It was close enough to the wagon now that he could discern a shape huddled just behind the flaming hydrogen tank.

Isbell wondered what outrageous plan of survival must be running through the Indian's head at this exact moment. Whatever devious strategy Winterhawk was now concocting up in the *Excelsior* would soon be interrupted by his own murderous ruination.

In a few short minutes, Isbell would become a rich hero.

It was going to be a good day, indeed.

CHAPTER 26

Hunkered down inside the *Excelsior*, Winterhawk winced as the second rifle shot tore through the rope basket just inches from his head.

He felt anger course through him. Nothing was going according to plan.

Let me see if I got this straight, son. You hijacked a military balloon that you can barely fly, and are now engaging in a shooting match without a gun. This is really your idea of a plan?

Winterhawk shifted around the rear of the balloon, crouching low as he stretched a hand towards the altitude control device. So far, he had been lucky in his guesswork with guiding the *Excelsior* back to the location where he had first been captured.

Navigating to the actual coordinates to the Van Duzer Forest had been relatively easy. Although it had been disconcerting at first locating the familiar trail landmarks from his vantage point several hundred feet in the air, he had soon become adapt at the art of minor course corrections.

Although he had faith in his limited ability to bring the balloon back, he had still felt a wave of relief wash over him after he had first sighted the two surviving aeronauts and the supply wagon.

As the hours had stretched on, he had believed that he had drastically overshot his mark; or, even worse, that Isbell and Tucker had double crossed their companions and taken off with the gold themselves. Along with the locket that would lead them straight to his family.

What he hadn't anticipated was how fast those men would figure out that Toomey and Walker were no longer piloting the *Excelsior*. He had hoped that he would have been able to land before they realized what had happened. Being unarmed, the only weapon that he'd been counting on for the final confrontation with the aeronauts was the element of surprise. And now, he didn't even have that.

Grimacing, he pulled down hard on the altitude control device.

Although he didn't have any confidence that he could successfully land the balloon, he needed to get it low enough above the wagon in order to attempt something else.

He was going to jump. There wasn't any other choice. He had to get onto that wagon and stop those men right here and now. Otherwise, he and his family would be looking over their shoulders for the rest of their lives.

Sounds like dead man's logic to me, amigo.

It just might be. But there was no other way.

Winterhawk felt the balloon descending. He shifted over to the edge of the basket, peering over the rim in order to get another visual bearing of his location.

He was close enough to the wagon to see Tucker holding onto the reins, looking intently forward. Isbell was beside him, the Henry repeating rifle clutched in both of his hands. Like Tucker, he was staring at a point somewhere just ahead of the charging wagon.

Winterhawk shifted his gaze to see what they were looking at.

His eyes snapped wide.

The Nelscott Flume and Lumber Company was coming up on them fast. He could see a dozen lumberjacks scrambling around the area. They appeared to be too intent on their arduous tasks to have even noticed the incoming danger. The 4500-pound Holbeer Steam Donkey grinded noisily in their midst, angrily snorting out huge plumes of white steam. Beside it, the massive Grafton crane was hoisting the large trunk of a Douglas fir from up off the ground.

Towering twenty feet over the Nelscott lumberjacks, the massive, reinforced flume stood out like an unnatural landmark. He saw the torrent of water steadily pushing logs down it, where they took a half-mile trip to the loading area situated on the Rogue River.

He looked again at the wagon.

The balloon was still engaging in its rapid descent, but it was hovering too far above the ground for him to jump safely onto the back of the wagon. There would be no way he could leap from the balloon at this height without breaking his legs, or worse.

But that was just *one* problem.

The other was distance.

Judging by how fast the balloon was covering ground, he estimated it would be less than two minutes before it completely overshot the wagon. If that happened, he would need more time to recalculate the flight path and try to intercept the wagon again.

But time was something he just didn't have.

Two rapid-fire rifle shots cracked loudly through the air.

Winterhawk jerked his head back from the edge of the basket, anticipating the bullets to once again tear into the fragile balloon. But they didn't.

There was the report of a third shot. It was followed by frantic yells coming from inside the lumber camp.

The distinctive, booming voice of Captain Isbell sliced through the air. It echoed across the forest like the blast from an artillery cannon.

What Winterhawk heard him yelling at the lumberjacks instantly chilled his blood, his heart hammering with fresh panic.

He had just flown himself directly into a trap.

Defenseless.

Airborne.

Helpless.

He was exactly where Isbell wanted him to be.

Without warning, the sky around the *Excelsior* was lit up with a barrage of explosive gunfire.

CHAPTER 27

"We're getting close to the Nelscott Flume!" Tucker yelled over the charging horses. "Whatever plan it is you've been hatching, the time for it is right now!"

Spinning around in the seat of the wagon, Isbell shifted the smoking barrel of the Henry away from the approaching *Excelsior*. The balloon was coming down fast behind them, but it was still traveling a hundred feet above the ground.

Isbell knew Winterhawk might be crazy, but he certainly wasn't dumb enough to risk a jump from that height. Besides, given how fast the balloon was moving it would probably overshoot the wagon long before it could land.

There were only a few seconds left for him to set things in motion.

He aimed the rifle at one of the lumberjacks standing closest to the wagon and pulled the trigger. The man jerked backwards, half his head instantly vaporized in an explosive puff of crimson spray.

Isbell sighted the rifle on a second lumberjack. The subsequent blast punched a ragged hole through the man's neck, flinging him high into the air like a dandelion caught in a windstorm.

Not missing a beat, Isbell swung the rifle up towards the elevated platform of the Grafton crane. He centered the barrel on the face of the confused operator. The man's frightened eyes locked onto the wagon, mouth an oval of shock as he tried to scream out a warning. The bullet from the

Henry caved in his lower jaw, splattering bone fragments throughout the cab in an explosion of dark red gore.

Before the trio of gunshots had even finished echoing throughout the area, the remaining lumberjacks yelled out in panic. The nine men scrambled for their firearms, heads craning to see whomever it was who had just declared war upon them.

Isbell began to wave his arms frantically at them from his perch on the speeding wagon. "It was the Indian!" he shouted. "He just shot three of your men! He's up in that balloon! Stop him!"

He could see some of the Nelscott lumberjacks staring at him with bewilderment before their eyes took in the sight of the *Excelsior* trailing close behind the wagon.

The men fanned out, taking cover where they could, training their weapons up at the balloon as they shouted excitedly at one another.

"I'll say this about you," Tucker growled, "you sure are a ruthless son of a bitch."

The horses galloped frantically into the lumber cutting area. The supply wagon careened dangerously behind the charging animals as the two riders clung for dear life.

"Just keep your head down," Isbell said. He motioned towards an open area in the woods just northwest from them. "Aim this heap towards that clearing. These idiots will be so focused on taking down that damn balloon that they'll hardly pay us any more attention."

Almost in unison, the nine surviving Nelscott lumberjacks fired upon the *Excelsior*. The crack of gunfire reverberated through the forest like a booming thunderstorm as multiple bullets shredded across the sky. Already coming in at a steep descent, the balloon jerked wildly from the impact of the multiple shots.

Snapping against the reins, Tucker began to whoop and holler with excitement. "Those boys are lighting his ass up! The *Excelsior* looks like a kite in a hurricane!"

Isbell had to agree.

The bullets were now punching into the *Excelsior* with ferocious force. The balloon swayed crazily as the blasts tore into it, the ropes which made up the basket quickly being turned into tatters.

At this rate, it wouldn't be long before the entire basket completely unraveled. Mere seconds, maybe. And when *that* happened, it would drop its traitorous occupant just as easily as a stone tossed from a high bridge.

Where are you gonna hide then, brownie? Isbell thought as a grin curled his lips. *When you hit that ground, you'll be as exposed as a stiff pecker waving hello on a nude beach.*

Another sound cut through the symphony of gunshots. It was a loud, screeching, mechanical hissing noise.

Isbell suddenly realized what it was.

The sound was emanating from the barometric contractor box located dead-center in the basket. A bullet had punctured it, which meant that the hydrogen tank would soon be unable to be properly regulated.

When that happened, the *Excelsior* would go up like a tinderbox.

Tucker had craned back for a quick peek at the balloon. He glanced over at Isbell, mouth curled up in excitement. "It looks like Lieutenant Winterhawk will be nothing but a burned marshmallow in the next few seconds!"

Isbell nodded triumphantly.

It now appeared that Major Toomey would taste his final revenge after all. And later, after he tracked down the Indian's family, Isbell would finally taste *his*.

Both men could feel sudden heat licking at the back of their necks.

The subsequent explosion was deafening.

Isbell jerked his body around, taking in the sight of the *Excelsior* burning as bright as a small sun. The entire balloon was now covered in flames from the ruptured hydrogen tank. It was spinning out of control, plummeting towards the ground at a frightening speed.

Isbell noted with satisfaction that the basket had unraveled. The hanging, burning strands of rope dangling below the balloon gave the impression of an ocean jellyfish being flung across a roaring campfire.

He then saw Winterhawk dropping helplessly down through the dead center of the flames, the raging inferno of the *Excelsior* trailing closely behind him.

"Burn in hell..." Isbell growled.

The supply wagon jolted, nearly throwing him off of it. Grunting, he whirled back around in the seat.

The horses snorted in panic. They were pulling the wagon sharply through the woods, their hooves trampling aimlessly through the thick underbrush.

Tucker was pulling frantically against the reins, but his efforts were having little effect on the frightened horses.

"Captain," Tucker cried out, his voice raising several octaves in panic, "I don't think I can stop them before—"

For a brief, sickening moment, the galloping horses appeared to be floating in midair. Their hooves were still in motion, but there was no longer any solid ground beneath them.

Isbell felt his stomach lurch as he realized what had just happened.

As incredulous as it might seem, there had been a massive hole hidden within the foliage in this darkened area of the forest.

And the horses and just run them straight down into it.

The wagon dipped sharply as the horses dropped from view, the momentum of their heavy body weight pulling the vehicle down with them.

Isbell was primed to jump when something stopped all of his limbs cold. It was a terrifyingly loud noise that easily eclipsed the frightened screams of the horses. It was emanating from out the depths of the darkness below.

Unholy growling.

It sounded just like...

Monsters.

His mind briefly flashed back to the massive footprints he had seen back in the clearing. His every instinct burned with the sickening realization that whatever was waiting for them down in that hole would be far worse than anything he could have possibly imagined.

And then there was no more time for thought as both men were toppling forward, screaming in tandem as they rode the wagon into the yawning maw below.

CHAPTER 28

The distinctive sound of flying bullets sounded like a hornet's nest that had been accidentally trodden over by a clumsy mule.

Jolon Winterhawk was laying prone on the floor of the basket, arms wrapped around his head, shielding himself from the relentless onslaught of bullets. He could hear the slugs tearing into the balloon; felt the thick ropes fraying and unravelling all around him.

He grimaced.

Captain Isbell and his Balloon Corps lackey had certainly played the right card when they killed those three lumberjacks in cold blood and blamed him for it. Those men still shooting up at him down there wouldn't rest for even a second until they made sure that he was stone dead.

An ear-splitting mechanical hiss sounded loudly above his head. He snapped his eyes open, frantically searching for its source.

The noise was coming from the barometric contractor box placed in the center of the basket. It had been punctured by a stray bullet. His eyes shifted to the hydrogen tank below it. The flame was now fully unregulated, burning hotter as the width of the hydrogen spread out dangerously.

At any moment, the hydrogen tank would ignite, turning the *Excelsior* into the world's largest firework.

Winterhawk felt a large section of the basket totally unravel beneath him, his body jerking downwards as the thick ropes began to give way beneath his weight. It would be only a matter of seconds before the entire frame of the basket became nothing more than torn tendrils of unsecured rope.

Winterhawk felt the scalding heat from the hydrogen tank sweep out across the basket. Reaching down, he grabbed onto one of the unravelling ropes with both hands, pushing hard against the floor of the basket with his shoulder.

The ropes beneath him shifted precariously, but held his weight. Grunting, he slammed his shoulder down against the basket floor until it finally gave way beneath him.

Then, he was in a sudden freefall.

Death was now rushing up at him.

He caught quick glimpses of the lumberjacks shooting at the balloon. The tall structure of the waterfall-fed flume streaked past his peripheral vision. For a split second, he also saw the wagon careening off into the forest northwest of the Grafton crane.

Isbell.

The locket.

He had to catch up to that bastard before--

There was an incredible boom as the hydrogen tank detonated.

Winterhawk felt the thick rope in his hands go taut as it reached its full extension beneath the basket. He grunted as he felt the snapping of the rope pull hard against his shoulders, the momentum swinging his body backwards beneath the rapidly descending balloon.

A split-second later, the *Excelsior* became a huge ball of fire directly above him. It had now become nothing more than an aerial inferno.

With his hands still grabbing tightly onto the frayed rope, Winterhawk kicked hard with his legs, pushing his body forwards as the fiery basket completely disintegrated into a flaming freefall.

The explosive residue of the hydrogen tank was cascading downwards in a gigantic sheet of fire, the intense blaze was threatening to consume him.

Reaching the full zenith of his swing, Winterhawk let go of the rope with a savage yell. He was momentarily airborne, arms pinwheeling wildly before he dropped facedown onto the flume. His body was instantly submerged in the ice-cold mountain water as he was propelled forward down the wooden chute.

The flaming residue of the *Excelsior* landed behind him, impacting against the flume with a horrendous crash. The burning remains of the balloon wobbled hard to the left of the structure, paused momentarily as if stuck, then toppled over.

Even over the loud din of the rushing water cascading over him, Winterhawk could hear the screams of panic coming from the lumberjacks.

They were all yelling the same thing.

A single, solitary word shouted out in tandem.

"Dynamite!"

CHAPTER 29

The last remnants of the *Excelsior* had fallen to the west side of the flume. The burning carcass of canvas and ropes had dropped onto the back of a Nelscott lumber wagon that had been filled with various supplies and tools of the trade.

Including five cases of dynamite and blasting caps.

Blasting was a widely used method to clear a densely forested area of stone obstructions, as well as to clear a large wilderness area otherwise made impassable due to storm or fire damage.

The wagon had been placed near that area because, being tucked so close to the flume, it was thought to be the most easily accessible and safest area of the entire lumber site.

Safest...

That was just another in a long line of sick jokes.

The lumberjacks were still scattering, still running wildly, still shouting out their warning to each other.

"Dynamite!"

If bad luck was a city, amigo, I reckon you'd be Sodom and Gomorrah.

Winterhawk raised his head above the water and began gasping for air. He pressed both hands hard against the sides of the flume, futilely attempting to slow his wild, face-forward descent down the wooden platform. Behind him, the Nelscott supply wagon had gone ablaze, large spirals of fire licking up towards the sky.

He knew there was, in all probability, only a few seconds left before those fragile cases of dynamite would react to the scorching heat. He could only guess how large the subsequent explosion was going to be.

Winterhawk looked down the flume. There was a large log shooting down the chute just ahead of him. He was about ten feet away from it, and gaining fast. It was time to leave this watery deathtrap.

With a grunt of effort, he rolled onto his back. For a moment he was staring up at the dazzling blue sky, the rushing mountain water settling just beneath his chin.

Not wanting to waste another valuable second, he pulled his legs up to his chest, wrapping his hands around both knees. He shifted his shoulders hard to the left, the momentum spinning him around in the narrow chute. He was now once again facing the oncoming log.

Only this time, he was heading towards it feet first.

He could still make out the crackle of the burning lumber wagon roaring beneath the flume. Given the extreme panic he had heard coming from the men fleeing the area, he was all but certain that it must be packed to the rafters with dynamite.

That meant that the subsequent detonation would be considerable.

Winterhawk kept his legs bent as his feet impacted hard against the log cascading ahead of him on the flume. The jarring collision was enough to push his knees up against his chest, knocking the wind from his lungs.

Gasping for air, he pulled his body forward, reaching out for the log with both hands. He needed to get some sort of handle hold on it before—

BOOM.

The explosion sounded like it could have come from an erupting volcano. The ground shook beneath the wooden beams of the flume as a massive fireball tore through the air. The wagon was instantly obliterated, the gigantic explosion punching a ragged crater twelve feet down into the earth.

Still ravenously hungry, the fireball chewed savagely into the flume, ripping a hundred feet of the structure to pieces in seconds.

Scattered around different areas near the flume, the fleeing Nelscott lumberjacks threw themselves to the ground. Hundreds of chunks of wooden shrapnel ripped through the air all around them.

With his hands grasping the sides of the log, Winterhawk pushed himself out of the water. He somersaulted onto the thick mass of the moving trunk, rolling to his feet.

The concussive blast continued to push itself forward and upwards. Tendrils of fire had already ignited the limbs of more than a dozen surrounding trees, while the sheer force of the explosion had effectively toppled a dozen more.

The surviving structure of the flume lifted off the ground as if cupped from below by an invisible hand. It tore itself away from its waterfall host like an umbilical cord ripped from the womb.

Incredibly, the chute swung upwards through the air, briefly resembling an L-shape before proceeding to topple forward back onto itself. The beams supporting the structure snapped like matchsticks as the flume began to collapse.

Winterhawk splayed out both of his arms for balance as he stood upright on the rushing log. Looking down the length of the chute, he could see an entire section of the flume disappear right before him as the structure dropped from view and to the ground.

He could feel the intense heat from the fires pressing against his back. His every instinct was to jump from his precarious perch on the flume and run for safety. But he knew a jump from this height was too dangerous. The landing itself might not prove to be fatal, but he was all but guaranteed to break a few bones in the process.

And given that he was surrounded by so many hostiles, *that* would probably be just enough to ultimately kill him.

That would make for a mighty peculiar obituary, wouldn't it? "Jolon Winterhawk. Husband. Father. Warrior. Survivor of countless battles and skin-of-his-teeth escapes. Death by twisted ankle after he couldn't limp away from a murderous group of lumberjacks."

The steam donkey was a dozen feet ahead. He could also make out the blood-splattered interior of the Grafton crane control room, as well as the dead operator hunched lifeless over the controls.

If he could just ride the log at least parallel to the steam donkey, then he could jump onto the top of the Hobart and scale safely to the ground.

It was as good a plan as any.

Until it wasn't.

Without warning, the flume suddenly collapsed directly in front of him.

From the location south of the Grafton crane and down to the timber staging area along the Rogue River, the flume remained upright and intact. But north of the crane, the remaining chute structure was dropping like dominoes.

Instead of looking down the runway of the flume, Winterhawk was now facing what amounted to a wooden cliff. He crouched low on the log, placing as much of his body weight on his hamstrings as he could; outstretched arms still frantically maintaining his balance.

A split second later, the log sailed off the edge of the flume.

It careened through the air before tilting sharply into a rapid descent, falling towards the ground at a forty-five-degree angle.

Winterhawk remained crouched on the back end of the log, shifting his entire body weight forward as he fought against the punch of air threatening to rip him from his perch.

Finally, one end of the log slammed hard into ground, piledriving itself into the loose soil with a wallop. It remained upright for a half-second before its weight began pulling it backwards.

Throwing his body forward upon impact, Winterhawk rolled down the moving log in a series of somersaults until his feet hit the ground.

Sensing the crushing weight coming down fast on top of him, he launched his body into the air. The massive log slammed onto the ground behind him, missing his body by mere inches.

The twisted and broken frame of the flume had now collapsed, cascading torrents from the waterfall gushing through the underbrush.

Winterhawk landed hard on the ground, grunting with the impact. Before he could even react, he was hit by the force of the flume water, rolling him for several feet across the forest floor.

The fire continued to rage around the flume area as more trees burned under the ever-widening scope of the explosion. The sky was already darkening as thick plumes of black smoke curled upwards.

Given how rapidly the fire was spreading, it wouldn't be long before the entire Nelscott lumber area would be completely consumed by it.

Winterhawk pushed himself off the ground, shaking the mass of water-drenched hair away from his eyes. His shoulders burned from the exertion of swinging beneath the *Excelsior*. His right arm ached from the severe rope burn he had received from the mail hook. He could feel the sharp jabs of pain across his exposed upper torso where he had received burns from the numerous explosions he had survived.

I've never been a shitter-is-half-empty kind of guy, and neither have you. Let's just point our tribal feathers towards the bright side of things, shall we? You're almost home! All that is left now is for you to survive a raging forest fire, escape the angry clutches of these bloodthirsty lumberjacks, take down two trained soldiers, steal back your precious locket, and possibly square off against those mythical Nu'numic beasties. Nothing but easy-peasy, lemon squeezy, am I right?

No. There was definitely nothing *easy* about it. Nothing was ever easy in this life. Especially surviving. What *was* easy enough to do in this world was to operate under the pretense of objectifiable sanctification.

Instead of recognizing that mankind was inherently the problem for every solution, humanity had somehow convinced itself over the millennia that everything in life had been set out just to serve them. As if God had made the universe as nothing more than a church potluck for His creation to pick and nibble at.

If a man is hungry, simply put whatever you want on the plate. If a man should covet another man's possessions, use any means necessary to claim what should be rightfully yours. Depending on the color of one's skin, what is mine is mine, and what is yours is mine.

White makes right. This is the way of the world. You're a big boy now, Jolon. I thought you understand all of this already.

Winterhawk *did* understand. Only all too well. He recognized long ago that it was easy enough to follow a moral compass when the direction it invariably pointed was always back at oneself.

Well, well, well. Let's roast some marshmallows around that grand old campfire of irony. Before you had the silly ass notion of suiting up in armor and clanking off to the Crusades, you were just some snot-nosed little boy who allowed Chief Joseph to double down on your daddy issues. He promised you honor, didn't he? Well, don't you think Colonel Smythe was promised that very same thing by his very own group of lying elders? Oh, his particular kind might not hang out around wigwams and pick flecks of peace pipe out from between their teeth, but their breath still smelled like bullshit, just the same.

It wasn't as simple as all that.

Chief Joseph had bartered with the United States government for the betterment of his people. Sending a handful of his warriors to fight in the Civil War an act of cooperation, not desperation. Men like Winterhawk had known the risks. They had known what was at stake.

And what about the families of these so-called warriors? What about Chenoa? Do you really think she'll understand your noble sacrifice when Captain Isbell decides to make good on his horrific promise?

Winterhawk felt fresh rage swelling up inside him. Even if it became the very last thing he would ever do, he vowed Isbell would die today.

A pair of rifle shots rang out, the report cracking close above his head.

It was time to move. He sprang to his feet as another volley of shots tore through the air above him.

Although the entire area was now seemingly ablaze from the explosion of dynamite and the collapse of the flume, the Nelscott lumberjacks were still entirely hellbent on taking him out.

Winterhawk squinted hard through the smoke that was starting to envelope the forest. From his previous vantage point free falling from the *Excelsior*, he had last seen the gold-laden supply wagon careening due west about a hundred feet from the edge of the waterfall that flanked the remains of the flume.

If the wagon had somehow kept moving through all of the chaos and destruction, then his chances of catching up to them now were pretty much non-existent.

He shook the thought away. He couldn't have come this far just to fail now.

Winterhawk broke into a dead sprint. He could hear the frantic shouts of the lumberjacks coming from behind him as the men saw him bolting away. They followed in pursuit, opening fire as they ran.

Winterhawk swerved to the right, then cut sharply to the left. He hoped this zigzag pattern would temporarily throw off their aim. So far, it was working.

He ran blindly into the thick smoke, reflexively holding up an arm and shielding his face from the intense blasts of heat erupting from the dozens of burning trees in his path.

The roaring waterfall could still be heard above the crackle of the fires. That landmark was his compass west. As long as he followed the sound of the waterfall, he could traverse the same path he had seen Isbell and the wagon take earlier.

Winterhawk pushed himself to run harder through the bourgeoning forest fire as the heat threatened to blister his exposed skin.

The loud snapping of cracked limbs succumbing to the tremendous heat and crashing down to the ground sounded off like cannon fire. He realized that if just one of those flaming limbs landed atop of him, then this frantic chase would be a very short one indeed.

The noise of the waterfall was behind him now. Soon, he would see the indentations of the wagon tracks and ascertain which direction—

Screams.

Coming from somewhere just ahead of him.

The sounds were muffled; distant. It was almost as if they were coming from deep within the ground.

Winterhawk bolted through a large mass of bushes, then stopped. His breath was heaving in his lungs, eyes wide as he stared down at the ground.

He saw the deep grooves made from the supply wagon. They ended in front of a massive hole in the forest floor.

Isbell and Tucker had driven the wagon right over the precipice and down into that large pit.

That's precisely where the screams had been emanating from.

And then Winterhawk caught something else.

The stench of rotted and decaying meat wafted up from the pit, assailing his lungs. Whatever was living down in that cavern had amassed a lot of dead flesh.

There was a deep growling echoing upwards from the darkness of the cavern hole. It was followed by a monstrous roar.

Does that sound like a bear to you, chief? No? Well, how about a Bengal tiger that somehow escaped from a traveling roadside carnival? No, I don't believe that's what could have made those noises, either. Whatever could it be? Wait! I think I know. Remember those obscenely large moccasin prints you encountered earlier? Those are the footprints of the Nu'numic. From the sound of those screams, I would guess that Isbell and his butt-mate just might have gotten themselves a close-up look at your fabled Ancient Ones. That deep, dark abyss you're staring down into? It's the entrance to the lair of legends, hombre.

Winterhawk then heard something else that made everything he was taking in seem that much worse.

It was a second roar. But it wasn't coming from the same creature. The two distinct sounds were overlapping now. The Nu'numic was definitely lurking down there. And now, there was more than one of them.

Winterhawk stepped closer to the edge of the hole, peering intently into the blackness of the immense cavern. Generous rays of sunlight shone down into the pit, casting pools of light twenty-feet below him.

He could see the supply wagon laying on its side on a stone floor. Its frame had been broken into three sections, bags of ore strewn all around it. Laying nearby were the corpses of both horses, their necks broken from the fall.

Isbell suddenly stepped backwards into the light. He was visibly shaking, face pale, trembling fingers loading shells into the Henry repeater.

Tucker appeared beside him. His shoulder was slouched obscenely to the left, the collarbone obviously shattered. He was clutching his Colt with an unsteady right hand, the barrel shaking.

"Get away!" Tucker wailed, voice cracking with fear.

Two massive shapes could be seen walking across the stone ground of the pit towards them. He caught a glimpse of matted black fur in the sun, as well as a horrifying flash of teeth—

"There he is! Kill that Indian bastard!"

A volley of gunshots rang out.

Winterhawk whirled around and saw a trio of Nelscott lumberjacks running towards him, pistols blasting. He felt hot lead streak dangerously close to his body.

It's time to make a tough decision, son. Either stand here and get taken out by this country bumpkin firing squad, or jump down into the lair of legends and pray that the Nu'numic only eats white meat.

Winterhawk gritted his teeth.

As the Nelscott lumberjacks once again opened fire, he turned back towards the yawning maw of the cavern that lay spread out before him.

If he stayed topside and faced those gunmen unarmed, eternal glory would be waiting for him in just a matter of seconds. But if he descended into that lair, he would be potentially encountering a gruesome fate worse than anything he could ever imagine.

There wasn't any other choice.

Letting out a savage yell, Winterhawk leaped into the chasm.

In the blink of an eye, the dark pit swallowed him whole.

CHAPTER 30

Jolon Winterhawk could see the floor of the pit rushing up at him.

With his legs pulled towards his chest, the momentum of his descent speed was maximized. To counterbalance, he immediately leaned slightly forward, extending his legs to get into a better position to absorb the impact.

The stone floor looked absolutely unforgiving. He was all but certain to break a leg or fracture his ankle when he landed.

You have to focus; think about your field combat training. You spent months back at Chompuunish learning how to leap off the back of running horses. The same rules apply here. When you first hit the ground, don't land on your heels. Land on the balls of your feet, knees slightly bent. Don't be too tense, but don't be too relaxed. Target that sweet spot just between the two.

Winterhawk landed on the stone floor, knees slightly bent.

Absorbing the full impact, he tucked his legs and immediately transitioned into a roll. Pulling down his right shoulder and pressing his head protectively against his chest, he rolled onto his back, continuing the rapid somersault until he was finally crouched on both feet.

The wreckage of the supply wagon lay directly before him.

He looked around, quickly trying to get his bearings. He estimated that the cavern stretched back well over a hundred feet. In the distance, he could hear the dull roar of the waterfall that had once fed power to the Nelscott flume. That must have been the primary way that the Nu'numic had traversed into their lair.

He immediately sensed the terrifying presence of the two creatures. They had a pungent, animalistic odor that mixed sickening with the putrid stench of rotted corpses that thickly permeated the air of the cavern.

Isbell and Tucker had been too intent on aiming their weapons at the advancing monsters to even have taken notice of his arrival.

The two legendary creatures roared in a display of utter dominance; the cacophony of noise absolutely terrifying within the confines of the cavern. Even the rocks appeared to tremble in abject terror.

This was their domain. This cave, even the vast wilderness above, had been their hunting grounds for centuries. For them, the men who had just invaded their sanctum weren't a threat--they were dinner.

Winterhawk eyed the broken remains of the supply wagon scattered around his feet. He saw a familiar shape laying among the bags of gold ore. With his heart pounding, he dove towards it.

Deafening gunshots rang out in the cavern the two surviving members of the United States Balloon Corps made their last stand.

Tucker had fired first.

The pistol cracks were deafeningly loud inside the cavern. The muzzle flashes illuminated his ghostly, pain-stricken features. His shoulder injury had made him unbalanced, and his fear had made his aim unreliable. Even with two massive targets, his shots went wild; bullets impacting against the rocky walls of the cavern and ricocheting wildly.

Isbell had much better control of his fear, but the Henry repeater was too cumbersome a weapon for close quarters combat. He had shouldered the rifle, but the monsters had already recognized the threat coming from the firearms.

They pushed away from one another with a speed that defied their size. One had moved backwards, retreating into the darkness until only its red eyes shown. The other pressed its back hard against one side of the cavern wall, swiping out with a muscular, clawed arm.

Isbell fired the Henry at the nearest monster, but the rifle was caught by the massive hand of the creature. Knocked off its initial trajectory, the bullet sheared a large chunk of rock from the ceiling.

Isbell grunted as the creature knocked the rifle free from his grasp, sending it clattering uselessly against the ground.

Tucker screamed with unbridled fear. His voice was raising in sharp octaves as he emptied his pistol, the chamber clicking empty.

His wild volley of shots had just struck the wrong target.

Crying out in pain, Captain Isbell dropped hard to the ground. One of the bullets had sheared a deep chunk of flesh from the meat of his left thigh.

"You stupid asshole!" Isbell screamed, clutching his bleeding leg.

No longer able to control the shaking of his body, Tucker moaned as the Colt dropped helplessly from his grasp. He staggered backwards, his broken shoulder appearing to droop even lower.

"God, please help me..." he muttered, eyelids fluttering as he blinked with dumb fascination at the nearest monster.

Several feet behind him, Winterhawk was snaking his way through the scattered bags of gold ore. What he was seeking had been buried beneath the hindquarters of one of the dead horses. It was the folded blanket where he had previously hidden his weapons.

He was close enough to it now to reach out a hand and--

There was a sudden chorus of excited shouting coming from above. The three lumberjacks were perched on the edge of the hole, peering down at the utter chaos spread out across the floor beneath them.

"What the hell is going on down there?" one of the men shouted down into the cavern.

Isbell craned his neck, staring up at the men with stunned disbelief. "Help! There's something down here with us!"

Hearing the new voices, the first creature cocked its head and began making low, ominous clicking noises.

The second monster turned sharply, responding with a series of low whistles, and beating chest thumps. This was obviously the male attempting to protect its mate.

It looks like even the Ancient Ones will have themselves a marital spat or two. It's such a cozy little thought, isn't it?

It was just the kind of animal hierarchy he'd seen displayed before in coyotes. Those animals mated for life, and would often engage in bickering behavior whenever threatened. The male would participate in a form of mate guarding, forcefully protecting the female from danger.

It appeared that the Nu'numic were endowed with those same survival instincts of mate protection. The Creator undoubtedly gave it to every living thing.

Nearly as soon as it had started, the conversation between the two creatures ended. Grunting some sort of farewell communication, the female moved quickly backwards through the cavern. It lumbered noisily until it reached the waterfall; then, there was silence.

But only momentarily.

The first monster flung itself out from against the wall, stepping into one of the pools of sunlight. It stared up the lumberjacks, arms outstretched, roaring loudly in a grand display of its dominance.

The lumberjacks took an involuntary step back from the edge of the cavern, faces awash with shock and horror at what they had just witnessed.

Winterhawk threw his body against the carcass of the horse. He frantically grabbed the edge of the blanket and pulled hard, feeling its contents sliding out from beneath the weight of the dead animal.

Tearing his eyes away from the monster, Tucker stared up at the three men. Before he could add his own cries for help, he clumsily backed into one of the ore bags, losing his footing. With his good arm waving wildly for balance, he tipped forward.

Sensing the movement, the enraged monster spun around, snatching Tucker in midfall. The man barely had enough time to choke out a gargled scream before the creature had savagely unscrewed his head, severing it from his neck with a sickening plop. A geyser of blood pumped upwards, spraying the walls with a sheet of red.

Tucker's headless body took a lurching step forward as his legs responded to the last electrical impulses that had been fired from his brain. He performed a ghastly two-step before his body finally crumpled to the ground.

Still clutching onto the decapitated head, the monster spun it around. Tucker's eyes were moving. His lids blinked rapidly, taking in the full face of the monster staring at him. His mouth moved in a silent scream.

The creature brought Tucker's head up to its face, sinking its teeth into his forehead and grinding down with a sickening crunch of bone. The Nu'numic pulled its mouth back, savagely peeling the skin completely off Tucker's face like the rind of an orange.

There was a hideous slurping noise as the monster cracked through Tucker's skull and began sucking up his brains.

"Shoot it!" Isbell screamed.

"We're gonna do better than that!" one of the lumberjacks shouted down at him. "Just get your puckered ass out of the way!"

With one hand still grasping the wound on his leg, Isbell used the other one to pull himself painfully across the floor.

Winterhawk had finally yanked the blanket free. He rapidly unfurled it, the bow, quiver, and Girandoni war club clattering to the ground.

He snatched up the Girandoni and fastened it securely around his left leg.

Crouching down, he opened the quiver. There were only two remaining copper-tipped dogwood arrow shafts nestled inside. He pulled one out, slinging the quiver across his back.

Above him, the distinctive sound of a lit dynamite fuse could suddenly be heard.

It was death from above.

CHAPTER 31

Winterhawk looked up towards the top of the cave entrance.

One of the lumberjacks had ignited a stick of dynamite, holding it away from his body. The other two men had cautiously stepped away from him, pistols still trained on the monster below them.

The only reason you're still drawing breath right now is because that big hairy bastard hasn't had the time to sniff you out yet. You can thank those lumber boys for that precious little gift.

The Nu'numic dropped Tucker's half-devoured skull. It hit the stony ground with a sickening plop.

Winterhawk scooped up the Hornbeam bow, eyes frantically darting between the lumberjacks moving twenty feet above him.

His stare settled onto a large stone that sat on the ground near the far-right side of where the three men were standing.

He gritted his teeth.

He had an idea. He was going to need something to draw the monster's full attention away from him. What he needed now was a distraction.

Isbell was grunting with exertion as he continued to pull himself along the ground, moving as far away from the creature as he could. He took a quick glance over his shoulder, eyes going wide with surprise as he saw a familiar figure scurrying from out of the far reaches of the cave.

"Winterhawk?" he muttered with absolute shock. "How many damn lives have you got?!"

Sliding forward across the stones onto one knee, Winterhawk rapidly knocked one of the arrows, aiming it up at the lumberjacks.

You've got just about ten seconds left before that dickweed up there drops his boom stick.

As if hearing his cue, that lumberjack leaned over, dangling the dynamite over the cavern. "I hope your ass is still hungry," he grinned down at the monster, "because we got something for you now."

The Nu'numic let loose a thundering roar, hands savagely beating his massive chest, red eyes flashing with uncontrolled rage.

Winterhawk shifted the Hornbeam, sighting the arrow onto the large stone that was near the three men.

The other two lumberjacks standing near the precipice suddenly saw him. Their voices rose to a shout as they swung their pistols around, fingers curling around the triggers.

Winterhawk released the bow string.

The medieval archers referred to is as rooking. During field battles, it was all too common for the top-ranking member of an attacking battalion to shield himself behind a row of armor-wearing defenders as he proceeded to give orders. This individual, typically a field commander or even a king, would be wearing minimal head armor in order that he would always be recognized by own troops during battle and summarily always protected. The most skilled enemy archers soon realized this and planned a strategy that would circumvent that limited battlefield protection.

Rooking was achieved by means of angling an arrow so that it struck an enemy's armor chest plating and ricocheted. The most skilled archers could bullseye a seemingly harmless strike on one attacker, but kill an intended target by calculating the direction the arrow would bounce after being deflected against a hard surface.

It required a punishing degree of skill.

While performing archery training at Chompuunish, Chief Joseph had tested his warriors rooking technique by having them fire arrows into rivers, where ostensibly they would practice skipping bolts across various sized rocks.

Winterhawk had been the only warrior among the group to have truly mastered it. The trick, he had soon realized, was all in the angle.

When a bullet strikes a solid object, it ricochets because of a combination of velocity and size. An arrow has neither of those distinct advantages. When a bolt strikes against a hard surface, it has the possibility of bouncing off its intended target, but it loses ninety percent of its power after that occurs. Apart from sheer luck, an arrow that inadvertently ricochets becomes useless as a means of taking down an opponent. To purposefully fire an arrow into an obstruction with the intention of striking a target required equal parts audacity as it did desperation.

Winterhawk had fired the arrow after aiming precisely for the upper left side of the stone. While a typical shaft would descend an average of five degrees for every ten feet before reaching its intended target, these copper-tipped dogwood shafts had been crafted for a weighted buoyancy needed while firing from horseback. They were anchored to maintain a steady flight trajectory amidst the chaotic shifting variables of the archer.

The arrow struck the stone at the precise spot that he had been aiming for. While a direct bulls-eye against the hard rock would have propelled the shaft immediately backwards, the sharp angle in which the bolt landed shifted its trajectory sideways. The copper-tip momentarily dug into the stone before rapidly angling its way to the left. The momentum of the arrow was more than enough slide it forcefully across the stone, the noise sounding like a dull razor carving its way through several weeks of grizzled chin stubble.

The rooking maneuver continued on for a full second before the arrow reached the edge of the stone and was once again launched airborne.

The tip punctured the cheek of the lumberjack who had been standing closest to the stone. His eyes fluttered in shock as he felt the shaft push into his mouth.

The lumberjack's head whipped sideways as the streaking arrow ripped a gaping hole through the other side of his face. The man let out an explosive gagging noise as the nock of the arrow imbedded itself against his teeth, anchoring the bolt to the inside of his mouth.

The forceful momentum of the arrow's sudden stop was enough to fling him totally off his feet. He careened sideways, the copper-tipped shaft protruding grotesquely out from the side of his face.

He collided roughly into the second lumberjack beside him, both of their heads smashing painfully together.

The second man instantly let loose a high-pitch scream as the protruding arrow slid deeply into his right eye socket and lodged against the bone. The men were unnaturally pinned together now, waltzing along the edge of the cavern like a pair of drunken dancers.

The third lumberjack cried out in surprise as the two men stumbled into him, throwing him off balance. With the lit dynamite stick still clutched in one hand, he waved his arms, trying desperately to regain his footing.

It was a futile gesture.

Screaming in tandem, all three intertwined lumberjacks tumbled forward into the mouth of the cavern. They landed in a messy pile on the stone floor, various limbs akimbo.

"Glad you boys could drop in," Winterhawk muttered.

The monster threw back its massive chest, roaring with an uncontrollable rage at the unexpected presence of more unwanted visitors.

The two lumberjacks who had been pinned together by the arrow landed closest to the monster. They had a dozen broken bones between them, their bodies writhing and contorting with mutual agony as blood pooled thickly beneath them.

The Nu'numic leaped on top of them, stomping down against their bodies with a ferocious intensity. Both men began mewling with agony as the creature's feet repeatedly smashed them into a pulp. The horrifying sounds of splintering bone and tearing flesh consumed the cavern.

The third lumberjack landed nearest to the supply wagon, a half-dozen bags of gold ore breaking his haphazard fall. He landed with a loud grunt as the air was pushed from his lungs.

The dynamite stick immediately flew out of his grasp, bouncing against the stone floor and rolling fast.

Dropping the Hornbeam, Winterhawk made a long dive for the rolling dynamite stick. Seeing him in motion, the lumberjack also made a move for it. Both men collided together on the floor, exchanging a fast volley of punches.

The lumberjack came out on top.

"We have to kill the fuse!" the man screamed, savagely pinning Winterhawk to the ground by his neck with right arm. His left hand stretched out towards the dynamite. "You plan on dying down here?!"

"You first!" Winterhawk said, bringing both knees up to his chest, planting his feet in the man's midsection. He pushed his legs out with explosive force, launching the lumberjack high into the air.

Rolling over, Winterhawk snatched up the live dynamite stick.

Crying out, the lumberjack continued his airborne journey for a full five feet across the cavern floor before he was snatched in midair by the Nu'numic.

Pulling out the last remaining arrow from the quiver behind his back, Winterhawk reached down and scooped up the fallen Hornbeam.

Bellowing with rage, the monster lifted the lumberjack high over his head, holding the screaming man up by his arms and legs.

Winterhawk carefully pushed the copper-tip arrowhead through the bottom of the dynamite stick.

Letting loose with an ear-splitting, primal scream, the Nu'numic wrenched outwards with both of its enormous arms. The lumberjack was torn completely in two at the waist in a huge spray of blood. Both quivering halves of the man flopped in the creature's giant hands like salmon that had just been yanked from the river.

Winterhawk nocked his final arrow, quickly pulling back the bowstring and taking aim.

The monster finally saw him. Flinging the gory remains of the lumberjack to the floor, the creature lunged forward with frightening speed, razor-sharp teeth flashing.

"Rest in pieces, asshole!" Winterhawk shouted, firing the bow.

The dynamite-tipped arrow streaked into the monster's oncoming maw, finding its bullseye in the back of its throat. The creature reflexively swatted upwards with one massive hand, fingers briefly touching the bolt protruding outwards from its mouth.

The faint sizzle of the fuse went silent.

The subsequent detonation sounded like a mini thunderclap inside the confines of the cavern. The Nu'numic was instantly blown into dozens of ragged, furry chunks of meat that sprayed in all directions.

Winterhawk was blown backwards by the explosion, the Hornbeam spinning away from his grasp. Most of his upper body was splattered with the steaming wet viscera of the Nu'numic.

Landing hard, he slid backwards on the stone floor, his battered body coming to a stop after his head bashed against one of the walls.

And for a merciful moment, the silence in the lair was deafening.

CHAPTER 32

Jolon Winterhawk lay on the floor in a total daze, breath heaving in and out of his lungs. His muscles twitched against the strong pull of absolute exhaustion that was threatening to overwhelm his body.

The bloody remains of the Nu'numic pressed thickly down onto his upper torso like a grotesque second skin.

Well, I guess you can now add Legend Killer to your long list of sordid accomplishments. The Nu'numic had survived for countless generations in these woods under the guise of myth. It took you all of a single afternoon to change all of that. I wonder how the other monster out there will react once it finds out you just turned its mate into cavern chili?

He heard the roar of the waterfall somewhere off in the distance. The sound was almost soothing as it echoed off the cavern walls. Just behind the din of the water, he could make out something else.

It was another kind of roar, but this one was much more dangerous.

It was the sound of an uncontrolled wildfire. Soon, it would surround this whole area, blocking any chance he had of escape.

He couldn't help but think that things had finally come full circle now.

The burning of the forests seemed representative of the last decade of his life. It was systematic of the war raging within himself as he straddled the appeasement of two entirely different cultural worlds. He had only recently learned that it was the sort of war that doesn't herald a victory. In this sort of battle there was no winning, just degrees of losing.

There's nothing new to see here, chief. It's what happens whenever you seek out the Heart of the Monster. Our people have known this sad truth for ages.

The Heart of the Monster.

There is a creation story at the center of every culture in the world. For the Nez Perce, the story of the *nimíipuu* people began at Kamiah in Idaho. It was here where a sacred coyote named Iceye'ye killed a monster who was consuming all living creatures in the region.

Discovering that the monster had devoured all the people in the land, Coyote tricked it into eating him, too. But once he was inside the belly of the beast, Iceye'ye killed it by cutting out the monster's heart. Afterwards, Coyote had sprinkled his bloody paws across the valley of the region, and the Nez Perce people came into being. Without Coyote's act of supreme bravery, the people and animals of the world would still be imprisoned in the Monster's belly.

As the stories had been passed down across generations, the legend of Iceye'ye had been further endowed with human characteristics. Coyote was both a hero and trickster, as well as being a fool and a savior.

The monster had been slain, but its bloodlust continued to beat in the heart of those men who took up the mantle of attempting to erase all the Indian tribes from existence.

Winterhawk thought of the recent Mankato Executions, where hundreds from the Dakota Sioux tribe had been sentenced to death. That particular tribe had been accused of starting the Little Crow War of 1862, in which 490 settlers, mostly women and children, had been killed. The truth was that promised provisions given to the Sioux through government treaties had been reneged upon, leaving the people starving through a vicious winter. Desperate for food and supplies, the Dakota Sioux had launched an attack against neighboring white farms that had turned deadly. Eventually, President Lincoln had sent in soldiers. Over 300 of the Dakota Sioux people were arrested and, after a mass trial, those men had been sentenced to death.

While Lincoln had ultimately commuted the majority of the sentences, 38 Dakotas were still hung. It was reported that upwards of four thousand people watched the execution, many of them bringing along picnic baskets.

The heart of the monster was still very much alive.

Winterhawk felt a deep sadness close around his spirit.

It wasn't all the senseless bloodshed that weighed so heavily upon him. It was that everything that had transpired seemed inevitable. There appeared to him a fatalistic nature in everything that had come before, and with all the great unknowns that lay stretched ahead along the crooked path of time.

That was the purest definition of fate. It meant accepting that the road ahead and the road behind shared the same shitty map.

By all means, please continue to take all the time you need pontificating on the sinful nature of mankind. But while you bathe in generational self-loathing, don't forget to scrub between your own toes. You might be surprised what you'll discover is crammed up in there. You'll find the dirt on your feet from after you decided to walk away from your family. The soil of Malheur has now become the caked-on dirt of your choices ever since. You might have left as a warrior, but you sure-as-shit are coming back as nothing more than a stone-cold killer.

That was certainly true. But what was *also* true was that he had done whatever it took to adapt. He had embodied whatever was necessary to overcome. That was as much the key to survival as the weapons you fired during combat.

You could be as battle-hardened as you truly wanted, but there was nothing quite as painful as the agony of living with regret.

Regrets? Is that what we're calling it these days, amigo? That sounds pretty fancy. When your father was alive and kicking, that kind of thinking was better known as mistakes. *Your poppa made a big one when he left his family; you made one when you left yours. The big difference is that death is what snatched your father away; blind faith is what sent* you *packing. Misplaced allegiances are the mistakes both of you shared.*

He noticed something coming from outside of the lair now.

The encroaching wildfires had drastically increased in volume.

It was time to move.

Rolling to his feet, Winterhawk untied the Girandoni from his leg. He hefted the heavy war club in his hand, staring angrily down at it.

With a yell, he spun towards the broken remains of the wagon. He hacked savagely at the gold bags until their innards were bleeding out onto the floor. After a few moments, he finally lowered the war club.

He stared at the mounds of ore that had spilled onto the ground. The sight reminded him of a long-forgotten moment back at Chompuunish.

Chief Joseph had been speaking to his warriors along the riverbank. Winterhawk recalled the moment with such clarity because it had occurred on the eve of his Army enlistment. Five sleeps later, he would be fully adorned in the uniform of the white man.

"Our first agreement with our Creator was to tend to the land he provided to our people," Chief Joseph had remarked. He had scooped up a handful of riverbank sand for effect. "The Western heart values nothing but the gold. To the Nez Perce, every grain of sand beneath our feet is like gold. It's those very grains of earth that you'll be fighting for. Restore to us what the Creator has provided."

Winterhawk grimaced at the thought.

There was nothing down in the cavern that needed restoration. The lair needed a cultural burning, which was the ancient tribal philosophy of fire as medicine. When it's prescribed, fire acts as a Messenger, a holy gift from the Great Spirit. Fire represents cleansing and renewal because from out of the ashes comes new growth.

Winterhawk once again secured the Girandoni to his leg.

He dipped a hand into his pocket, pulling out the Army discharge papers and the tin matchbox. Pulling out one of the matches, he ignited it against the tip of his thumb. He moved the discharge paper across the burning match, holding it over the flame until it caught fire.

He tossed the smoldering paper into the air, watching it land onto the nearest pile of ore. It ignited instantly, spreading rapidly. The flames mercifully consumed what remained of the three dead lumberjacks.

Winterhawk turned away from the fire as the stench of burning flesh reached his nostrils. He thought briefly of Briggs, the soldier back in the dining car of the *Goose*. The man's dying wish was that the gold wouldn't fall into the wrong hands. Well, it certainly wouldn't now.

Mission accomplished.

Not so fast, chief. There's still a bit of unfinished business left to attend to. More than a bit, actually.

Winterhawk stared at the trail of blood on the cavern floor.

He felt fresh rage well up inside of him.

Isbell had signed his own death sentence when he had threatened the lives of Chenoa and Kaya. When he had stolen the locket, he had made a pact to hunt down and destroy his family. And for making that threat, the soldier was going to pay.

Isbell represented the worst of humanity. He had somehow survived the Nu'numic, but he would not survive what was coming next.

Just like any rabid animal, Captain Isbell needed to be put down.

Winterhawk began to follow the trail of blood further down into the darkness of the cave.

CHAPTER 33

Captain Thomas Isbell realized that his entire life, however little now remained of it, hinged on the faintest glimmer of hope that he would find the strength to pull himself free from the nightmare that he had left behind.

Those things...

Tucker had been totally devoured.

The man had been ripped apart, eaten alive by one of those unholy monsters. His old friend had died while watching his very own brain matter being chewed up like a handful of ripe huckleberries.

The pain in Isbell's leg was excruciating.

He should have tied some sort of tourniquet on it already, but he was worried that if he stopped to even do that, he might not have enough strength to keep moving.

Moving?

That was being overly optimistic about things.

He didn't need to even look to confirm that he had left a huge amount of blood trailing behind him on the cavern floor.

Isbell also understood something else.

He did not believe that the second monster he had encountered was still in the cave. He had seen it moving towards the direction of the waterfall moments after the two beasts had communicated with one another.

One had made the decision to stay and fight, while the other had decided to flee and survive.

Smart strategy.

It was the exact same thing he was doing.

The question now was how to get out of this cave.

He guessed the monsters had been using the waterfall to gain access in and out of the cavern. The large hole that he and Tucker had tumbled into must have been something akin to a side door.

So, if the waterfall acted as some sort of animal exit, then that's exactly where he needed to go.

Isbell was suddenly overwhelmed with coldness, teeth chattering, the sound echoing loudly inside his mouth. It was hypothermia. Bleeding trauma. He had seen it happen countless times on the battlefield. Severely wounded soldiers usually succumbed to it within moments after sustaining a life-threatening injury.

He glanced down at the jagged stones he was pulling himself across. Those rocks weren't conducive to heat; instead, they were refracting the cold emanating from the darkness of the cave.

If he was going to make it out of here alive, then getting off of those stones needed to be his first priority. Even if he could only clutch the dirt walls for support and limp like a snail, that might be just enough forward motion to raise his body's core temperature.

But first, he had to get back on his feet.

Grunting with the exertion, Isbell flattened his whole body against the ground. Pulling his arms back towards his shoulders, he curled his hands into tight fists, pressing the knuckles down against the rocks.

He pushed up with shaking arms until he could find leverage with his good knee, tucking it beneath his body for balance. His wounded leg throbbed with agony as he slowly climbed to his feet. Screaming with pain and unable to keep his balance, Isbell stumbled hard against the cave wall, fingers digging into the soft dirt for leverage.

Remarkably, he was able to stay upright.

His chest heaving with exertion, he glanced into the darkness ahead of him. There was light. He could see the waterfall now, situated at the end of the cavern.

The massive edge of the flume jutted through the water near the very top of the cave entrance, providing the runoff necessary to power the logs down to the river below. It's wide lip provided a respite from the crashing force of the water cascading all around it, offering a clear passage in and out of the cavern.

Isbell could barely make out the shimmering light behind the steady roar of the water. At first, he thought it must be the afternoon sun trying to push its way through the waterfall. But there was something not quite right about what he was seeing.

Isbell squinted hard, slowly realizing what was wrong.

The light source behind the waterfall was flickering with a dark orange hue. That could only be the result of one thing. There was a massive forest fire out there, and it must be raging close to the cave entrance.

A blood-curdling roar erupted from behind him. The monster back there was obviously in a state of total rage. Something else was provoking it now. Moments later, he heard several men screaming. They sounded consumed with agony.

Whatever fiery chaos was happening outside, he knew certain death lay behind him if he didn't press forward.

Isbell pushed his shoulder hard against the cavern wall for support as he began limping towards the waterfall. He noticed that the floor had been become thick with mud as the water seeped its way into the first section of the cave.

He was close now, just a few dozen steps away from his escape.

An explosion suddenly ripped through the air behind him.

The concussive blast walloped into him, knocking him completely off his feet. His body crashed down hard. Isbell cried out in agony as his bleeding leg slapped against the muddy floor. The pain was agonizing. He fought the urge to black out.

Gasping wildly for air, he still felt the intense heat rolling against his back. He could smell the distinct scent of burning nitroglycerin and powdered shell sorbents.

That blast...

It had been the dynamite.

The lumberjack who had been perched on the lip of the cavern hole must have finally gotten around to detonating it. Judging by those screams he had heard, the explosion had probably been more of a mercy killing.

He strained his ears, but couldn't make out anything beyond the sound of his own labored breathing. Whatever had ultimately gone down in that bloodbath he had just crawled away from, it was apparently over.

Isbell refocused his gaze on the waterfall. He had to manage the strength to not only reach it, but to pull himself out from beneath the flume and find help amidst the fires raging outside of the cave.

Even without a serious injury, it was a difficult task; *with* one, it seemed nearly impossible. There was only so much his body would take. There was only so much that he could endure before the smoldering embers of his will went cold forever.

But impossible or not, he had to try.

Isbell once again pulled himself up onto a single knee, doing his best to ignore the blistering pain that coursed through his bleeding leg. Grinding his teeth together with agony, he felt another wave of coldness blanket his body.

He needed to get warm, fast. He had to slither his way out from beneath the flume, pull himself out from this cave, and to find some rest under the gaze of the sun on a field of soft grass. Right now, he could even envision himself staring into the flames that were consuming the forests outside.

He could almost imagine how the heat would feel against his skin.

Isbell blinked in a moment of confusion.

He felt that heat right now.

As he felt the warmth pushing against him from behind, Isbell shook his head to clear the fog of delirium that must be consuming his mind.

And then he realized something.

There were fresh shadows bouncing against the walls of the cave now. Created from a new source of light. The shadows were jagged, looking not unlike mountain peaks. But those peaks were in constant motion, almost as if they were—

Flames.

Crackling sounds echoed loudly inside the cave.

There was a large fire growing somewhere in the cavern.

In this new firelight, Isbell could see piles of skeletal remains stacked against either side of the cavern walls, the source of the putrid odor that he had been inhaling. Most of the bones had been picked clean; however, strips of rotted, tattered flesh still gripped many of the gnawed-on skeletal pieces. The bones belonged to man and animal alike.

Just then, a new shadow appeared on the walls of the cave. It dwarfed the dancing flame peaks that had consumed his vision. This new shadow was broad, huge, and moving.

Isbell felt a surge of fresh panic clutch him.

It had to be that *thing*. Somehow, it had survived the blast and it was coming for him.

No.

He realized it was something else.

It was *someone* else.

The shadow spoke, the voice sounding hard and savage. "Do you know what I've learned about life, Captain Isbell? It ends."

Hearing those words frightened Isbell more than the ravenous creature that he had already encountered. He was terrified because he now understood that the voice belonged to the *real* monster.

And with that realization, all hope of escape finally slipped out of his grasp.

CHAPTER 34

Jolon Winterhawk understood what it felt like to be terrified in the coldness of a confined space. It was tantamount to being buried alive. That feeling of enclosure was akin to the wood paneling inside of a coffin, the sickly smell of pine consuming your nostrils as you scratched helplessly against the unforgiving sides that pressed in tightly all around you.

He had experienced it before.

Ten years ago: June, 1864. Navigating his way through the scorched trenches in Mechanicsville, Virginia. The fateful Battle of Cold Harbor, which had claimed over 18,000 casualties.

The Union had formed a defensive line behind Boatswain's Swamp, located two miles north of the strategic Chickahominy River. After confederate cannons had relentlessly pounded their position for three solid nights, the order had been given by Brigadier General Fitz John Porter that all remaining Union soldiers were to retreat. The Union army was commanded to fall back onto the south side of Chickahominy, where it was thought that the Rebels would not engage in pursuit.

Serving as one of the senior reconnaissance members of the Army's 3rd Armored Cavalry Regiment, Winterhawk was among the first soldiers to depart the Union stronghold at Boatswain's Swamp. He and a dozen other men had traversed the water-logged terrain as a constant barrage of shells continued to rain down around them. They were looking for the safest path forward, they were searching for the quickest way out.

What they uncovered was the fastest way *down.*

With the inky blackness shrouding their vision, the seasoned reconnaissance unit had been relying on sense memory of the land. As they had edged ever closer to the Chickahominy, they allowed the sound of the roaring river to guide them closer still.

Winterhawk hadn't heard the first man cry out until it had been too late. For the briefest of moments, he had thought they might have walked into some kind of Rebel ambush. That perhaps the Confederates had somehow delivered a pincer attack from both sides of the river.

As several other cries of panic sounded out, Winterhawk had turned towards the source, bounding forward across the brushy terrain, hand reaching for his holstered Colt.

He then had realized two things in rapid succession.

The first was that his legs had become immobile, all his forward momentum ceasing. It had been almost as if a divine hand had reached down from the sky to hold him perfectly in place.

Almost immediately, he had realized the second thing. That his body was still moving. Only he wasn't going in a forward direction any longer. He was sinking *downwards*. The thick mud was up to his knees before he understood what had happened.

Quicksand.

Underground sources of water are typically behind the formation of quicksand. If an underground reservoir flows upward through loose sand, particle friction is compromised and the hard ground soon becomes nothing but a floating suspension bridge of muddy soil.

This phenomenon is typically caused by vibrations within the ground, which increases the pressure of the shallow groundwater liquefying the soil through intense shaking. This can occur with such seismic events as earthquakes or—

Cannon blasts.

Because the water seeps in from the bottom, the top layer of mud is often deceptively dry, causing it to look like any normal stretch of soil. That's why there hadn't been any signs of danger. The ground had been safe right up until the moment that it wasn't.

Within seconds, the entire reconnaissance regiment had become snared in the quicksand. The dozen men were shouting out in panic, arms thrashing wildly as they began to sink lower into the sucking mud.

"Stop!" Winterhawk had screamed at them. "You have to stop fighting against it!"

But nobody had been listening. The soldiers had all been smothered by the cold darkness, their midnight world punctuated only by intermittent explosions of Confederate cannons and rifle blasts. And now, the very earth was swallowing them whole.

Winterhawk had encountered quicksand plenty of times before. The fast and hard rule was that the harder you struggled, the worst you'll get trapped. The trick was to relax. If you didn't, if you just continued to flail your arms and legs, then you'll only succeed in forcing yourself deeper down into the unforgiving mud.

But the men continued to thrash wildly, crying out for help as the mud seeped past their waists.

Winterhawk had taken a deep breath to steady his nerves.

If he was going to get out of this alive and save however many of those men that he could, then he was going to have to focus his energy on a near-impossible task.

He needed to go swimming.

Winterhawk moved into a horizontal position, leaning onto his back until he felt the shockingly cold mud lapping against the back of his neck. Once his body weight was more evenly distributed, he started floating.

He kicked his legs, gently bringing his feet up towards the surface. He began a determined backstroke, methodically paddling with short strokes on the surface. He had to be careful not to submerge his hands down in the mud because of the incredible risk of getting them stuck.

Once all of your extremities are submerged beneath the mud, the chances of being able to extract yourself from the quicksand become nearly untenable.

Winterhawk had come across men who had died after only being submerged chest-deep in quicksand. Exhausted from their struggles, they had simply been unable to pull themselves out from beneath the heavy sand and mud. They eventually succumbed to dehydration.

Of course, there were also those who drowned. The irony was that most quicksand pits were rarely deeper than six feet. But once panic sunk in, it wasn't long before the individual in the quicksand was gulping lethal doses of mud.

He wouldn't let that happen to these brave men he had fought alongside for months. They had survived countless Confederate assaults. Heroes like that don't die because they drowned in mud.

Winterhawk stared up at the night sky, the frantic splashing sounding off all around him. He guessed the quicksand was at chest level for them by now. For some of those soldiers, maybe even higher.

There wasn't much time left.

He felt solid ground pushing up against the top of his shoulders, signaling the edge of where the quicksand trap was. Grunting with effort, he had kicked hard with both legs, propelling his body out of the mud, allowing him to slither backwards onto firm soil.

He had stared up at the night sky, attempting to rest for just a moment and catch his breath.

But there would be little chance of that.

Seeing how he had extricated himself from the quicksand, the Cavalry soldiers started to scream at him. Their tortured cries for help booming louder in his ears than the myriad of cannon blasts peppering the area.

Winterhawk had rolled over onto his side, climbing carefully to his feet. He gasped briefly as he momentarily slipped, coming dangerously close to toppling right back into the mud.

He held is footing.

The quicksand pit was briefly illuminated by a fresh volley of cannon fire blasting down from the hilltops. He could just make out the line of soldiers thrashing in the mud. It appeared that they had traversed across the unstable ground in nearly a single formation. If he didn't do something to try and get them out, they would be dead soon.

"Hold on! I'm going to get you out of there!"

He turned sharply, eyes scanning the surrounding area. His gaze fixated on a nearby row of trees. One of the younger ones had been toppled by a recent explosion, its splintered trunk sagging into a V-formation onto the ground.

Without hesitation, Winterhawk had rushed towards the fallen tree. It was unwieldly and cumbersome. But it would have to do.

Having reached the shattered trunk in a dead sprint, he slammed his shoulder hard against the one side of the split tree. He grunted at the impact, his shoulder smarting with the sharp pain of the collision. He stumbled forward as one half of the tree collapsed onto the ground beside him.

He swung around, grasping one end of the splintered trunk and heaving his body backwards. Roughly fifteen-feet long, it was too heavy to maneuver effectively, so he had proceeded to drag it backwards.

Reaching the spot where he had pulled himself out of the pit, he dropped the heavy trunk to the ground. Moving fast to the opposite end of the broken tree, he once again hefted up one end. He pointed the trunk towards the screaming soldiers and shoved it into the quicksand with as much force as he could muster.

The trunk sunk briefly into the thick mud before casting off through the dark morass. It skimmed the surface of the pit for several feet before losing its momentum, floating in place, but within reach of the frantic soldiers.

"Grab onto the log!" Winterhawk had yelled at them.

Most of the trapped men began to pull themselves onto the log, draping their arms onto the trunk with tremendous difficulty. The log sunk beneath the combined weight of the soldiers, but it remained buoyed atop the thick mud.

Another brilliant explosion lit up the night sky, completely illuminating the quicksand pit. For a brief moment, Winterhawk had thought that all of the soldiers had grabbed onto the floating trunk. Seconds before the fresh light had totally vanished, he saw that he had been mistaken.

There were two Cavalry soldiers who had been stuck too far away from the log to have been able to reach out for it. He could just make out the tops of their bobbing heads, their arms pointing upwards as the mud seeped past their wide, terrified eyes.

Those men were going to drown. They were going to die less than twenty feet from him. He had to do something.

He made the decision without thinking.

Running forward, Winterhawk dove back into the quicksand. He felt the sludge cover his entire body, threatening to pull him under. Forcing himself to remain calm, he kicked forward with his legs, arms sweeping in a steady arc over his shoulders as he propelled forward.

He focused on the momentum of his body. Concentrated on how many strokes it would take to reach those soldiers. Ignored the fear that he hadn't gotten enough air in his lungs to sustain him.

Moments later, he had reached the area of the pit where he had last seen the two soldiers. He allowed his legs to drift down, arms fanning laboriously through the thick mud around him, head whipping around, eyes peering into the darkness.

He couldn't see them; in fact, he couldn't see anything at all.

He felt a tugging on his right leg. Then, fingers clasping onto his left arm. The men had found him. They were clawing against him, pulling at his body in absolute panic.

Then, Winterhawk had found himself submerged in the quicksand. He inadvertently snorted mud up his nostrils. He pulled free from the soldiers. He needed air. He needed to get above the surface. He kicked hard with his legs, felt a bump of resistance against his head.

He realized something with a rush of panic.

He had just collided with the hard layer of ground beneath the quicksand. He had somehow gotten himself turned completely around. Down was up, and up was down.

The mud pressed against him from all sides now.

Fingers belonging to one of the drowning soldiers began scraping against his face. Before he could pull himself away, the digits wormed their way lower, pressing hard against his lips, inadvertently prying his jaw open.

Thick mud seeped into his mouth.

He couldn't control his next reflex.

His body had already reacted.

It was independent of his thoughts.

Trapped several feet beneath the surface of the quicksand, he inhaled.

Deeply.

Soon, the darkness was an all-consuming entity. And for this sort of pit, there was no bottom.

CHAPTER 35

The past is never really past. It stays with you all the time. Decisions and consequences are but mirror constructs of thousands of individualized moments that meld together in the fabric of our memories. They offer the illusion of choice when, in fact, the path was always laid down for us.

The past isn't a milestone, Jolon. It's really just a stepping stone. Be careful that you don't lose your balance while crossing it, amigo.

Jolon Winterhawk snapped his eyes open, breath hitching in his throat. His heart hammered a relentless beat within his chest. His hands were clasped so tightly into fists that the nails digging into his flesh drew small flecks of blood.

He quickly took in his surroundings.

The cavern was cold, and dark. The heady combination of dampness and blood made his nostrils twitch with distaste. The massive waterfall was crashing just ahead. The relentless noise of the pounding water smashing against the rocks sounded not unlike the distant call of tribal drums.

Winterhawk glanced down at his feet. He noticed with distaste that he was standing in a thick pool of mud.

The mud must have pulled hard against him when he had walked across it; acted as some sort of emotional trigger. There must have been a distinctive sound the mud had made sloshing against his boot that had set him off. Or maybe, it had been the temporary feeling of being trapped in a place when he had inadvertently set his foot down in the muck.

Whatever it had been, the memories had unexpectedly flooded over him. They had briefly taken full control.

Mechanicsville, Virginia. The Chickahominy River. The Battle of Cold Harbor. The men he had saved; the men that he hadn't. The quicksand filling his lungs. The boggy deathtrap he had barely escaped from.

Maybe you didn't survive everything *that night. To say that anyone walks away from the battlefield unscathed isn't telling the whole truth. We* both *know what happens when the darkness falls. That's when the nightmares like to come out to play. Like taking a leisurely swim in a quicksand pit while dying soldiers pulled you beneath the surface. They wanted you to join them that night. I think maybe they still do.*

Winterhawk pushed that thought from his head.

The past was *not* the present.

The intense heat of the burgeoning ore fire burning in the cavern behind him was a stark reminder of the current reality. The sticky, wet viscera of the slain monster covering his upper body was a harbinger of the ferocious battle that still might lay ahead.

Might?! I understand that being monumentally naïve is one of your strongest traits, but don't take advantage of the situation. You just blasted one Nu'numic into bite-sized chunks. You don't think the other one is going to take that personally?

Winterhawk felt waves of exhaustion again. The urge to lie down on the floor of the cave beside the vast collection of rotted skeletons was almost overwhelming. For the first time in his life, he truly understood what it was like to lose your grip on the will to press forward.

Experiences can weave themselves together in your mind until they become nothing but a heavy blanket that you're unable to push yourself out from underneath. You can suffocate beneath the weight of things from the past if you allow it.

No.

That was enough.

He had to focus on the present, on the *now*.

Pulling away from his thoughts, Winterhawk fixed his cold gaze onto the mortally wounded soldier crawling across the muddy floor. "Do you know what I've learned about life, Captain Isbell? It ends."

Isbell stopped inching forward along the cavern. His face was drenched in sweat, skin shockingly pale. Groaning with pain, he turned over onto his back. His left hand snaked down to his waist, shaking fingers curling around the handle of the sheathed Bowie knife against his belt.

"I'm going to gut you like a pig."

Winterhawk wanted nothing more than to walk over and grind his boot heel against the man's throat until he was incapable of speaking. Instead, he took a long, deep breath. He willed himself to remain in control of his anger. When he finally spoke, he was surprised by how weary his voice sounded.

"What exactly happened to you, Major? How did you end up like this?"

"What happened?!" Isbell snorted. "Your filthy kind killed my wife and baby boy, *that's* what happened! Some sort of chickenshit raid from the Shoshoni while all the men in my town were out fighting in the Great Rebellion."

His eyes flashed angrily as the painful memory consumed him.

"They killed my wife quick. Shot her in the head because she tried fighting back, not hiding in fear like all the others. But the same couldn't be said for Travis. One of those Indian bastards bashed his head against his crib until his brains had leaked out from his nose."

Winterhawk imperceptibly winced at the image.

"That's how I found my baby boy," Isbell continued, struggling to a kneeling position on the floor. "You end up seeing a lot of blood and guts on the battlefield. But smelling your own son's brains? That sort of shit just hits different."

"I'm sorry," Winterhawk said.

"What are *you* sorry about, brownie?"

"The Shoshoni Tribe," Winterhawk answered. "Some of their people helped the Confederates gain a foothold in Eastern Oregon. My father was murdered during one of those later skirmishes."

"Good," Isbell spat. "One less Indian in the world taking a shit on this glorious land is a great damn day."

Right now, I bet you're feeling like the hospital in the ghost town: out of patients.

"Give me back the locket, "Winterhawk said. "Give it me right now or I will kill you...right now."

Isbell attempted to climb to his feet. Incredibly, he managed to make it onto one leg before the wounded one gave out. Crying out with a mixture of pain and frustration, he staggered sideways across the cavern floor.

He slammed his shoulder against the cave wall, chest heaving with exertion. The large Bowie knife dangled precariously from his shaking hand, but he kept his grip on it.

"Tell you what," Isbell said, "I'll trade you that locket for the rest of that gold ore back there. We both get what we want. We can both just walk right out of here."

"You won't be walking very far," Winterhawk answered. "Not with that wound bleeding out the way it is. Tucker killed you with that shot. The thing is, you just don't know it yet. As for your idea of a trade, there's nothing left for either of us back there. Not anymore."

Isbell looked down the long end of the cavern, eyes taking in the shadows of the dancing flames splayed out across the rock walls. Sickening realization spread across his face. "You didn't. There's no way that you would have just torched a half-million dollars..."

"That's the trouble with the whole thing, isn't it?" Winterhawk replied. "We're either spending our lives trying to dig something out of the ground, or placing tombstones right on top of it."

Isbell stole a mournful glance back at the waterfall. His body began shivering again with the effects of hypothermia. A fresh sheen of cold sweat coated his face.

"The locket, Major. NOW."

Isbell turned his head back, facing Winterhawk with a death grin. "Being that you torched the other end of this cave, going through that waterfall is the only way out of here."

Winterhawk nodded. "I reckon you're right."

"That other *thing* will be out there, too. It'll be waiting for you."

"That isn't your problem," Winterhawk answered, fingers lightly touching the Girandoni. "*I* am."

"Your filthy hands aren't going to touch me, brownie."

"I don't see that you have a choice in the matter."

"That's where you're wrong," Isbell said. "We all have choices. That's what brought you and I together, isn't it? I chose how I came here, and I'll damn well choose how I'm going out."

You see that look in his eyes, amigo? That's the look of someone who isn't afraid of death because he has finally accepted his own fate. Those aren't the eyes of the defiant; they are the eyes of the defeated.

"Drop the knife, Isbell. Give me the locket."

Isbell flashed another grin, staring at the far end of the cavern. For an eerie moment, Winterhawk could see the ore fires flickering in the man's eyes. The flames were getting closer to them both.

"They'll probably discover my ashes down here someday," Isbell said. "But when they do, I ain't looking for some kind of big military funeral. I hope they know that. All I want is for them to climb to the highest spot and throw my ashes into the clouds. Hope there's a strong wind blowing that day. I always wanted to travel the world."

Isbell turned away from the looming fires. There was something different about the expression on his face now. There was a mournfulness that shown through the sheen of sweat and the ghastly-white complexion. When he opened his mouth to briefly gulp air, the flash of teeth was tantamount to a row of weather-beaten tombstones standing crooked on a muddy hill.

Winterhawk could see how this was all going to play out. When you are facing the end of the line, there are only two possible outcomes for a soldier: death in battle, or a new perspective on fear.

Isbell had been right. Life *was* all about choices. And he was about to make his very last one.

Taking another large breath, Isbell raised the Bowie in front of his face. He jerked forward, sliding the blade into the side of his neck. He slammed sideways against the cavern wall, body convulsing, pushing hard against the handle of the knife, driving the blade deep into his flesh.

He was dead before his body folded onto the ground.

Winterhawk stared down at the corpse for a long moment. "I am truly sorry about your family," he whispered. "They didn't deserve what happened to them."

He strode over to Isbell's body. Bending down, he rummaged through one pocket, then the next. He felt the locket and pulled it out. Snapping it open, he stared at the picture.

"No families ever deserve it," he said.

The hardest part about war isn't in the dying. The hardest part is pinning that burden of grief onto the uniform that your family will adorn for the rest of their lives. That's the ultimate sacrifice that a dead warrior will never fully understand: grief.

Clasping the locket around his wrist, Winterhawk rose to his feet. He could feel the intense heat of the burning ore edging closer down the cavern. It would reach the skeletons lining the cave walls before too much longer. When it did, the remains of all that rotted flesh would feed the hungry flames.

Those bones back there, they mark the way of those who came before you. In the end, that's what death really is. It's a path we all trod upon until it's our time to show others the way forward. That's the mystery of the lair of legends, amigo. We all enter into it; only not many ever really leave.

Winterhawk began walking towards the backside of the waterfall. Ducking beneath the tail edge of the flume, he moved beneath the massive wood structure. In just a few short steps, he found himself out of the darkness and into the blazing light.

It was now his time to face the heart of the monster.

CHAPTER 36

Jolon Winterhawk scurried out from beneath the safety of the flume. Even with the large waterfall roaring behind him, it wasn't enough to drown out the burning forest spread out before him.

The wildfire might have had its epicenter at the *Excelsior* crash site, but the flames had already engulfed the forest in a quarter-mile in every direction. Aided by strong gusts of winds, the blaze continued expanding at an alarming rate.

Through the dense, black smoke, he could just make out the unnatural metallic shapes of the Holbeer Steam Donkey and the attached Grafton crane. In the distance behind it, the Rogue River stretched out like an oasis. The remaining section of the flume wound its way down to the water like an artery.

Reaching the river would allow him to navigate the fastest way back home. All he had to do was somehow commandeer a boat, and he would be well on his way in reuniting with his family.

There's no way you can make it through that fire; not alive, anyway.

That was accurate enough.

Large fires like this one were totally unpredictable. He could be making his way through an unincumbered route one moment, and the very next find himself pinned in all directions by trees felled from the savage heat. Making his way south to the Rogue River was definitely out.

That left north.

Pushing his way further into the dense wilderness before nightfall was not ideal, especially when he didn't have access to a full complement of provisions.

But what choice did he really have? He could either face the unknown of the wilderness, or he could risk navigating an unpredictable wildfire.

His body tensed.

There was now something else.

Sounds...

Coming from somewhere behind him. He could hear it beneath the roaring of the waterfall and the cacophony of the massive fire. His muscles reflexively tensed, head cocking to one side as he attempted to make sense of what he was hearing.

It was animalistic, and terrifyingly savage.

It was the Nu'numic.

A strong, pungent odor filled his nostrils. He could no longer smell the copious smoke wafting over the decimated logging area as this new scent overpowered him.

A massive growl reverberated through the air.

As panic took an immediate grip, he resisted the strong instinct to turn sharply and face whatever was coming his way. He needed to be reactive, to assess the threat, and formulate a plan to survive what would come next.

He turned around, eyes tracking to locate the creature.

Judging by the proximity of the growl, Winterhawk had gauged that the Nu'numic was within a thirty-foot radius of his present location. The sound had also been directional, meaning that it had been coming from somewhere not directly behind him.

But from *above*.

He squinted hard through the dense smoke.

The large rock formation stacked on either side of the waterfall. It had scaled the stones after exiting the cave earlier. The monster must have gotten into a vantage point immediately after escaping from the cavern. It had been lying in wait. Surveying the breadth of the fire. Feeling hope that its mate would soon emerge victorious from the darkness. Overwhelmed with rage when, instead, it had been only Winterhawk. The man who had brought destruction to its lair, and was painted with the blood of its kind.

Winterhawk could sense the massive form of the creature poised on the rocks. The heat of its blind rage burned more intensely than the wildfires. Although it had the girth of a grizzly, the monster was exhibiting all the cunning of a mountain lion. While it understood that it had full advantage over its prey, it was still assessing the threat level that it might be facing.

The monster had dealt with the unpredictability of man before.

The creature moved confidently to the end of the rock formation, standing to reveal its full height. Out of the confines of the cavern it looked even more massive. It was well over eight feet tall, weighing at least a thousand pounds. Its muscular frame was matted with dark, coarse hair. It had crimson-tinged eyes. It began to beat against its chest, head pulled back, exposing a frightening array of teeth.

It was asserting its full dominance now, letting everything in the animal kingdom know that death was coming soon.

Winterhawk had few options left.

His first thought was to run back into the cave and make his way back to the rear of the cavern. There might be a chance that one of the lumberjack's fallen weapons hadn't yet been touched by the burning ore. He could still make a final stand in the lair against the Nu'numic.

You know what I think, chief? If you're seriously contemplating this strategy, then your picnic basket must be short a few sandwiches. Remember, the Nu'numic has survived for countless years because it is not *as dumb as you are.*

Winterhawk gritted his teeth.

If he had a gun, he realized that it would take more than just a few well-aimed bullets to bring down the massive creature. Even if he was to risk his survival on a single kill shot, he didn't have any firearms on him. The only weapon he did have was the Girandoni strapped to his thigh.

Not really sure what the monster would do with that big stick, amigo. I suppose it might use it as a toothpick to get pieces of you out of its teeth.

Conventional weapons would be of no use.

While it would take something of equal proportion to stop the charge of the Nu'numic, it would undoubtedly take something even bigger to finally bring it down.

His shoulders stiffened, muscles bunching together.

There was something out there that would make what was coming next a fair fight.

The Holbeer Mini Steam Donkey. It was indeed a marvel of the industrial age, but it wasn't the only hulking metal behemoth lurking within all of that smoke.

While the steam donkey had the amazing capacity of dragging logs up and down the mountain slope with relative ease, it was the Grafton crane that flexed the most mechanical muscle. Tasked with hoisting the logs up onto the flume, the Grafton was built to withstand several thousands of pounds of load pressure as it performed its duties.

If he could somehow lure the Nu'numic into the metal claws of that crane, he might be able to trap it. It would allow him time to either kill the creature or find a way to escape.

It'll be that easy, will it? Just like playing a little friendly game of hide-and-seek? You cower inside that 4,500-pound steel contraption while the Nu'numic covers its eyes with those massive claws and counts to ten. If you're lucky, that big beastie might even want to play another *game after it finds you. Something like tug-of-war, but with your intestines.*

Winterhawk stared up at the Nu'numic.

The monster had stopped roaring. It's red eyes were now slitted with rage, teeth flashing as if it were grinning.

Winterhawk suddenly pounded his fists against his chest, head thrown back as he let out a guttural scream of rage.

It was a language both of them understood.

The creature stood motionless on the rock outcropping, momentarily unsure of what its defenseless prey was doing. It had always encountered man to be in a terrified state, constantly laying down in fear and allowing himself to die by the hands of the monster.

"You want me?" Winterhawk shouted. "Then come and get me!"

He pivoted on the soil, once again facing the direction of the flume. He could just make out the odd beetle-shape of the Holbeer Steam Donkey amidst the thick black smoke carpeting the lumber ground, with the tall Grafton crane looking like the head of some prehistoric monster.

Winterhawk broke into a wild sprint, arms pumping furiously.

Roaring with unbridled rage, the Nu'numic bounded off the rock outcropping and chased after him.

CHAPTER 37

Winterhawk could hear the massive thudding of the Nu'numic landing heavily a short distance behind him. The thunderous impact shook the ground with a small tremor.

Even with the brief head start, Winterhawk knew it would only take the monster a few powerful strides to catch up to him. Still at a distance of 160 yards, he would never be able to reach the elevated platform of the Grafton crane before the creature would take him down.

It was time to make a small detour.

He veered sharply, heading directly towards the large wall of fire that was still burning on the collapsed section of the flume.

The Nu'numic had broken into a lumbering run as it began gaining on him. It was close enough now that he could smell its putrid odor. Any moment, he would feel those razor-sharp claws sinking deep into his back.

The wall of fire was upon him now. The blasting heat was almost unbearable, forcing him to close his eyes. If he didn't change course in the next few seconds, the wildfire would begin to flay off his flesh.

Winterhawk could feel the sickening breath of the monster on the back of his neck. The creature was undeterred by the oncoming flames, its pure bloodlust had overpowered all survival instincts.

NOW!

Winterhawk propelled his body sideways. Throwing himself hard to the ground, he rolled away from the fire. The ground beneath him was blazing hot, the soil burning his exposed flesh. He screamed out in pain.

The Nu'numic charged forward, missing trampling right over him by inches. The creature yelled in confusion, unable to react quickly enough to avoid the fire.

The monster crashed into the wall of flames, letting out a piercing scream as sections of its matted fur immediately caught fire. It lumbered through the flames, momentarily blinded by the intense smoke. It began wildly swatting at various sections of its burning fur, massive hands putting out the flames as it spun around in wild circles.

Winterhawk was already back on his feet and charging forward.

The twin machines were 100-yards from him now, but the ground between him and the crane was fraught with obstructions.

When the burning *Excelsior* had detonated the wagon of dynamite, it had left an enormous crater that was fifty feet in diameter. Scattered around it were various sizes of the exploded section of the flume; each of the pieces ablaze, some protruding out of the ground like burning sacrifices to a petulant god.

Winterhawk maneuvered around the fiery obstacles, sprinting his way down and through the smoking impact crater.

He was close enough now to see up into the open front cab of the Grafton crane.

The dead operator was slouched at an unnatural angle in the seat, a third of his head missing from the impact of the Henry repeater. The machine itself was still running, puffs of white steam contrasting against the black smoke of the forest fire. Stretched out a quarter-mile behind it, the remaining section of flume wound its way to the Rogue River and the crowded log staging area below.

The crane had its talons spread around the massive girth of a Douglas fir. The trunk had been raised halfway from the ground to the flume before its movements had been stopped short by the death of the operator.

Winterhawk stared up at it.

With that tree hanging from the crane, he knew that the likelihood of him being able to use it to grab the Nu'numic was impossible. But if he could position the creature beneath the crane, he still might find another way of killing it.

If only he could get some help out here!

Ironic, isn't it? Where's the Cavalry when you really need them?

As for any sign of the surviving lumberjacks, there were no traces. He couldn't even detect the sounds of yelling. They must have already made their way down to Boscombe to begin evacuating their families.

That left him alone on this battlefield.

I hate to be the one to break the bad news, but you're not really alone out here, amigo.

He heard the deafening footfalls seconds before he could pinpoint from exactly which direction they were coming from. He had been running south towards the steam donkey, but this sound was coming in fast from the northeast.

It was the Nu'numic.

The monster was executing some sort of pincer maneuver. It had circumnavigated the same fiery obstacles that Winterhawk had just been traversing, utilizing its superior strength and speed to take a different route in pursuit.

Through his peripheral vision, he could see its enormous girth racing fast towards him. He was trying to comprehend the fact that the creature was actually running while simultaneously trying to shove that terrifying image out of his mind.

With breath heaving in his lungs, Winterhawk had finally reached the bottom platform of the Holbeer steam donkey.

Although it was classified as a mini version of its giant mechanical brethren, this model still towered twenty feet off the ground because it was attached to the Grafton. The cab of the crane itself was situated flush against the flume, with a metal ladder hooked beside the operator's chair providing the only access to the machine.

He noticed that the blood from the dead lumberjack in the cab had dripped down each rung, a harbinger of the violence yet to come.

Winterhawk leaped upwards, his body crashing hard against the ladder.

His hands quickly grabbed onto the blood-soaked rungs as he began frantically pulling himself up towards the cab. In just another few seconds, he would be safely climbing inside the--

With a savage roar, the monster slammed into the frame of the steam donkey with an earth-shattering impact.

Winterhawk immediately lost his grip on the ladder, feeling himself momentarily dropping. He grabbed onto one of the rungs with his right hand as he fell, his body dangling precariously, legs kicking the air in a desperate attempt to find a foothold.

The Nu'numic stood directly beneath him, growling ferociously. It began swatting at his swaying legs, massive claws coming within mere inches of his feet.

Winterhawk grabbed onto the ladder with his left hand, preventing his body from sinking any lower. His shoulders throbbed with exertion, hands aching as they held his entire body weight. His feet frantically scrambled for purchase on the rungs, boots maddeningly slipping against the dead lumberjack's spilled blood.

The Nu'numic jumped into the air, halving the distance between itself and Winterhawk with a single push from its muscled legs. It attempted to grab onto one of his kicking feet, but barely missed. As it plummeted back towards the ground, one if its hands scraped hard against his left leg.

Winterhawk screamed in agony as he felt the sharp claws raking deep into the thick flesh of his calve. The pain was excruciating, like a hot poker searing against his skin.

Below him, the Nu'numic landed hard, momentarily thrown off-balance as it attempted to regain its coordination. In a moment, the monster would attempt a second jump.

And this time, it would not miss.

Winterhawk was clinging desperately to the ladder, feeling his strength slowly ebbing. His fingers went numb as he felt his grip on the rungs loosening.

This is your final battle, Jolon. Don't you dare lie down like this.

As he tried fighting through the pain that threatened to overpower him, something unexpectedly swung through his line of vision. It was metallic, catching the sun with a sharp glint.

The locket fastened tightly around his wrist.

Kaya and Chenoa.

Those battlefield graveyards of the Civil War are behind you now. While you've shed blood for Chief Joseph and the Nez Perce tribe, the truth of the matter is this, Lieutenant: All that you've ever done as a soldier, as a proud warrior, it was only for them. Nothing else in this world matters anymore. The only mission you have left now is to get home. And to do that, you have to do one last thing: survive.

Winterhawk finally found a foothold on the slippery rung.

He looked up, seeing that the cab of the crane was still a good five feet above him. Holding onto the ladder, he pushed back with his hips, squatting down onto the rung he was perched on, moving his body into a tight V-formation.

The creature launched itself back into the air with an ear-piercing roar. Its massive frame was hurtling up the side of the ladder at an incredible speed, both arms splayed out in anticipation of grabbing onto its helpless prey.

Winterhawk swung his torso forward, letting go of the ladder as he drove himself up from the squatting position with explosive force. As the motion flung him momentarily airborne, he twisted his body, landing inside the open cab of the Grafton.

The monster smashed hard against the side of the steam donkey, grunting with surprise that its prey had moved so quickly to elude it.

Displaying incredible reflexes, the Nu'numic grabbed onto the ladder a second before gravity would have yanked it back to the ground. It dangled over space for a long moment before determinedly climbing up towards the cab.

Twisting inside the small confines of the elevated platform, Winterhawk grabbed onto the body of the slain crane operator and pulled the corpse around to the open side of the cab.

A second later, the Nu'numic appeared in the exposed frame of the steam donkey. Its massive head poked through the opening, jaws opening wide as it finally sighted its prey.

"Hope you like leftovers!" Winterhawk yelled, pushing the corpse of the crane operator against the monster. The Nu'numic was caught by surprise as the dead weight of the man pressed up against its face, temporarily blinding its vision.

Winterhawk kicked hard, his boots impacting with the corpse. The momentum was enough to push the creature backwards as the monster lost its grip on the ladder.

The Nu'numic and the slain lumberjack plummeted to the ground.

The monster landed hard on its back, groaning with pain as its head bounced off the dirt. The dead man plopped down beside him.

Winterhawk turned towards the controls of the Grafton crane, eyes scanning the sparse console, trying to make sense of what he was seeing.

You didn't know a tinker's damn about flying a military balloon until today, chief. How difficult do you think playing with this toy crane could be?

The noise of the engine was deafening behind him, the twin tanks blasting out jets of white steam in tandem with each other.

Catching his full attention, Winterhawk glanced back at the large tanks. His eyes tracked along the rotating gear shaft and steel pulley chain that was tethered to the tanks, noticing that the thick coil of chain stretched out far beyond the elevated platform. It ended somewhere just outside the cab.

He had a sudden blast of realization.

The chain was connected directly to the crane.

His eyes darted back to the console. Amidst a host of knobs, there was a metal wheel set between a large wooden handle and a two-pronged metal lever.

"Those have to be the controls for the crane," he muttered to himself, hands moving to the metal wheel.

Twenty feet below, the Nu'numic growled and opened its eyes. Breathing heavily, it sat up.

Winterhawk spun the metal guide wheel to the right, smiling with satisfaction as the lumbering crane began to move. The pulley chain creaked noisily beside him as the platform begin to shift.

He could feel the tremendous heat from the surrounding wildfire pressing in closer around this area of the flume. In less than an hour, the entirety of the Nelscott Flume and Logging Company would be nothing but ash.

The creature had climbed to its feet, totally oblivious to the momentum of the Grafton crane swiveling into position above it. It was still heavily disorientated from the fall, shaking its head as it proceeded to take a few lumbering steps forward.

It turned suddenly, nostrils flaring.

The creature had finally taken notice of the dead crane operator laying at its feet. Thinking the corpse was Winterhawk, the monster savagely pounced. It began digging its claws deep into the shattered body, pulling out large strips of flesh.

Inside the cab of the Grafton, Winterhawk stopped spinning the guide wheel. The platform came to a lurching stop as the crane swung into place, the Douglas fir swaying uneasily inside of its talon-like grip.

He moved his hand over to the two-pronged metal lever.

He recognized it as being the same concept as a standard railroad frog, the mechanical structure that enables trains to cross from one track onto another. When a train comes into the switch from the curved or diverging side of a turnout, the railway operator uses a similar two-pronged lever to engage the track mechanism.

With this device built into the Grafton's control panel, squeezing one handle would activate the chain to close the crane, and squeezing both handles would pull against the chain and open the talons.

Winterhawk glanced down at the frenzy of violence happening on the ground. The Nu'numic had already ripped the crane operator into dozens of unrecognizable pieces; now, it began pulling long strips of flesh from the man's exposed ribcage.

The monster's thirst for revenge would be very short lived.

After the crane released the massive trunk, thousands of pounds of falling timber would crush every single bone in the body of the raging Nu'numic. The weight of the tree would probably bury it three feet deep in the soil. Then, the creature would be totally consumed by the encroaching fires. Soon, there wouldn't be a trace left of its existence.

Winterhawk closed his hand on the lever, squeezing both handles.

And absolutely nothing happened.

Gritting his teeth, Winterhawk repeatedly worked the two-pronged lever. Beside him, the guide chain lurched once, then froze. The twin steam engines let loose a horrendous screeching noise and began rattling.

Winterhawk felt panic rising in his chest.

The guide chain had malfunctioned. The release mechanism was stuck. Judging by the sounds the steam engines were making in the cab of the platform, he was now officially dead in the water.

Winterhawk looked down, eyes going wide.

The noises coming from the malfunctioning steam tanks had been loud enough to catch the attention of the monster. It was now straddling the mutilated body of the crane operator, attention completely riveted on the cabin of the Grafton.

Its crimson eyes were locked onto him.

He could see a flash of animalistic recognition reflected in them.

Moving with a burst of frightening speed, the Nu'numic moved towards the platform ladder and began to climb.

CHAPTER 38

With his left calf throbbing with agony, Winterhawk pushed himself away from the control panel of the Grafton crane.

He whipped his head around, hearing the Nu'numic making its way noisily up the ladder. The monster would be inside the cab in a matter of seconds. In that span of time and with his leg injury slowing him down, there wasn't anywhere he could go.

The twin tanks made another loud rumble, white puffs of steam now pouring unabated from the engines. It sounded to him like the entire Grafton crane was rebelling against itself now. In fact, it was almost as if...

The whole steam engine was going to blow.

Winterhawk unfastened the Girandoni from his thigh. He hefted the weight of it in his hand. The razor-sharp whale bone fitted against the back edge just might be sharp enough to hack its way through both steam tanks.

Winterhawk swung hard. The back edge of the war club impacted with one of the steam tanks, puncturing it with a lengthy gash. A geyser of scalding steam immediately shot out, spraying against the control panel.

Winterhawk ducked beneath it, moving fast towards the second tank.

An ear-shattering roar filled the platform as the Nu'numic pulled itself off the ladder and squeezed its considerable girth into the confines of the cab.

Winterhawk advanced on the second tank, hacking repeatedly with the Girandoni until jets of steam were pouring out. He hurriedly backed away, heels teetering dangerously on the edge of the platform.

The monster remained hunched on the opposite side of the cab. It growled menacingly at Winterhawk through the twin blasts of steam now shooting out from the tanks. The heat from those blasts had made it cautiously pause when its every instinct had urged it to charge forward. Only twenty-five feet of metal platform was all that stood between them.

The twin tanks rumbled, shaking as if an earthquake was happening right beneath them. It was only a matter of moments now before they would split apart. The detonation would undoubtedly take down not only the Holbeer steam donkey and the Grafton crane, but whatever was still standing in its way.

It's time to take the high ground now, Jolon. Sometimes to find a way through, you first have to find a way up.

Winterhawk glanced at the ceiling.

The operational platform of the crane was shielded from the elements by a thick slab of steel. He could easily scale it. The trouble was, where exactly would he go from there?

There was really only one way to find out.

Winterhawk rocked backwards on his heels, feeling gravity pulling at his back. He tossed the Girandoni up onto the roof, hearing it clang hard against the steel as it slid from view.

The Nu'numic charged forward, crying out with pain as the twin steam blasts scorched its already burned body

Jumping up, Winterhawk grabbed onto the edge of the steel roof. With his muscles screaming with the exertion, he pulled his body up onto the top of the crane platform.

The charging creature had missed grabbing onto him by less than a few inches. Roaring with anger, it began to pull itself up onto the roof in pursuit.

Winterhawk scurried across the top of the Grafton crane platform. From this vantage point, he could see the wildfire burning in all directions. The sheer scope of the devastation was enormous. Thick, black smoke permeated the entire landscape. It would take a millennium before this land had healed itself.

The Grafton swayed dangerously in the intense winds of the fires, the trunk in its grasp swinging back and forth like a pendulum. The curved back of the crane was positioned ten feet away, sitting at a slightly lower elevation than the roof of the platform.

Keeping his eyes locked onto the crane, Winterhawk bent down and retrieved the Girandoni.

He knew that remaining on this roof would only bring death to him in two different ways. Either the steam tanks would blow and he would perish in the explosion, or he would be torn limb-from-limb by the vengeful Nu'numic.

He had to get onto that crane.

Survive, soldier. That's the name of the game. So far, you have a one-hundred percent success rate in doing just that. But we're at the end of the line now. It's time to double-down on those odds. It's time to bet on yourself.

Behind him, the Nu'numic had pulled itself onto the roof. It stood to its full eight-foot height, breathing deeply as it growled. Large splotches of its massive torso revealed burned areas from when it had run through that wall of fire; matted, coarse fur splotched with viscera from the mutilated body of the crane operator. It raised back its head, roaring loudly, the sound echoing throughout the valley.

Winterhawk stood his ground, facing the monster.

Beneath them, the two tanks shook uncontrollably. The hissing of the escaping steam rose in a sharp pitch. It would only be a few more minutes before they finally detonated.

And then he heard something else.

It was an echo of a long-distant memory. It was the voice of his father. He closed his eyes. For the briefest of moments, he could see himself once again as a young boy sitting by a cascading stream. His father was beside him, staring into his eyes.

"What is life, Jolon? It is the flash of a firefly in the pitch-black night. It is the breath of a buffalo in wintertime. It is the small shadow which runs across the grass and loses itself in the sunset. Life is just moments, my son."

Sometimes an entire life can come down to just a single moment. In the end, that's the only truth any of us can every really know for sure. Moments strung together is what constitutes our memories, validates our very existence. Your father died protecting you and your mother. His legacy still breathes inside of you, Jolon. If this is truly your final moment, if this is the last memory you'll ever have, then I suggest you make it really...fucking...count.

Winterhawk snapped opened his eyes.

He raised the Girandoni high above his head, letting loose a piercing battle shriek.

Then, he charged straight towards the monster.

CHAPTER 39

Even the Nu'numic appeared temporarily confused by the strategy.

Its weaker, wounded opponent was now charging at it like some kind of runaway train. It went against all of its natural hunter instincts. The primordial rage that had been fueling it for ages was momentarily stifled; briefly overtaken by an animalistic coda of self-preservation. It took a solitary, defensive step backwards, teeth flashing in defiance.

Running towards the monster, Winterhawk was once again struck by how massive it was. While it did tower a full two feet over him, it wasn't the actual height of the creature that was so daunting. It was how powerful it appeared.

Each limb was a construct of muscle, the matted fur barely able to conceal ropey tendrils of vascularity. It exuded the authority of an animal used to being at the very pinnacle of the food chain. It had no natural predators because the Nu'numic had existed for millennia in the shadows of its own legend.

It didn't fear man, it consumed them.

The monster had been badly burned while traversing through the wildfires and pushing its way through the twin jets of steam, but it wasn't afraid; it was beaten, but far from being defeated.

Winterhawk understood exactly how it felt.

He should have already been dead dozens of times over.

Yet, he kept pushing forward.

Even now, with death roaring before him, he was running towards a certain demise.

At least, that was the *partial* plan.

He had banked on the strategy that his mad rush across the steel rooftop would somehow catch the monster in an unguarded moment. That his offensive maneuver, however suicidal it might be, would force the creature into a defensive position. That it might have bought him just a few extra seconds. Because that's what his entire strategy hinged upon: seconds.

And it had worked.

The creature took a confused step backwards, arms sweeping across its body as if to wield off an attack that it knew was coming soon.

Those were valuable, precious seconds indeed.

If the monster had come charging across the Grafton rooftop first, he would have had no choice but to have died swinging. He could have gotten in a wounding thrust with the Giardini, maybe even gotten in a successful parry or two against those slashing claws, but he would have fallen in the end.

He could never beat the Nu'numic in a head-on physical battle. To vanquish the creature, he needed something with much more strength and power than he was remotely capable of.

He needed to harness the power of what drove the mightiest of rivers, and sustained the largest of oceans. The Creator might have endowed water as the lifeblood of the planet; however, today it would be a form of water that would be the source of his salvation.

The large engine powering both the Holbeer steam donkey and the Grafton crane had already been mortally wounded. The grinding of the guide chain he heard earlier was akin to a heartbeat entering its final rhythm of life. The punctures he had given to the twin steam tanks had hastened the machine's demise.

And when the machine died, Winterhawk planned on it taking the monster down with it.

He continued his wild charge, ignoring the fiery pain burning at the back of his left calf. The wound was deep, but not incapacitating. His adrenaline was overriding everything else. But like the very structure he was now running on, he knew it would not last very long.

Survive, soldier. Whatever it takes. That beastie took its best shot in trying to take you out. Now, you're going to take yours.

The Nu'numic looked behind it, saw the long drop that awaited its next step. It flashed its teeth, remembering the last time it had fallen from this height. It stood its ground, facing its attacker. It was done retreating.

Winterhawk was nearly upon it now, still letting loose with his high-pitched battle cry. His vocal cords were strained, voice cracking. He was close enough now to smell the stench of rotted meat on its fur.

He turned sharply in mid-sprint, continuing his momentum as he began running in the opposite direction. He was now once again facing the Grafton crane. He increased his speed as he raced across the steel roof.

He could hear the creature roar in confusion. He knew that the indecisiveness wouldn't last long. The hunter's natural instinct would soon recognize its fleeing prey and give chase. But this was a fight that would either be won or loss by a matter of seconds. And for now, he still retained the advantage.

Winterhawk was fast approaching the edge of the platform.

The crane was ten-feet away. Clutched in the metallic talons, the Douglas fir swayed a good five feet beneath the curved apex of the structure.

That was his target.

He had to count his steps now. He needed to make sure he bounded off his right foot for maximum lift, as well as to minimize the loss of strength from his wounded calf.

Three steps away.

The timing was critical. A miscalculation here would cost him his life.

Two steps...

The Nu'numic roared to life behind him, charging in pursuit. Below them, the steam engine began to emit a high-pitched whine.

One step.

NOW!

Winterhawk soared off of the platform, throwing both arms high into the air. Using the Girandoni for additional momentum, he swung it around like a windmill, driving his body forward towards the oncoming crane.

He was airborne for a full second before gravity began tugging at him. Fighting against the unpredictability of the rapid descent, he pulled both legs together for stability, hunching forward against the wind.

The Douglas fir offered itself as a big landing target, but safely navigating the sharp forty-five-degree downward angle while in-flight was a challenging endeavor.

When jumping horizontally between two parallel locations, the trick was to extend both arms to potentially catch yourself on a ledge or outcropping should the jump come up a little short.

But this wasn't as simple as jumping between two stationary points. Executing a vertical leap between areas of different heights represented an entirely different set of dangers.

Because of the downward trajectory of the jump itself, landing firmly on your feet was critical to survival. If the individual misjudged the trajectory and came up short on the landing spot, trying to grab onto a ledge while falling would have catastrophic results. The additional weight of the falling body combined with the acceleration of the fall would most likely rip the arm out of its socket.

Even after managing to land on both feet, you needed to tuck your head and tumble sideways, resisting the instinct to roll forward onto your head. Because of the angle of the downward incline, the jumper risks breaking their neck if they roll straight forward. Throwing your body sideways and allowing the shoulders to absorb the impact of the landing.

Of course, leaping from an elevated roof onto a tree trunk held within the clutches of a swaying crane was next to impossible.

When you are betting with your life, sometimes the only thing you can do is double down.

Winterhawk had timed the jump perfectly.

Landing on both feet, he sunk down, letting his legs absorb the initial impact. As he felt pain from his bleeding calf rip straight up his left leg, he threw his body sideways, crashing down onto the trunk on his right shoulder.

He rolled to his feet, crouching, holding the Girandoni across his body like a broadsword. The trunk shifted uneasily beneath his feet, the ground below seeming to move in tandem with the crane.

He turned sharply to look at the Holbeer steam donkey and the Grafton crane platform. He saw thick plumes of white steam shooting out in all directions. The shrilling from the steam tanks was getting more urgent. In just a few moments, the entire structure would detonate.

One reason he had risked the jump from the platform onto the Douglas fir was to give him enough distance to survive the blast. The other reason was that he knew the monster was much too big to emulate his dangerous leap.

It would remain trapped on the roof and be destroyed.

Out of his peripheral vision, he caught sudden movement.

It was a shape large enough to block the sun.

Winterhawk stared with stunned disbelief as he watched the impossible sight of the Nu'numic soaring through the air towards him.

CHAPTER 40

Winterhawk frantically scurried along the trunk.

When that big beastie lands on this floating log, it'll look like a cannon ball just got tossed onto one end of a playground teeter-totter.

The center mass of the dangling Douglas fir *would* be the safest place to be once the monster set down upon it. He was primarily concerned of how well the crane would actually hold once it did.

Dealing with his additional weight was one thing, but throwing an extra 800-pounds of snarling flesh onto the Grafton's load was asking for nothing but trouble.

The monster thudded onto one side of the trunk, the log dipping dangerously. The creature remained in a crouched position, massive hands splayed against the tree as it regained its balance. Its crimson eyes were locked onto Winterhawk, teeth flashing as it readied itself to pounce.

The roaring wildfire had now encircled the entire platform area. The heat was pressing in from every direction now, thick clouds of black smoke darkening the skies like an eclipse.

Winterhawk hefted the Girandoni with one hand, holding onto the crane chain with the other. While he still had the advantage of mobility over his larger attacker, there wasn't anywhere up here he could maneuver to.

As long as he remained on this floating tree trunk, he was trapped.

When the Nu'numic finally moved, it was much faster than he had expected. One second, it was still crouched on the log; and the very next, it was in full motion. It bounded across the trunk, maintaining perfect balance as it quickly honed in on its prey.

Still maintaining his tight grip on the chain with one hand, Winterhawk launched himself off the log.

The monster lunged at the spot he had been standing on just a second before, claws slashing uselessly against the empty space.

Winterhawk swung around in a wide arc high above the forest floor, using his handhold on the chain to pivot his body completely around. He planted his feet once again on the log, now standing directly behind the surprised Nu'numic.

He brought his right arm down as hard as he could, burying the Girandoni dead-center into the monster's thick back. The whale-bone edge sunk through the creature's fur and embedded itself six inches deep into the flesh.

The Nu'numic roared with agony from the blow.

Planting his boot firmly against the monster's lower back for leverage, Winterhawk reached forward and grabbed onto the handle of the war club, yanking it free from its body.

The creature swiveled its massive body around, feet clamoring for support on the shifting log.

Winterhawk was already in motion.

He brought the Girandoni around in a wide, swinging arc. It embedded deeply into the meaty left side of the Nu'numic. It struck hard against the monster's ribcage, lodging itself between the bones with a sickening thunk.

The monster wailed, swinging its arms around in pain.

Winterhawk was hit by one of its flailing hands, the blow knocking him completely off his feet. He landed hard on his back, body skidding across the log from the force of the impact. He stomped both boots down against the trunk in an attempt to slow his movement, fingernails frantically scraping against the wood for traction.

For a single terrifying moment, he feared he would slide right off the side of the trunk and drop down into oblivion.

While his upper body stopped inches from toppling over the side of the trunk, his head and shoulders dangled precariously off the edge. He inhaled a large lungful of smoke, coughing as he pulled his shoulders back onto the relative safety of the log.

The monster was staring down at its chest, hands batting against the Girandoni protruding from its fur. With each swipe, the whale-bone sunk deeper into its flesh, blood spurting.

The Nu'numic raised its head and locked its eyes onto Winterhawk. With its chest heaving, the creature let loose a thunderous roar and charged towards him.

He was out of options.

There was nothing else he could do, and nowhere to hide.

This was truly the end.

Just then, two things happened simultaneously.

The high-pitched whining coming from the punctured steam tanks became eerily silenced.

And then, the steam engine of the Holbeer donkey finally detonated.

The subsequent explosion was deafening.

The elevated platform immediately crumbled. The guide chain that was threaded to the Grafton crane jerked wildly as the falling steel roof severed it like an umbilical cord.

The crane itself was temporarily pulled backwards as the collapsing platform plummeted to the ground. The sound of screeching steel reverberated through the air a second before the guard chain was yanked off of the crane. It pushed forward with such momentum that the suspended Douglas fir began to roll within its clutches.

The monster had still been in motion when the explosion had happened. The concussive blast knocked it sideways, the massive creature attempting futilely to keep its balance as it careened across the trunk.

When the crane itself had been pulled backwards by the force of the collapsing platform, the Nu'numic tumbled into the air.

The talons of the crane finally gave way beneath the sheer weight of the Douglas fir. With a loud snap of metal, the gigantic log dipped vertically, dangling wildly over the ground.

Winterhawk began sprinting up the trunk as it swung downwards. In a few short seconds, the talons of the crane would not be able to hold its load.

The creature landed on its back on the forest floor, one of its legs twisted at an unnatural angle beneath it. The monster let loose with a guttural cry of agony as dozens of its bones snapped on impact.

Winterhawk continued his crazed near-vertical run up the Douglas fir as the crane's talon began to disintegrate beneath him. He was desperate to reach the other end of the log before—

The talons finally crumpled apart, dropping the log into space.

Winterhawk took a running leap into the air as the gigantic trunk vanished beneath his feet. His body slammed hard against the curved peak structure of the Grafton, hands grabbing onto the steel.

The entire crane toppled forward as its fractured base decided to give way.

The Douglas fir plummeted towards the ground, spinning entirely end-over-end before landing with a massive thud onto the forest floor.

The screams of the monster were instantly silenced as the log smashed directly on top of it, driving its body a foot into the dirt.

Winterhawk continued to grip onto the crane as it tipped forward. Seconds before it impacted with the ground, he hurled himself off the structure. He landed hard, rolling for several feet before his body collided with one of the flume's legs.

Behind him, the crash of the Grafton shook the ground with enough force to rattle his teeth.

Groaning with pain, Winterhawk slowly sat up.

He looked over at the fallen Douglas fir. Both arms of the crushed Nu'numic were stretched out from beneath the massive trunk.

"Tree hugger," he muttered.

CHAPTER 41

Jolon Winterhawk was exhausted. Every pain sensor in his body was firing off simultaneously. He could barely breathe amidst all of the smoke. He felt more dead than alive; yet, he had miraculously survived.

He glanced again at the remains of the Nu'numic protruding out from beneath the trunk. Once the wildfires totally wiped the whole valley clean, there would be no trace of its existence.

Back in the lair, only unidentifiable pieces of its mate remained.

Soon, the fires from the ore would consume those, too.

The Ancient Ones would return to the realm of legend now. He would be the only living witness that it had even existed. It would be a truth he would confess only in his nightmares, if at all.

But the Nu'numic did not need a witness in order to sustain its own legend. Stories had already been passed around for centuries; in all likelihood, they would be a part of tribal lore for many more millenniums to come.

The Yupik and the Inupiaq tribes had been absolutely correct about the Ancient Ones. They had proven to be fierce protectors of the forest. Their savagery had increased the closer man had encroached onto their domain. Their bloodlust heightened as their land had been threatened. In the end, the Nu'numic had been forced to defend their very home.

And they had perished in that fight.

He felt a great wave of sadness at that realization.

The why's that are behind these things doesn't mean too much. Dead is dead, chief. Don't matter what the justification for it all might be.

Winterhawk glanced down towards the direction of the Rogue River. He could barely see glimpses of it through the thick smoke that continually swirled around him. Before, he had hoped to make it down there and somehow secure a boat passage back home. Now, that was completely impossible.

Circling high above him, an eagle squawked loudly. He tilted his head, cupping a hand over his eyes as he sought it out. He soon located it. The majestic bird was making a long pass above the burning forest that used to be its home. Then, it soared off in the direction of the waterfall.

Winterhawk stared after it for a long moment.

Watching the eagle had sparked something.

A few moments ago, it seemed that the best course of action was to put the wildfire at his back and walk out of here. To place his chances of survival on somehow navigating his way through some of the most difficult terrain the Creator had seen fit to place on this world.

The eagle had reminded him of something else.

A grin stretched across his face.

Walk?

He could do a whole helluva lot better than that.

CHAPTER 42

The wind had been favoring the flight of the *Intrepid* for the last hour. The final remaining vestige of the Army Balloon Corps had been traversing over the top of the wilderness landscape for miles now, its rope basket skimming mere feet above the endless sea of trees.

Winterhawk had stationed himself behind the balloon's automatic altitude control device, recalling once again how Captain Walker had operated it on the *Excelsior* during their fateful flight back to the wreckage of the *Golden Goose*.

Later, his own return flight back to confront Isbell and Tucker had been achieved by nothing but guesswork and prayer.

Had that entire ordeal been really confined to just a single day? He marveled at how only a few hours could seem like literal years had passed. There were some experiences that, no matter how brief, achieved a lifetime of significance.

He glanced briefly at the setting sun, marking his directional bearings for the hundredth time. As long as he could navigate the *Intrepid* in a northeasterly course, he knew that eventually he would make it home.

He squinted at the small speck of a mountain range that was just now appearing on the horizon. He knew he was finally looking at the Wallowa Mountains. Nestled behind the impressive eastern spur of the Blue Mountains, the peak of the Wallowa cleared just over 9800 feet. His destination lay at the very base of that mountain range: the Malheur Reservation.

Home.

Winterhawk turned the locket over in his palm, snapping it open. He stared down at the picture of Kaya and Chenoa, his heart swelling as if it was the very first time he had seen it, and not the millionth.

They'll never truly understand what you endured to come back to them. But I suppose you'll never fully understand what they *had to endure waiting for you to come home.*

Winterhawk grimaced as he felt the wind shifting, pushing the balloon slightly off course.

He had done everything he could to navigate the *Intrepid* as far as it had already gone. He supposed that the remainder of the flight would once again be back to guesswork and prayer.

The hydrogen tank sputtered loudly. He felt the balloon dipping slightly, the sensation of his stomach dropping as it sunk even further.

The tank stopped sputtering, and the balloon mercifully halted its frightening descent.

Borrowed time, chief. That's exactly what's going on here. You know it, and I know it. The odds of being able to land this contraption at Malheur are about as high as the amount of hydrogen left in that tank: next to zero.

That was true. He had overheard Ambrose telling his men to syphon as much hydrogen from the *Intrepid* as they could before embarking on that final trip. How much they had actually taken and how much had been left in the *Intrepid*, he could only guess.

He remembered all of this as he had trekked away from the wildfires and made his way to the nearby clearing where he had first been captured. There, he had found the balloon still tethered to the tree.

He believed it would take him home. He had faith that it could. His battered body left him with little choice. Sometimes, it was the hope in the thing that made everything that followed possible to endure.

Yes, hope. That's where it all begins, and where it all ends.

Soon after he had cast off the mooring ropes, the balloon had risen quickly. The wind had immediately pulled and tugged at the basket with great force, but he had fought hard enough to remain upright and adrift.

After a while, he was able to inhale great lungfuls of clean air. Behind him, the fire had continued to swallow up large parts of the forest. It was still advancing steadily towards the Rogue River when he had traveled far enough away to lose sight of the flames. The huge clouds of smoke stayed with him for much longer; however, even they had now dissipated from his vision.

His left ankle was throbbing with incredible pain. The adrenaline his body felt for hours had slowly begun to ebb. Soon enough, the nerve endings would shift from stabbing hot slivers to icy numbness. There was already a cold sheen of sweat developing on his face. He would be experiencing the full effects of hypothermia before too much longer.

He pushed all of that far from his mind.

What *might* happen was of no present concern to him.

He just had to have faith in the wind at his back.

. . .

ALMOST THREE HOURS had passed since he had lifted off.

Winterhawk glanced again at the setting sun. He felt the coldness of the altitude beginning to sap his strength. He looked around the basket of the balloon, hoping to find something to wrap around his bare torso. He hadn't seen anything before, but maybe an item would materialize now. He had certainly experienced stranger events than that over the last several days.

But the basket remained empty.

There had been nothing left for him on board.

Winterhawk looked away from the sun, staring at the approaching Wallowa Mountains.

He had drifted several miles closer. The peak was beginning to loom large. He could not yet make out the Malheur Reservation spread out around its base, but he knew it was there; more importantly, *they* were there. His wife and daughter, protected somewhere down in that mass of trees that swallowed up the landscape.

Chief Joseph would be there, too. Would he be proud of his greatest warrior? Would he regale in the tales of his exploits? Would the Nez Perce tribe welcome him with a grateful embrace?

There was that hope again. It was the last weapon he had.

Crouching down, Winterhawk stroked his hand down the back of his ankle, whetting his fingers in blood.

In the Nez Perce culture, the face of a recently deceased individual would be painted red before being buried. It was used to symbolize that peace had been achieved in death.

He wasn't dead yet, but he felt at peace.

He traced lines of his own blood across his cheeks.

His mind was on Kaya and Chenoa, but he was also thinking about something else.

He had once thought that ghosts represent the guilt of still being alive.

Sometimes they come back because of love, Jolon. Isn't that a hoot?

They say that a fallen warrior may choose to return from the other side in order to guide the path of the living. People who have experienced this describe it occurring during near-death encounters, sharing memories of *something* guiding them away from imminent danger. These people say that the ghosts of these fallen warriors weren't represented in spirit, but in—

Voice.

Winterhawk closed his eyes.

He should have recognized it all along.

Don't be too down on yourself, Jolon. There's a lot of things I didn't see, either. But that's the tragedy of life, ain't it? We miss what's standing right in front of us because we're too busy looking at what's behind.

His father—

Died while protecting you and your mother. I would have liked to have said "gallantly protecting," but we both know what a shit job I made of that. But there's something you need to know, Jolon. There is something you need to understand. Even more importantly, there's something you need to believe. *Are you all ears now, amigo?*

He nodded.

When I ran that fateful day, I wasn't fleeing from those Confederate assholes. I was drawing their bullets away from you, and from your mother. I was trying to bide time to give our own warriors a chance to fight back. And did they ever.

"But you were taken," Winterhawk whispered.

Why do you think I had to come back, Jolon? To make sure that you weren't taken, too. After you enlisted, I knew that I had to guide you safely back home. It's been a long road for both of us.

"I'm almost home now, father," Winterhawk said, keeping his eyes squeezed shut. "What happens now?"

For a long moment, all he could hear was the sound of the wind shaking against the canopy of the balloon.

Your mission is over, Jolon. And so is mine. I get to finish out the rest of my peaceful journey. You are just now starting yours, son. If you have to make the same decision that I did someday, I trust that you'll be the same guardian and protector of Chenoa that I have been for you.

"Thank you," Winterhawk said, his voice barely above a whisper.

But there was nothing else to hear but the roaring of the wind.

His father was finally gone.

The loud sputtering of the hydrogen tanks echoed loudly.

Winterhawk snapped his eyes open, noticing that sunset had now begun to totally blanket the sky. Even the Wallowa Mountains had gotten so much closer now. He figured that he was within five miles of the Malheur Reservation.

Close enough for him to walk safely, even at night.

With a loud, sputtering gasp, the tank blew out its final blast of hydrogen. Winterhawk grabbed onto the edge of the basket for support as the balloon began to wobble crazily in the air before beginning its rapid descent.

The *Intrepid* was batted violently between two large trees as it fell from the sky, the thick branches doing their best to shred the balloon before it could land on the ground.

The *Intrepid* stopped in midfall with a sudden jolt.

Winterhawk grunted, losing his grip as he was flung to the floor by the sudden stop. Panting, he pulled himself to his feet, noticing the basket swaying uneasily beneath him. He looked up and saw that the *Intrepid* had become ensnared in the grip of a massive branch.

Scooting over to the edge of the basket, he peered down, wondering with trepidation how far it would be down to the forest floor.

He didn't have to worry.

The ground was only a foot beneath him.

He swung his legs up over the basket, carefully hoisting himself over the side. Dropping to the ground, he felt the sharp pain igniting the nerve sensors on his left ankle.

That was good. The pain would keep him awake. It was what he needed to focus on as he picked his way through the underbrush. The wound from the monster would help push away his exhaustion, if only temporarily.

Turning sharply, he took one final look at the sun before it slipped behind the ragged peaks of the Blue Mountains. The sky was bathed in a beautiful orange hue, offering the world the last moments of light before darkness smothered everything.

Winterhawk knew it would be a difficult walk through the forest to Malheur at night, but he wasn't afraid. There had been a time when the dark woods would bring along with it trepidation and fear. But those days were far behind him now.

He had fought the most savage foe that the wilderness had ever concealed. He had gone to battle against a legend and come through the whole experience bloodied, but victorious.

He then thought briefly of Colonel Smythe. That had been a man of conviction and courage. He represented the very best of his people, someone whose memory would continue to stand tall in his own life for the rest of his days.

He would make sure that Kaya understood the full measure of the men whom he had proudly served alongside. There had certainly been evil men spreading hate among them, but that was the reality in every culture. Even his own.

He already missed the voice of his father. The remainder of his journey would feel lonely without him.

The darkness had absorbed yet another light, but that light was never meant to shine in this world. It was meant to radiate in the next life, a place where brave warriors found the peace they had always been seeking. His father had returned to be a guide; now, he had taken his rightful place in eternity. The courage he left behind was for his son to pick up and carry. It wasn't a burden, but a responsibility. He could feel the weight of it settle deep in his heart. It was comforting.

Casting one final look at the *Intrepid*, Winterhawk walked into the clutching embrace of the massive forest.

In the distance, he thought he could see the tendrils of smoke from the dinner campfires that would be scattered around the hundreds of teepees. If he listened hard enough, he believed he could make out the faint melody of songs as the elders serenaded their children to a restful sleep.

Home was close, as close to him at this very moment as it had been in years.

Jolon Winterhawk smiled warmly.

It wouldn't be too much farther now.

Love never traveled far. It didn't have to.

EPILOGUE

Cemetery
Joseph, Oregon.
1903

"When I first hired you as a guide," Theodore Roosevelt remarked, eyes twinkling mischievously, "I never imagined that *this* would have been part of your famed Oregon hunting expedition."

Shifting the strap of the Zieg A-8 Australian hunting rifle across her back, Chenoa Winterhawk couldn't quite stifle the smile that spread across her face. Admittedly, this *was* an unusual place to take the President of the United States, even someone as decidedly adventurous as Teddy.

"Slight detour," she replied, striding purposefully through the dilapidated main gates of the Malheur Indian Cemetery. Like everything else about the land that used to belong to the Nez Perce tribe, the cemetery was in a state of environmental disarray.

After Chief Joseph's surrender near the Canadian border in 1877, nearly the entire populace of his people had been taken to eastern Kansas before being forced to relocate in Oklahoma. Part of the terms of those negotiations had been contingent on their sacred land being divided up by the United States government. Over the intervening years, members of the Nez Perce tribe would slowly migrate back to the western states, where they hoped to reclaim all the ancestral land that had been taken from them.

But not everyone from the tribe had been forced to leave Oregon.

The United States had drafted the Treaty of Nez Perce, wherein a small percentage of the original tribal descendants were allowed to live upon a government-sanctioned reservation in eastern Oregon. The treaty had diluted thousands of miles of Nez Perce land into a stretch that barely covered several thousand acres.

Given his dedicated and heroic service to his people, her father had been granted permission by Chief Joseph himself to stay behind with his family and live on that reservation.

This had been her home since she was a young girl. It was really all that she had ever known. To her, it remained a paradise on earth.

"I trust we are here to pay respects to your father," President Roosevelt said as he dismounted from his horse. As his boots touched the ground, he caught stern looks from the three Secret Service riders who were flanking his side. He gave them an indifferent wave as he followed Chenoa into the cemetery. The riders glanced uneasily at each other, hefting large-caliber rifles, eyes scanning the horizon for potential danger.

"Yes," she answered softly, "we are in the place of respect." It had been far too long since she had been here last. Years, possibly. But she could still trace the winding path through the tombstones that led to her father as easily as she could the day he had been buried.

"I had read up on your family history before employing you as my local guide," Roosevelt commented. "Lieutenant Jolon Winterhawk was a great soldier."

"Chief," Chenoa corrected sharply. She hadn't meant for the edge to come out in her voice like that. She thought she had learned to mask all of that anger years ago. Apparently, she hadn't.

"I'm sorry?" Roosevelt said, brows slightly arched.

"Chief Winterhawk. My father was given the title shortly after his return from Cavalry service. I was seven when the ceremony happened."

That had been thirty years ago now.

In the veritable lifetime since, Chenoa had grown into the greatest tracker that her tribe had ever seen. Some even say that her hunting skills surpassed those of her own father. Of *that* particular accolade, she remained dubious. In any event, it was how she made her living now.

They had finally reached her father's tombstone.

Chief Winterhawk might have led the life of a brave soldier, but he had died as a peaceful farmer. Apart from the need to hunt and provide food for his family, she never once saw him pick up a rifle after his return home from the war.

Although it was a life he never really talked about, sometimes, in the middle of the night, she could hear when the nightmares of the war had returned to him. Her mother had told her once that she believed those nightmares had been fueled by something more than battlefield trauma.

Although he had never spoken about it to either one of them, her mother had always thought that there had been something *else* that had terrified him. What that something might have been was a secret he took with him to his grave.

"Is this it?" Roosevelt inquired, motioning to the blank gravestone she was now standing beside. "There's no inscription."

"Yes, there is," Chenoa answered quietly.

She pulled up on the chain of her necklace, revealing a battered silver locket hung below. She grasped it tightly in her hands, knowing that, for whatever reason, this locket had been the most precious antique her father had owned. The picture inside had become washed-out and faded, but it had meant something special to him.

Nodding reverently, President Roosevelt lit a cigar. He turned his back while he smoked, allowing her a moment of privacy as she stood at the foot of her father's gravesite.

Chief Winterhawk had been gone for over half her life now. But there were still moments when she felt his presence; times when she swore she could still hear his voice. It was almost as if he was still--

Her head suddenly snapped up, eyes tracking the line of trees that flanked the cemetery.

Something large had just moved across her peripheral vision. She stared intently into the thick clusters of shadows, trying to make out exactly what it might have been.

It felt like she was being watched.

Detecting her unease, Roosevelt studied her features. "What is it, Chenoa? Did you see something?"

Let's snap to attention here, Pocahontas. It's not every day that the President of the United States wants to engage in a little chit-chat with a lowly hunting guide from Oregon.

"I don't know, sir," Chenoa answered distractedly.

Way to really inspire confidence there, chief.

A strong wind gust wound its way down through the hills, rustling the branches of the nearby line of trees.

She thought she could detect a strange, pungent odor.

"Are you sure?" Roosevelt asked, dropping his cigar onto the ground. He crushed it beneath his boot, following her gaze out to the surrounding trees.

The wind was gone, and the unusual smell had vanished right along with it.

"Yes. I'm sure."

Chenoa let out her breath, forcing her heart rate to return to normal. Whatever it was that had been out there, it was obviously gone now.

It was probably nothing.

ACKNOWLEDGEMENTS

Going the distance.

For a writer, that could certainly mean many different things. For *this* writer, it is the culmination of various strands of the same dream that have, after many decades, finally come together in a spectacular way.

I would like to thank Reagan Rothe and the entire Black Rose Writing team for believing in me. That you are reading "In the Lair of Legends" is a testament to their unwavering commitment in fostering fresh literary talent and taking chances on bold stories. Receiving that book contract was an overwhelmingly emotional experience that I will never forget. Special mention to David King for his brilliant cover design!

A huge note of thanks to some of the talented authors who read my early manuscript and offered notes, advice, praise, and encouragement: Jeremy Engel, Lena Gibson, Michael Fletcher, Randolph Harris, Tom McCaffrey, Michelle Weinfeld, Karen Brees, and Jay Levin.

David Morrell. My favorite author. Your craft first inspired me to become a writer. Forget all about the footprints of the Nu'numic. Your footsteps are the biggest ones I want to follow after.

To my brother Mike, and his family: Marianne, Cora, Max, Jake, and Claire. You live the adventures that I can only write about. Love you all!

To my mom and dad. My biggest supporters, my greatest cheerleaders, and my personal heroes. Never once, not a single time, did they ever cast even a shred of doubt that I would reach my dreams. There's absolutely no way that I can express how much I love you both.

To my beautiful wife, Deborah. Thank you for your unwavering support. Thank you for your patience for years on end while I worked all day, then would often write throughout the night. You understood my dream better than I did some days. Love you, Snuggie.

Fulvio Cecere. You believed in my potential so much. No matter what setbacks happened along our creative journey, you endured and pressed on. You remain a profound inspiration. No surrender, pal.

Serena Hunt. Our thirty years of friendship is something that kept me going more times than you'll ever know. You are fearless in so many areas of your life, particularly in your unshakeable support in my writing. Thank you for always being there for me.

And I definitely would not be here without the friendship and support of so many others: Vanessa Padgett, Philip Whitfield, Lindsey Stark, Kelsey Famous-Stirling, Tapi Gibson, Tobin Elliott, Sheila E. Young, Jason Dillon, Bob Stewart, Phillip Grombacher, Rob Beguelin, Jim Voss, Russ Beguelin, Dan and Kathy Geib, Karen Bennett, Sigfried Seeliger, Liz Loomthong (and Camo), Jason Holborn, Loretta Billon, Peter Papas, Lynda Hughes and Deanna Hughes ...and so many, many more. You know who you are!

Jolon Winterhawk was right. Hope *is* a long road to travel.

My sincere wish is that knowing the struggles it took for me to reach this point might bring encouragement to others who find themselves stuck in the creative trenches. I hope that it might bolster the spirits of those who have worked so hard for years and feel that there's nothing at all to show for it.

I implore you to not give up. Keep going. If you get knocked down, climb back onto your feet again. Investigate other creative outlets. Feed that part of yourself before it starves.

Hope is a superpower. Never take off that cape.

No Surrender,
Dave Buzan
(January 2023)

ABOUT THE AUTHOR

David Buzan is an optioned screenwriter. He's also had work published in American Cinematographer, Film Score Monthly, This Week Magazine, among several others. David is a graduate of the Vancouver Film School, and also holds a Bachelor of Science Degree in Psychology from Liberty University. He and his wife currently reside in Keizer, Oregon.

NOTE FROM DAVID BUZAN

Word-of-mouth is crucial for any author to succeed. If you enjoyed *In the Lair of Legends*, please leave a review online—anywhere you are able. Even if it's just a sentence or two. It would make all the difference and would be very much appreciated.

Thanks!
David Buzan

We hope you enjoyed reading this title from:

Subscribe to our mailing list – *The Rosevine* – and receive **FREE** books, daily deals, and stay current with news about upcoming releases and our hottest authors.
Scan the QR code below to sign up.

Already a subscriber? Please accept a sincere thank you for being a fan of Black Rose Writing authors.

View other Black Rose Writing titles at www.blackrosewriting.com/books and use promo code **PRINT** to receive a **20% discount** when purchasing.

Made in the USA
Coppell, TX
05 September 2024

36883334R00163